To Jon,

Reservation Point

by

Robert Farago

email: <u>robertfarago1@gmail.com</u>
Instagram: @robertfaragowriter

*My
friend!

R. Farago
2019*

Chapter One

"Hey Lieutenant," Officer Swanson asked, "why'd you become a cop?

My partner looked troubled. His face told me he'd made "the realization."
The rookie had finally come to the conclusion that his job sucked. The
hours sucked, the coworkers sucked, the boss sucked, the general public
sucked, the union sucked. Everything sucked.

Officer Swanson's expectations of excitement, camaraderie and respect had
smashed against the sharp, immovable rocks of reality. He'd come face-to-
face with boredom, indifference and hostility. As his superior officer, it was
my job to remind him of his sacred duty to serve and protect the good
people of Providence, Rhode Island.

"It's the paperwork," I told Officer Swanson. "I became a cop because I
love paperwork."

I'd been messing with Swanson's head for a week— more than enough time
for the rook to realize that half of what I told him was bullshit. The question
he wrestled with: which half?

"I'm serious," I lied. "Writing's a compulsion."

Officer Swanson didn't have a clue what "compulsion" meant. As far as I
could tell, "Lieutenant" was the only three-syllable word in his vocabulary.
But he did hear the word "writing."

"Do you do stories?" he asked.

"Fiction? Most of my reports answer to that description. I've written a
couple of novels. Nothing published."

"How would you describe me?" Swanson asked. "If I was in one of your books?"

I stared at the battleship-grey triple-decker house in front of us, pretending to rack my brains for inspiration. A stiff breeze pushed needle-nosed rain sideways, stripping the few leaves defying the approaching winter, forcing me to turn on the windshield wipers every minute or so.

"Officer Swanson's facial features were as half-formed as his character. His bovine expression and receding hairline reflected his genetic suitability for a lifetime of monotony, interrupted by periodic episodes of senseless violence and bureaucratic stupidity."

"That's good right?" Swanson asked. "Can I read one of your books?"

"*Can* you?" I replied.

Swanson didn't get it. Or maybe he did. I'll never know. A rail-thin guy in blue jeans and a white T-shirt interrupted our confessional. He emerged from a ground floor apartment carrying a severed head by the hair, dripping blood onto his sneakers and the cracked concrete below.

"Well there's something you don't see every day," I observed, in case Officer Swanson thought otherwise.

The perp walked up to one of the plastic wheelie bins haphazardly arranged in the front yard. He opened the hatch and dropped the head inside. I swear I could hear it bouncing around. Mission accomplished, the perp turned and walked back into the building.

I can't remember how I called it in— there isn't a specific radio code for decapitation. I requested backup, steeled myself against the biting cold and opened the cruiser's door.

"Yo Swanson," I said, popping the collar on my ugly ass coat, leaning into the patrol car. "Time to go to work."

"I'm ready," Swanson said with false bravado, fiddling with his gear, adjusting his Kevlar vest. I half expected him to check his hair in the mirror.

"Shouldn't we call SWAT?" Swanson asked, his hand resting on his holstered gun as we walked towards the perp's front door. "What are we going to do?"

"I'm going to apprehend the suspect. You're going to try not to shoot anyone. Especially me."

Swanson slowed slightly, hanging back. I climbed the rotting stairs leading to the decapitator's porch. Fearing electrocution, I passed on the cheap plastic doorbell barely attached to the water-stained wall by a couple of thin wires. I knocked on the door.

I stepped back at an angle to the entrance, in case the perp decided that a shotgun blast was the best way to greet his visitors. The thin guy opened the door, stepped into the threshold and smiled. I smiled back, happy to see two empty hands. I was less happy to see blood spatter on his white T-shirt. He had a bright blue neck tattoo. Anna Nicole Smith? Santa Anna? The Santa Maria? Something.

"Good afternoon. My name is Lieutenant John Canali. How you doin'?" I asked, initiating the call-and-response routine that somehow survived the TV show *Friends*.

"I'm doin' OK," the perp replied, as if I was genuinely interested his well-being, as if he hadn't spent a good part of the morning sawing off a man's head.

I heard a metal button snapping free and the swish of metal against leather. Officer Swanson had unholstered his GLOCK.

"I was wondering," I said, trying to keep the bloody perp's attention focused on me, rather than Swanson's gun. "Did you dump a severed head into that trash can over there?"

"Which one?" he asked, peering at the row of plastic bins.

"Second from the left."

The perp narrowed his eyes like a Jeopardy contestant trying to remember the name of a Shakespearean sonnet.

"Let's try that again," I said, maintaining my smile and pleasant tone of voice. "Did you dump a head into *any* of those bins?"

"I might have," he answered cautiously. "Who wants to know?"

"Sir, is there anyone else in your apartment?" I asked with a weary sigh. "Anyone *alive*?"

"No," he said simply.

"Would you mind if I have a look inside?"

"I'm kinda busy right now," the perp replied, glancing nervously down the street.

"I understand," I said quickly, laying on as much mock sympathy as I could muster. "Sir, can do you do me a favor? Step forward, turn around slowly and put your hands behind your back."

"Why?"

I couldn't tell if the bloody bad guy was dumb or just playing dumb. Alternatively, insane. A strong possibility, all things considered.

"Sir, if you *don't* follow my instructions, you're gonna get shot. Either by Officer Trigger Happy behind me or one of the twenty cops about to roll up."

The perp swallowed hard, thinking, peering over my shoulder at the gun pointed at his chest.

"If you want to commit suicide by cop I'll just *step out of the way*," I said, emphasizing the last part in case Officer Swanson's trigger finger got itchy. "You have five seconds."

It's hard to regain the element of surprise when you're a cop facing someone facing a cop. A fake countdown isn't a perfect solution but it's better than nothing.

"Five . . ."

I grabbed the perp by the shoulders, spun him around and ran him off the stairs as hard and fast as I could. Imagine a surfer launching himself into the waves on top of a long board. If you've never heard the sound of a ~~cornered~~ *UNSORTED* ~~pinned~~ criminal hitting cement face down with a cop on his back, it's an impressive combination of crunching and squelching.

The bad guy screamed and thrashed on the concrete like a freshly landed flounder. Before I could get to my cuffs something black darted into my field of vision, followed by a flash of light and an almighty crack.

It took me a fraction of a second to realize that Swanson had shot the perp in the back of his head, not a foot from my face. In the remaining part of that second, Swanson put a second bullet into the bad guy's brain.

On the positive side, most of the perp's gray matter and skull fragments ejected forwards, away from me. Only a light red mist blew into my face. On the negative side, I was instantly deaf and blind.

I jumped off my human surfboard, wiped my eyes, drew my gun and scanned for threats. I looked down and saw Officer Swanson cuffing the virtually faceless dead guy.

I remember wondering whether to add "resisting arrest" to the official report, and an EMT shouting at me like a Brit trying to speak English to a French waiter, telling me that the hellacious ringing in my ears might or might not go away. Other that that, the immediate aftermath was something of a blur.

When I regained my wits, I found myself sheltering from the biting wind and freezing rain behind an oak tree, wrapped in a space blanket, watching the police and media circus from a distance.

Swanson was holding court with a bunch of officers, hyped-up on adrenaline and adulation. He pointed at the trash bin and retraced his steps, miming the sequence of events that led to a double homicide. Contaminating the scene.

I couldn't hear what Swanson was saying — or anyone else for that matter — but he was doing enough talking for the both of us. Until the rookie sashayed into the apartment, came stumbling back out and threw-up at the bottom of the stairs. An officer consoling Swanson looked over at me accusingly, as if I'd exposed Swanson to nauseating gore to teach him a lesson.

A couple of detectives herded the uniformed gaggle to one side, making room for late-to-the-game crime scene technicians. Deputy Chief Jack "Double D" Johnson separated himself from the group and waddled towards me.

"Double D" for Dunkin' Donuts. Don't get me wrong. I sympathize with people who've lost the battle of the bulge — sugar, carbs and crack are kissing cousins. But Johnson's obesity was a clear signal to the public that their local police didn't give a damn about professional standards. Not that it was a secret.

"Lieutenant," Johnson said, acknowledging my existence.

"Chief Johnson" I replied, hoping that would be the end of our little talk.

"I'm taking my kid to the new *Star Wars* movie tonight," Johnson said.

At first I thought he was testing me; the conversational equivalent of holding a few fingers in front of someone who'd been hit in the head, asking them to count digits. I reminded myself that the Deputy Chief Johnson cared less about my mental health than his friends' parking tickets. As in removing evidence of their existence.

"The Jedi are the bad guys," I said.

Johnson looked at me as if I'd summarized a lecture on nuclear particle physics.

"The Jedi knights are a religious cult fighting to restore a monarchy," I explained. "How much of a reactionary do you have to be to root for them?"

"Junior's a smart kid," Johnson said defensively.

"Chip off the old block," I said pleasantly.

Normally, a verbal exchange with Johnson led to an expletive-filled tirade, complete with threats of suspension, demotion, a pay cut and a beat down. This time the Deputy Chief stopped dead in his tracks and smiled — a more frightening reaction than his spittle-ejecting tantrums.

"What do you know about what happened here?" he asked slowly.

"Nothing," I said. "We were told to park and look out for trouble."

"Witness protection," Johnson said, as much to himself as me. "Then what?"

"The suspect came out of his shit hole holding a head like a handbag, dumped it in the trash and went home to watch *High School Girls in Trouble*. I called for backup and moved in to arrest him. My rookie shot him in the head. Double tap."

"He made a move," Johnson said, somehow forgetting to make the words sound like a question.

"Don't they all?" I said, pausing to honor all the poor bastards who dared threaten a Providence police officer.

Johnson shrugged his shoulders and looked around, as if the answer to my question was hiding behind a tree.

"Hey Chief, just out of curiosity, which one of the dead guys was our witness?"

Johnson snorted like a bull who suddenly realizes the guy in the funny hat carrying the sharp pointy things is not his friend. He looked across the street, gathering his thoughts.

"The one your partner shot," he said. "Unfortunately," he added without a trace of regret.

I followed Double D's gaze to the house. Chief Lamar, the boss of bosses, stood in front of the crime scene tape surrounding the perp's porch, bathed in the harsh glow of police lights. He looked straight at us.

"He wants to talk to you," Johnson said, assuming I was both stupid and blind.

I nodded my thanks and crossed the street. Providence's top cop stood a good 6'5"; the Chief towered over all but professional basketball players. His uniform was always squared away, his ramrod posture never less than dress parade ready.

"Chief," I said, nodding at Lamar, offering the same respect I lavished on meth dealers.

"Canali right?"

Chief Lamar had a photographic memory. He remembered names, faces, personal histories, winning lottery ticket numbers, the batting statistics for the Boston Red Sox and anything anyone ever emailed, texted or told him. The Chief's memory was so good he pretended to forget names so he could seem vaguely human.

"Yes Chief," I replied. "A lowly Lieutenant on his way to retirement."

"You OK?" he asked, noting the blood stains on my uniform.

"Sure, I'm fine. We got lucky today."

The Chief stepped forward, inches from my face. His shark eyes looked down into my baby blues. Armani Code cologne assaulted my nostrils. I knew it was only a matter of time before Lamar poked me in the chest.

"Shallow men believe in luck," Lamar pronounced, saying the words with Charlton-Heston-as-Moses-like solemnity. "Strong men believe in cause and effect."

I was impressed. The Chief dissed me quoting Ralph Waldo Emerson.

"To be yourself in a world that's constantly trying to make you something else is the greatest accomplishment," I replied, matching him Waldo for Waldo.

Chief Lamar flashed a magnificent, entirely fake smile. He clapped my right shoulder with his hand — a move that resembled a friendly gesture like a rabid dog resembles a family pet.

"So Canali . . ." he began, trying to inject some suspense into the proceedings.

"So Chief."

"Congratulations," Lamar said, releasing me from bondage. "You're our new SWAT team negotiator."

"Thanks," I said, forgetting to fall to my knees and kiss his shiny shoes. "What happened to the old one?" I added, expecting to hear something about an officer retiring in the face of a criminal indictment.

"The guys trade-off."

The Chief shrugged, unfazed by the inadvisability of asking random officers to try to talk hostage takers out of shooting people.

"Well there goes my dream of being the head of parking enforcement. Wait. Don't you have to *listen* to people to be a negotiator?"

"Oh you listen alright," the Chief said, shaking his head condescendingly. "You just don't like what you hear."

"You got me there Chief," I admitted.

"Give your statement tomorrow," Lamar instructed, "then take a few days off. I'm sending you to the FBI for training, then Atlanta to see their SWAT team negotiator do his thing."

"The City Too Busy to Hate."

"That was before they met *you*," the Chief said, delivering the anticipated chest poke.

Lamar winked at me. I tried to make my grimace look like a smile as the Chief headed off to debrief his coronary-courting second-in-command. Not seeing anyone interested in interviewing a material witness to two homicides, I looked for the squad car where I'd left it, parked in front of a U-Haul. Both vehicles were gone.

Under union rules, I had a day to "gather my thoughts" before submitting my report or participating in an official interview. Not knowing what else to do, I called Mia.

"*Caro*," she said, her musical Italian accent having its usual rejuvenating effect.

"You heard about the shooting?" I asked.

"The *decapitazione*? You were there?"

"I was there. And now I'd like to be somewhere else."

"With me."

"I'll send my location to your phone."

"I may be a few minutes," she said, unsurprisingly. "Don't lose your head."

Funny girl, Mia.

Chapter Two

"Hi honey, how was your day?"

Mia asked the question in her best imitation American accent. For an Italian immigrant raised by her grandmother in a small Sicilian village, it wasn't bad.

I should have answered with some witty banter. I was too tired. So I ignored the question and punched-up Albinoni's *Adagio in G Minor* on the Bentley's stereo. A silent motor gradually reclined my seat; it was like nestling into a well-worn baseball glove. I closed my eyes, let the classical music swell around me and surrendered to the chair's warm embrace. I was out in seconds.

"So dear, how was your day?" Mia said again, American-style, easing me back to consciousness.

"Awesome," I said yawning. "Best day ever."

"*Dolor comunicato è subito scemato,*" the twenty-eight-year-old real estate agent said.

"Wait. I got this. *Subito* means fast right?"

"A problem shared is in half," Mia said with characteristic impatience.

"Hey Oprah, can we talk about this later?" I asked, returning the chair to its original, upright and locked position.

Mia's jet black hair framed angular features, flawless skin and dark eyes. Despite the fact that her beaver fur jacket was closed — the hot-blooded Italian kept her car at Arctic temperatures — she could no more hide her perfect figure than I could hide my distress at the bright red marks on the wrists holding the hand-stitched steering wheel. Mia saw me looking. Her jaw set. Her eyes focused down the road.

"How was *your* day," I asked.

"How do you say it in English?" she asked. "The heart wants what the heart wants."

Mia said the words so fervently I expected her to make the sign of the cross. Instead, the barest hint of a smile crawled across her ruby red lips. I couldn't tell if she was admitting weakness or remembering the activities that had left their mark.

"So your heart wants someone to tie you to a bed, call you a whore and whip you," I said.

"Yes. And since you don't do it, somebody else does."

"What are friends for?"

Mia paused, gathering her thoughts. It was like watching a line of thunderstorms rolling across the Bay.

"*Who are you to judge me?*" Mia demanded, slamming her right hand onto the steering wheel. "I don't remember *you* being a *gentile amante*, You want to see the bruises? I'm happy to pull you over and show them to me."

"You. Show them to you. Mia —"

"Your last girlfriend, how old was she? You cradle robber!" she spat.

"She was legal," I said defensively.

"*Testa di cazzo!*" she yelled. "You think you're better than anybody."

"Mia, I hate to play the sympathy card," I said, playing the sympathy card. "I just watched my partner cap a guy who played basketball with a severed head. Can we talk about house prices or something?"

Mia nodded and bit her lower lip, hard. The expression on her face had nothing to do with guilt, embarrassment or anger. It was a look of steely-eyed determination. I'd first seen "the look" about a year before, when my default rookie and I rolled-up on a run-down Victorian pile just below Thayer Street.

Officer Jefferson Jackson Brown Jr. and I were responding to a code 273D, domestic violence. It was a perfect spring morning. We'd lowered the cruiser's windows, airing out the ammonia masking the stench of alcohol, vomit, piss and fear; replacing it with the bright sharp smell of nature renewed.

I saw Mia from a distance, leaning against the Bentley's burgundy hood, her arms crossed, motionless. The closer we got, the more beautiful she became, moving straight from drop dead gorgeous to completely irresistible. As we approached and parked, Mia's face remained impassive. On closer inspection she looked . . . dangerous.

"He who dares not grasp the thorn should never crave the rose," I declared.

Officer Brown's raised eyebrow revealed his interpretation of the Charlotte Brontë quote: Officer Canali wanted to screw the lady in the black skirt. Which was fair enough.

Mia sized us up as we made our way to her perch. Her dark eyes revealed *niente*. When we were close enough for conversation, she remained silent, simply nodding towards the house.

Officer Brown gazed at the elegant mini-mansion like it was the Bates Motel. To his credit, he made a move towards the door — until he saw that

I was in no hurry. The ex-footballer looked for something to lean against that wouldn't crumple under his weight. He settled for an enormous red oak pushing up bits of pavement surrounding its base.

"Who's in there?" I asked, showing the young lady I was capable of speech and at least some measure of rational thinking.

"Who you think?" she said in a lilting Italian accent. "Quasimodo?"

"Now that's not very helpful Miss . . .?"

"Charles and Elaine Goodrich are in the house," Mia said, ignoring my question. "Recently divorced."

"Goodrich," Officer Brown repeated with a hearty laugh.

Mia's dark eyes flicked over to Jr., clocking him for the oversized idiot he was. She returned her gaze to me, checking to see if she'd called-in a pair of morons.

"And you are . . . ?" I asked, adding a little cop juice.

Mia looked at me and smiled. And there it was: the look of pure unadulterated "don't fuck with me but I dare you to try."

"Mia Sporcatello," she announced.

"So, Ms. Sporcatello," I said, as if I didn't recognize the name. "What's going on? Inside the house."

"Mr. and Mrs. Goodrich are not agreeing on the price of this property to sell."

As if on cue, we heard the sound of glass breaking, shouting, swearing and screaming. Officer Brown pushed off the tree.

"Any weapons involved?" I asked, holding up a hand to signal my partner that I hadn't finished interviewing the witness.

Mia rolled her eyes and shook her head. Clearly, she considered the Goodrichs' domestic spat amateur hour.

"I'd appreciate it if you didn't arrest anyone," Mia said. "I have someone to see the house in half an hour."

I'd like to say I'm above compromising my sworn duty for personal gain. I'd also like to say I'm hung like a horse. But I'd learned that saying something doesn't make it true — even if someone else believes it.

"Dinner?" I asked.

Mia smiled. It was like the sun coming out from behind a cloud at a children's party.

"*Si*," she agreed. "*If* you take care of this business."

I did, calming the Goodrichs, negotiating a cessation of hostilities and somehow neglecting to arrest anyone for assault.

That night, Mia and I ate at Figidini, a small Italian restaurant serving next level wood fired pizza. I struggled to maintain control over the pie, not wanting to look *imbranato*. Clumsy.

How *could* I have kept it together? Mia's racehorse-sleek figure and coal-black eyes had me tongue tied and clumsy. I felt like I'd been sucked into a romantic comedy; I was the nerdy guy who somehow snagged a date with a sexy girl who wanted to be valued for her intelligence.

Mia had plenty of that; our conversation ranged from the dangers of socialism to Amazon's catastrophic effect on main street America to

Ferrari's chances of regaining F1 glory. I can't say I was surprised by Mia's intellect. She was, after all, the daughter of Leo Sporcatello, the head of Rhode Island's resurgent mafia.

Sporcatello was known for his iron discipline and criminal cunning. "*La volpe argentata*" — The Silver Fox — hadn't been issued as much as a speeding ticket during his bloody rise to power. If Mia was half as clever as her father, she was twice as clever as me.

As we ate, drank and flirted, my guard slowly went down. By the time our spoons danced around each other above *stracciatella gelato*, it felt like we'd been lovers for years. Mia's mafia connection remained the elephant in the room — until she let it slip that "*babbo* owns three restaurants."

"Well it *is* a cash business," I said, without thinking.

Mia stared at me. I stared at her. I'm not sure who smiled first, but the next thing I knew we were both grinning like idiots, laughing at the world that had somehow put us together. Knowing that it wouldn't let us separate that easily, if at all. I broke eye contact first, looking down at the tomato sauce stain on my dress shirt.

"*Non ti preoccupare,*" Mia said, placing put her hand over mine. "You won't be wearing that long."

"Check?"

Sex with Mia was unlike anything I'd ever experienced: raw, savage, animal, desperate. At the end of it, two lamps were smashed, Mia's dress was in shreds and I had three new bookmarks in my browser.

So Mia was right that night in the car after Swanson shot the decapitator: I was on shaky ground criticizing her need for pain. Our sex sessions didn't qualify as "proper" S&M but they weren't exactly peace conferences. We both emerged from bumping uglies bruised and battered, one way or another.

Even so, I wasn't in the mood for a dressing down on the same day I'd seen a severed head tossed in the garbage and had my face splattered with the insides of a man's skull.

"What did they say on the news?" I asked.

"Hero cop shoots butcher killer," Mia said, flashing the Bentley's brights at a Volvo that dared block her triple-digit progress.

"That would be Officer Swanson," I clarified.

"They didn't use your name," Mia said, blasting past the cowed Volvo.

"It's just as well they kept me out of it," I said, peering out the Bentley's rain-streaked double-glazed window. "Where are we?"

"Getting lost in Rhode Island is like getting lost to your bathroom," Mia said. "What you are trying to say is 'where are we going?' We are going out to dinner, *naturalmente*."

"Mia. *Tigre*. I've got *blood* on my uniform."

"A badge of honor," she said with a laugh so infectious it put the CDC on alert. "There are some new clothes on the back."

I retrieved the bag from the back seat and extracted a pair of charcoal grey wool pants, a black polo shirt and a dark blue cashmere sweater.

"*Ermenegildo Zegna, Cara*, you spoil me."

Mia watched me out of the corner of her eye as I exchanged my uniform for the new threads, arranging my gear on the back seat. She glanced over at the finished product and smiled.

"*Perfecto!*"

"Until I have to explain it to Internal Affairs."

"Internal affairs," Mia repeated, trying out the words. "Aren't they all?"

Cosseted in luxurious fabrics, listening to Mozart oozing out of the German sedan's Bang & Olufsen speakers, I felt the day's tension ease. We'd soon be warm and cozy, watching the sun setting over Sakonnet River, a world away from the bloodshed in North Providence.

After a comfortable silence, we pulled off the highway and made our way to the road winding its way down to the waterside restaurant.

The maître d' was genuinely pleased to see us. Same for the gentleman wearing a diamond-encrusted Rolex at a table near the door — until his attention to my date earned him a swift kick from his dining companion. We settled into a table by the window. Our waiter introduced himself, handed us menus and promised his undying servitude.

As Mark popped the cork on a hundred-dollar bottle of Heitz Cellar Cabernet Sauvignon, Mia unleashed her full seductive repertoire: smiles, hair manipulation, eyebrow work, seemingly random cleavage displays and take-me-right-now-right-here body posture. I sat back, sipped the wine and enjoyed the show.

Every now and then I looked out at the river. The lights from the houses across the water sparkled in the dark. Mia's beauty, the wine, the gentle clinking of glasses, the low murmuring of surrounding diners; it all had a soporific effect, distancing me from the images of bloodshed and death that kept running through my head.

I may have been comfortably numb, but I was also famished. I demolished my beet *carpaccio* as Mia waited for her apple cider-brined chicken.

"You should have ordered oysters," Mia said, her eyes sparkling in their own special way.

"Oysters make you love longer, clams make you love stronger," I said, popping an orange segment laced with sherry vinaigrette into my mouth.

"Then you should have both," she said, a sly smile igniting my imagination.

When our main courses arrived — Mia's chicken with sweet potatoes, goat cheese gratin, swiss chard and red-eye gravy; my medium rib eye with mushroom demi glaze — the conversation turned to the day's events. Mia wanted all the gory details, right down to how much blood dripped off the disconnected head.

"*Macabro!*" Mia said. "How do you say? Ugly. Why were you doing there?"

"The guy in the house was a witness," I revealed, taking a break from my steak. "We were sent to keep an eye on him."

"What case?" Mia asked, reaching across to carve herself a piece of my dead cow. "Why did this *matto* cut off the other man's head? Why didn't he just shoot him and dump him in the swamp," she asked, ever the practical mob boss' daughter.

"Estuary," I corrected. "It was either complete craziness, a personal beef or someone taking care of business."

"So you're not going to tell me," Mia said, putting down her silverware, crossing her arms and pretend pouting.

"There's nothing to tell," I said.

Mia picked up her wine glass and contemplated me carefully. I had no idea what she was thinking. I hoped it was something carnal, but I suspected she knew more about the killing than she'd say.

"You need a break Gianni," Mia said, changing the subject. "You should take some time away."

"I've got a week off courtesy Chief Sociopath. You want to go up to the Cape? It's bleak but beautiful this time of year. I know a little place . . ."

"*Si,*" she said, with an 'I bet you do' smile.

"I forgot to tell you," I said. "I've got a new job. SWAT team negotiator."

"Doing what?"

"High-risk apprehensions. Taking out terrorists, busting down some crack head's door and shooting his dog, that sort of thing."

"I know what SWAT is," Mia said looking at me like I had pin lice in my eyebrows. "What do *you* do?"

"I convince the bad guy not to shoot anyone. Or anyone *else*, as the case may be."

"*I* negotiate," Mia reminded me proudly, not-so-patiently inviting me to ask her more.

"And you're damn good at it," I said. "What's your secret?"

"To know their *punto di riserve*. In English?"

"Reservation point."

"It's the point beyond who someone will not go in a negotiation."

"Which," I corrected. "Beyond which."

"Say a seller won't take less than two-hundred-thousand dollars for her house. That's their reservation point. The buyer? He won't pay more than one-hundred-and eighty thousand dollars. That's *their* reservation point."

"A twenty thousand dollar spread."

"Someone has to change their reservation point," she said, tilting her head slightly.

"Or?"

"Or nothing," Mia answered, once again staring at me as if I was an idiot.

"Different stakes," I said defensively. "Let's say a hostage taker wants to escape. What if that's their reservation point and they won't budge?"

"Then he's going to die," Mia said with a casual shrug. "Why you do this job Gianni?"

"*Someone* has to."

"And someone has to clean toilets," she said, holding up her empty glass for a refill.

"As far as I can tell, it's more like being a therapist with a bunch of guys with rifles standing by in case the patient doesn't want to change."

Mia and I laughed at the truth of my statement.

"After that job is finished, what?" she asked, looking down at the chicken bones neatly gathered on her plate.

I was taken aback by her question. I didn't talk about Mia's past or her father and she didn't talk about my future. Our future? That too. Mia saw my face and looked away, knowing she'd crossed the line.

"Are you looking at those murders?" she asked.

I paused. An Italian expression popped into my head: *tutta la strada porta a Roma*. All roads lead to Rome.

I had to assume that anything I said to Mia would reach her father. Leo Sporcatello was involved in just about everything nasty that happened in the Ocean State. He wouldn't be happy about a rogue cop — his daughter's boyfriend no less — poking his less-than-perfect nose into a high profile murder case.

I reached across the table, placed a hand on Mia's chin and gently tilted her head up.

"I'm not going to do anything more than look into your eyes as we make love."

"You're so old-fashioned," Mia teased, aligning her silverware on her plate. "Why do you think we will be facing each other?"

"I know this city," I said, watching the waiter evacuate our dishes. "People who pull up rocks end up dead."

"And I know you," Mia said accepting a small leather-bound desert menu. "You pull up rocks."

I held up my hands, pretending I was the kind of cop who was happy to mind his own business

Mia indulged her sweet tooth with a scoop of blackberry gelato with crushed peppermint. I ordered a double espresso, tanking up on caffeine for the night's activities, knowing Mia would insist I share her desert.

The following silence was uncomfortable. We both realized that looking into the *"macabro"* murder would put me on a collision course with Mia's father. It was only a matter of time before Leo Sporcatello and I butted heads.

I wondered what would happen. To me. To her. To us. One thing for sure: it wasn't going to be pretty.

Chapter Three

For a city cop, training with the FBI is like a little league baseball player practicing with the New York Yankees. Or so the FBI would have you believe.

FBI agents are sharper than a pimp's threads. But they're are also the worst kind of assholes: the kind who think they're the smartest guys in the room. *Any* room. Agents operated under the assumption that there was the Bureau's way of doing things and then there was . . . nothing. Well, nothing worth discussing.

Not that they wanted to have a discussion. Every FBI agent I met walked like they had a pole up their ass. They spoke in clipped tones, like a radio operator calling in an airstrike. They didn't talk *with* their students; they talked *at* us. Sure our trainers joked around. A couple even drank adult beverages. But I saw nothing to contradict my theory that the FBI is an off-shoot of the Mormon Church.

Agent Lacroix was our Bishop. The blond-haired thirty-year-old wasn't the kind of woman that men imagine naked. She was the kind of woman who'd be entirely comfortable naked, no matter what she looked like. Or who was looking.

Confidence. Gets me every time. Even when it waltzes over the border into arrogance. Agent Lacroix treated her students like fifth graders. She started day three of SWAT Negotiations for Dummies with a recap.

"What are the five steps of hostage negotiation?" Agent Lacroix asked.

My classmates — ten officers from around the country — knew the answer. They said nothing, intimidated by Agent Lacroix's comprehensive knowledge of tactics, complete mastery of the law and sky blue eyes.

"Number one," Agent Lacroix began. "Active listening. Listen to the suspect's side. Let them *know* you're listening. Number two, empathy. Understand where they're coming from and how they feel. Three, rapport. Empathy is what you feel. Rapport is when they feel it back. That's when they start to trust you."

"Influence," she continued. "Once the suspect trusts you, you've earned the right to help solve their problem. To get them to commit to a course of action. And finally," she said, like a dolphin trainer tossing a frozen fish to an obedient mammal, "Behavioral change. They act. And maybe come out with their hands up."

The class laughed dutifully. I considered putting both hands up, surrender-style. I settled for raising one.

"Yes Officer Canali," Lacroix said. "I'm listening."

More laughter.

"My father says people are motivated by two things: bribes and threats. How does that fit your model?"

"We call them incentives and disincentives," Agent Lacroix replied, her condescending tone reflecting the "fact" that the FBI had thought of everything long before we'd stepped foot on Quantico's sacred ground. "We encourage you to use incentives. Disincentives, threats as you call them, tend to reduce rapport."

"So you're saying I shouldn't tell the bad guy we're going to blow his brains out if he doesn't give up."

One of my classmates stifled a laugh.

"Absolutely not," Lacriox corrected. "Threats of violence destabilize a hostage taker."

"You mean make a crazy bastard crazier," I said.

Agent Lacroix glanced at her fellow instructors, making sure they'd recognized the Neanderthal in their midst. She turned her attention back to me, to see if I was jerking her chain. Once Lacroix concluded I wasn't playing her, once she figured I wouldn't crack under her silent interrogation, she blessed me with a "something like that" smile and moved on.

The rest of the morning's instruction featured videos of hostage negotiations, enlivened by examples where the process went badly wrong, graphic death resulting. After watching several episodes of *Hostage Takers Gone Wild*, we completed a multiple choice test designed to identify students too dense to realize that negotiators are a bad guy's best friend.

It was multiple choice, of course, with at least one completely ridiculous answer per question. I wondered if the Feds would certify anyone stupid, illiterate or uneducated enough to believe "empathy creates anxiety and lowers the chances of a successful resolution."

After handing in our papers, we retired to the conference room to feast on a selection of cardboard sandwiches. From there, we put on much appreciated FBI-branded winter jackets and headed for the Fibbies' fake town.

"We built Hogan's Alley during the Reagan administration," Agent Lacroix informed our little group of wannabe negotiators. The FBI's mock main street may have built in the late '80s but it was straight out of the mid-'50s. It was small town America, complete with bank, post office, drug store and dry cleaners.

The Mobile Command Center sat in an open field across from the Bank of Hogan. Out in the real world, the field would've been home to a used car lot. Only one vehicle occupied the space in Hogan's Alley and there was nothing "used" about it. The 10-wheeled blue-and-silver Mobile Command Center gleamed in the gloom, bristling with antennas and satellite dishes. It projected power with an enormous FBI logo and huge slide outs, emitting the kind of low-pitched hum sci fi films use to signal the audience that space is really, really big.

Entering the belly of the beast I wondered if the FBI loaned the vehicle to TV networks for football games; the interior was lousy with monitors, radios, telephones, computers and white boards.

"Follow me," Agent Lacroix directed, as if we'd bolt from the blissful warmth.

She led us through a security door into the "crisis room." We arranged ourselves around a mahogany conference table.

"We'll do this in shifts," Agent Lacroix instructed, hydrating from one of the plastic bottles gathered on the table. "Two at a time. We'll switch team members in the middle of their shift, then switch teams. Monitor what's happening in the control room and the crime scene from here. You'll find pads and pens in the cupboard. Make a note of what your brother and sister officers do wrong *and* what they do right."

A red-faced cop from the wilds of Nebraska handed out the writing materials.

"All you need to know at this point: there's a hostage situation at the Bank of Hogan. Canali and Stevens, you're up."

Officer Stevens was short, comfortably padded and completely forgettable; the kind of guy you'd never notice in a crowd of people. Or anywhere else.

The towheaded Michigander was also the youngest member of our class. From my forty-two-year-old perspective, he didn't look old enough to buy a shotgun, never mind talk a hostage taker into surrendering.

Stevens and I arranged ourselves at the Command Center's center console, donning headsets and getting comfortable in our chairs. The images coming from the bank were crystal clear; a faded poster promised 7.5 percent interest on a new savings account.

The pretend perp was in his mid-thirties, a scrawny white guy with a Hitlerian mustache and a cheap suit. He moved back and forth in front of the banking counter like a caged animal. The actor held a vintage flip phone in his right hand, a large revolver in his left. A row of five people sat on the floor behind the gunman with their backs to the counter: two black males, two white males and one white female. They didn't look like FBI agents but they sure looked bored.

As bank robbers don't usually wear suits, I guessed we were looking at workplace violence rather than a bank robbery gone bad. I was itching to find out. Officer Stevens was busy following the FBI playbook, starting with active listening.

"My name is Officer Stevens," the trainee said in the same tone I used to talk to kindergarteners about road safely. "I'm here to listen to what you have to say. What's your name?"

"Grayson," the hostage taker replied. "And I've got something to say."

"Go ahead Grayson, I'm listening."

"I'm sick to fucking death of being the bad guy."

"I don't think you're the bad guy," Stevens assured him. "But I understand how you feel. A lot of people feel that way about cops. They think *we're* the bad guys."

Stevens looked at Agent Lacroix for approval. She kept her eyes firmly fixed on the monitor.

"Stop with the empathy crap," Grayson snapped, scratching his head with his free hand. "I'm sick to fucking death of *playing* the bad guy. You know, *pretending*."

The five "hostages" suddenly paid attention to their "captor." Agent Lacroix didn't move a muscle, but she knew something was wrong. Stevens was oblivious.

"You don't have to pretend," he said soothingly, leaning towards the microphone. "You can tell me the truth. I'm here to help."

"The truth is you all think you're better than me. Well you're *not*."

Grayson walked up to the woman, pointed the gun at her chest and pulled the trigger. Her body jumped from the impact.

"Holy shit that looks realistic," Stevens said.

The male actors scrambled away from the gunman. In their hurry to flee, a couple of actors literally tripped over themselves, sprawling onto the linoleum floor. Grayson swung his gun around and fired a second shot, hitting a black man crabbing backwards on the tile.

An actor rushed Grayson. The shooter saw him coming and fired two shots, point blank. The man's head snapped backwards. His body dropped to the floor. As the bloodbath unfolded, Lacroix shoved Officer Stevens out of the way and pressed a button on the control panel.

"10-33! We have an active shooter at the Bank of Hogan. *This is not a drill.* I repeat, *this is not an drill.* We have an active shooter at the Bank of Hogan."

I could hear shouting and swearing coming from the conference room, mixed with the sound of chairs being pushed aside.

"Don't move!" Grayson shouted at the surviving actors, training his gun on each in turn.

Four shots from a six-shooter. Two left, unless "Grayson" reloaded.

"We have a *situation!*" Lacroix shouted at an unseen listener.

The comms link to the bank must have been open. Grayson cocked his head and turned to the camera.

"You call *this* a situation? You ain't seen *nothin'* yet."

Grayson lowered the flip phone and started punching numbers. I dove for the floor.

It's hard to describe what happened next, even though I see flashes of it in my nightmares. The short answer? The Mobile Command Center blew up. The next thing I knew I was looking at my breath rising up into the cold air, a tiny jet of carbon dioxide disappearing into a slate grey sky. It was a beautiful sight. Proof positive that I was still alive.

I had no idea where I was or how I'd ended up on my back. Even though I'd anticipated the explosion, I'd forgotten everything since I'd popped my morning multi-vitamin. I turned my head sideways. I looked straight into Agent Lacroix's dead eyes. And then I blacked out . . .

When I was a little boy, maybe six or seven, Mother kicked me down a flight of stairs. I don't know what I did wrong — there was so much Mother hated about me. But I remember her Gucci stiletto almost piercing my back, and the feeling of falling.

It was a dark day. The light that normally streamed onto the staircase from the stained windows was muted. I remember seeing the multi-colored glass as I fell; the look of pity in Saint Benedict's face as I headed for oblivion.

I saw the stairs looming up below me: hard, wooden slats with barely blunted edges. I saw my own death. It didn't scare me. It felt . . . inevitable. The logical end of a childhood spent cowering from the woman supposed to nurture and protect me. The mother who'd suddenly and irrevocably passed final judgement on the son she didn't want.

The actual impact was more of a sound than anything else. An explosion not unlike the one at the FBI's training grounds. I guess I tucked my head at the last second, saving myself from a snapped neck. But there was no escaping the sheer brutality, the otherworldly immensity of the collision. Bones cracked. Limbs flew in all directions. I entered a world of pain.

When I stopped moving, I could barely breathe. The attempt to draw oxygen into my body caused at electric shock in my chest that made me try *not* to breathe. To wish I didn't have to.

A small stream of red flowed across the polished mahogany step in front of my one functional eye. I watched it slowly cascade over the edge and drip onto the flat surface below. I heard mother's shoes coming down the stairs. Click, click, click — the sharp, steady drumbeat of evil.

In my childlike mind I thought Mother was coming to finish the job. Instead, she scooped up my small body. Ignoring my screams, she carried me to the car. I was barely conscious, but I knew she would be furious about the blood staining her silk shirt.

"You clumsy little shit," Mother said as we drove to the hospital to meet Dr. Gilligan, the family physician who accepted mother's flippant explanations for my bruises and broken bones.

I leaned my head against the Cadillac's window, watching raindrops gather and slide down the glass. I wanted to cry, to let my tears roll down my cheeks, to feel warmth on my face. *Something* other than the daggers trying to tear me apart from the inside. I lived a lifetime of misery before someone lay me on a hospital gurney.

"Hello Johnny, my name is Juanita. We're going to take good care of you."

The sympathy in the nurse's voice broke the dam; sobs joined my screams. How could anyone care about me? I didn't deserve it. I deserved to die.

"He fell down the stairs," Mother pronounced.

Drugs flowed into my arm, a cold river of relief. The pain was still there in all its terrible glory, but it felt like it belonged to someone else. Someone who was still moaning, crying and shouting "no!" when a nurse or doctor moved a body part.

Physically, I healed in a few months, happy to use my casts and concussion to avoid math tests and gym. Psychologically, I was more traumatized by Mother and Father's shouting matches. But I never forgot the utter helplessness of my endless journey through empty space.

I like to think Mother's abuse helped me empathize with crime victims. Deep down, I had a wound that would never heal. A fissure in my soul ready to re-open, leaving me prone to bouts of depression and anger.

Yes, anger. *Burning* anger. Returning to consciousness in the Mobile Command Center's remains, my brain boiled with an insatiable desire to kill the man responsible for the death and destruction. It was the first time in my life I felt complete, unadulterated hatred. An emotion that pushed all rational thought aside and left me determined. Painless. Fearless.

If I'd been in my right mind I would have checked myself for injuries and attended to the wounded. Instead, I struggled to my feet and walked towards the bank, towards Grayson.

Grayson was standing by the window, watching me walk towards him. He looked backwards for a moment, making sure he wasn't about to be jumped, then turned again to face me.

"It's over," I called out, hoping he'd come out of the bank so I could beat him to death with me bare hands.

I was standing in the middle of the street, defenseless, deafened and shivering. The acrid smell of charred flesh behind me curled my nostrils.

"Come out *now*!" I yelled.

Grayson's head tilted back slightly as he snorted at the suggestion. Then his face went blank, all emotion draining away. He slowly raised the revolver and aimed it straight at me.

A 5.56 NATO bullet zipped past my shoulder, pierced the bank window and entered Grayson's cranium, ending his crime. Once second he was there, the next he was gone.

"Fuck," I swore, trying to think of something to do. "Fuck, fuck, *fuck*."

A few hours later, the FBI's lead agent on the case took my statement in an interrogation room normally used for training. When I was done, after I signed my affidavit, Agent Smith chewed me out in a deadly serious monotone.

Smith said I'd put myself in danger unnecessarily, risking my life *and* the lives of the remaining hostages. My actions had forced the sniper to shoot, eliminating a source of information on a potential criminal or terrorist conspiracy.

All good points, noted and logged. But I wish I'd paid more attention to the bullet that had saved my life, the one that appeared out of nowhere. And considered the fact that unexpected shooters are more likely a curse than a blessing. As the Brits say, it's the bus you *don't* see that kills you. Advice that might have saved more than a few lives and kept me from falling into a Sporcatello-shaped rabbit hole.

Chapter Four

Every Friday, Rhode Island's Foxy Lady offers customers "Legs & Eggs." The strip club's Motel 6-style breakfast buffet features shrink-wrapped bagels and rock hard scrambled eggs. Unless you have a taste for horse meat hamburgers and food fried in stale cooking oil, that's as good as it gets.

Atlanta's Cheetah III served-up perfectly prepared Southern-style comfort food: chicken fried steak, meatloaf, chili cheese dogs, BBQ ribs, you name it. Sure it'll kill you. But at least you'll die smacking your lips.

Which is how I came to be eating blackened lobster tail with cheesy grits and fried okra, watching a young woman gyrating to a song telling players to put their pinky rings up to the moon.

My host, Sergeant Moses Drake, was a big man, and not in a cuddly way. The head of the Georgia State Police Department's Crisis Negotiations Team and Army vet was a genuine hard ass, a far cry from blowhard cops like Swanson who tell unruly perps to "stop or I'll say stop again." It took me the better part of a week to figure out why Sergeant Drake seemed so familiar.

At the end of Jackie Gleason's career, the comedian played Sheriff Buford T. Justice. *Smokey and the Bandit's* redneck cop was a good old boy constantly aggravated by his idiot son. Sergeant Drake was Sheriff Justice, only a lot bigger and a lot blacker. The idiot son-in-law frustrating Drake? Everyone he worked with, including me. At least at first. Once Sergeant Drake discovered we both had English degrees and shared a love of Hunter S. Thompson's gonzo journalism, it was Drake and Canali vs. the rest of the world.

That night, Sergeant Drake divided his attention between twerking females, a rare steak and a baked potato almost as loaded as the drunken executives gathered around the table in front of us. But not quite.

"You like her?" Drake asked in a lazy southern drawl, pointing his serrated knife at a buxom blond dancer whose carpet didn't quite match her curtains.

"Is that a trick question?" I asked.

Drake smiled as if I'd yelled *"Hell yeah!,"* unaware that I wanted to yell *"Hell no!"*

Strip clubs are a bad idea, generally. It's like being a kid in a candy store where leaving with your money isn't an option and leaving without candy is a solid win. That said, Sergeant Drake's money was no good at the Cheetah III — except for tipping dancers. Which he did in small amounts, reluctantly.

While I doubted Drake was pulling down steak, bourbon and stripper money, I wasn't about to ask the burly cop how such a lousy tipper came to be such a big deal at the mid-town strip club. At least not until I'd finished my lobster.

"You shoulda seen this place back in the day," Drake said, pausing to admire a piece of blood red meat headed for oblivion. "GLOCK was flying police chiefs into town from all over the country. Now *that* was a party."

I'd heard about the Austrian pistol maker's law enforcement sales: the hookers, blow and free guns. As a Rhode Islander, I'd filed that one under "business as usual." My business in Atlanta: following Sergeant Drake around during his monthly stint with the Atlanta Police Department's SWAT team.

My detail consisted of paperwork, shooting the shit with the SWAT team, more paperwork, equipment inspection and more paperwork. The only person in any real danger was me: I was dying of boredom. And then we got a heads-up from the Stone Mountain Police.

A man called 911 complaining of heart trouble. Five firefighters entered a suburban ranch house, ready to save his life. The caller welcomed his saviors with an AR-15. He threatened to shoot the firefighters unless they restored his gas, electricity, cell and internet. He instructed the public servants to have a seat while he waited for it to happen.

A hostage escaped out the back door. As the SWAT team gathered, the hyperventilating first responder calmed down enough to provide a detailed description of the bad guy, his house and weapon. Ten minutes after we rolled into the formerly quiet suburban neighborhood, it was Sergeant Drake's turn.

The APD's command vehicle was a lot less plush than the FBI's and, I hoped, a lot less likely to explode. Drake donned a headset from and called one of the captured firefighters' cell phones. I put on headphones and listened in.

"I want it back on," the perp demanded. "My phone, my TV, my god damn toaster oven. All of it. You hear me? Everything. On. Now."

"You want your phone, internet and electricity back on," Sergeant Drake repeated, doing the empathy thing.

"The fucking bank foreclosed on me," the perp said, and hung up.

"He's uncommunicative," APD's SWAT Commander announced.

"We're just getting started," Drake objected.

Drake tried calling the perp every five minutes or so. The phone went straight to voice mail. An officer handed him the other firefighters' numbers. Same result.

The Commander prowled the vehicle. His team delivered intel from witnesses, neighbors, the bank that pulled the plug on the bad guy's loan, a cousin in Ohio, his former employer, officers stationed within sight of the house and so on. After twenty minutes, Drake grabbed a megaphone and headed for the door. Before he could leave, the phone rang.

"I worked hard all my life," the kidnapper declared. "I did everything I was supposed to. I even went to church. I am *not* a religious person whoever-the-fuck-you-are."

"My name is—" Drake began.

"I couldn't give a *fuck* what your name is. I told you what I want and I don't see *none* of it happening. You're pissing me off."

"You're angry."

"Where's *my* cell phone? These fucking firemen, *they've* all got cell phones. *And* a fucking salary. Benefits, job security, a home and I don't know *what* the fuck else. Cars. Yeah, I bet they all have nice cars too. What kind of car do you drive asshole?" the perp asked a hostage. "A Toyota? Bullshit. I bet you drive a Lexus. What's that? Shut your fucking mouth or I'm gonna shoot you while your buddies watch."

"It must be frustrating," Sergeant Drake said, his voice sinking deeper into his vocal range. "Banks aren't very helpful when a hard working man falls hard times. They make you feel like you'll never get back on your feet."

"That's right" the bad guy agreed, his voice dripping with hatred. "The banks couldn't give a shit about me or anyone else. They just want to squeeze folks until they're squeezed dry."

"What can we do to make this right?"

"We? *I* can't do nothin'. There's only one way out of this mess and we both know it."

The words sent a chill down my spine. I could almost hear the bad guy punching the "end" button as he hung up — an imaginary sound that did nothing to steady my nerves.

Time passed slowly. I finished a bottle of water, checked my phone for messages, browsed the Providence Police Department's Facebook and Twitter pages and looked around the vehicle. It was the calm before the storm.

A shot rang out. The Commander ordered his men in.

I winced at the concussive sound of a flash bang detonating in the distance. I pursed my lips when I heard gunfire. Drake watched me closely, aware I was toughing out a serious adrenaline dump.

"You OK?" he asked over frantic radio chatter.

"Fear and loathing in Stone Mountain Georgia," I replied.

"Officer down!" a voice shouted in my headphones as the gunfire stopped. "Perp down. Hostages secure. I repeat we have an officer down."

The gunshot triggering the assault turned out to be a negligent discharge by a SWAT team member. His bullet pierced a back wall and disappeared into the housing development. The perp opened fire on the team as they breached his back door, shooting an approaching officer's gun hand. His colleagues answered the ballistic insult by firing a few rounds into the perp's chest, ending the incident.

Sitting in the Cheetah III strip club's main room, swirling the ice in my drink, I wish things had ended differently. As cops like to say to people who refuse to follow their instructions, "play stupid games, win stupid prizes." Even so, if the SWAT officer had handled his weapon safely, the confrontation might have reached a peaceful resolution.

No such luck. I sympathized with Drake's desire to drink all of Atlanta's bourbon. Through no fault of his own, the Atlanta cop had failed to defuse a hostage taker. I dreaded to think there would be days like that for me. I took comfort in the simple fact that not every hostage negotiation ends with a bomb blast.

I dipped the last of my lobster tail in drawn butter and scanned my surroundings. The Cheetah III was decorated like a modern whorehouse: shiny surfaces, spot-lit bottles and heavy red curtains. It probably looked like a bus station when management turned on all the lights.

Drake and I polished off our food and sucked down a couple more bourbons. We retired to one of the strip club's VIP rooms. I speculated about what I'd see if I fired up a black light and rejected a lap dance from a gorgeous red-head. Not to be rude, I tendered a twenty. The dancer accepted the cash with a practiced smile and tucked it into her G-string; I swore I saw Andrew Jackson wink at me.

After the redhead gyrated to songs by boastful rappers and a silken-toned Lionel Richie, Sergeant Drake introduced me to the self-proclaimed community college student, his gentle tone betraying more than casual familiarity. I was "a brother officer from Providence Rhode Island." Her smile disappeared faster than my twenty.

"What's the matter Destiny?" Drake asked, a look of concern furrowing his brows.

The bare-breasted redhead burst into tears. She stood on the raised platform bawling her eyes out; looking less like a stripper, more like a little girl who'd lost her teddy bear. She brought her right hand to her face, trying to wipe away the mascara and tears marking her otherwise flawless complexion. Drake grabbed a handful of cocktail napkins and extended them to the distraught dancer.

"I'll be alright in a minute," she said, her sobs slowing, holding the orange napkins by her side. "Please don't tell anyone."

"How long have we known each other?" Drake asked.

"A week," Destiny said, her laugh restoring some measure of control over her crying.

"Six months, seven days and twelve seconds," Drake said grinning. "You want to sit down?"

"I can't stop," she said, choking on her words, glancing at the one of the cameras in the ceiling panels. "I gotta work."

"You ain't gonna get in no trouble for talking to Moses Drake," he assured her.

Destiny crumpled onto a nearby velvet couch. She was all but motionless, lost in memories.She made no effort to clean off the mascara running down her cheeks; the black streaks like roads leading back to her eyes, where the walls she'd built to protect herself came tumbling down. Whatever she was seeing in her mind's eye, it wasn't good.

Drake walked over and kneeled by Destiny's side. It was quite a sight: the enormous cop crouching next to the tiny stripper, as if he was about to propose. I hadn't seen it at first but I recognized in an instant, like my stomach remembers food when it's hungry: everyone needs love. Even a tough-talking son-of-a-bitch like Drake.

Destiny's lifeless hand disappeared into Drake's gigantic palm. He pushed a strand of wet hair away from her face.

"Tell me what's going on," he urged

She looked over, trying to get a measure of my character, to decide whether or not she should or even could open up to a stranger. A Northerner, no less. I nodded reassuringly — which did precisely nothing to remove the skepticism in her green eyes.

"Lieutenant Canali's one of the good guys," Drake said.

Destiny's eyes searched Drake's face, silently asking him if such a thing existed.

"Make yourself comfortable in the main bar," Drake suggested. "Destiny and I are gonna have a little talk."

Twenty-three minutes later, Drake appeared, worse for wear. His clothes seemed to hang heavy on his frame. The spring had gone out of his step, along with the mischievous light in his brown eyes.

"You look like you've seen a ghost," I said. "Everything alright?"

"I've texted you an address," he said. "Meet me there at two. There's something you need to know."

I went back to the hotel, showered and put on some clean clothes. My Uber driver cruised into a huge apartment farm just outside I-285. It took us a good five minutes to find the right building. As I climbed the stairs, an *Imagine Dragons* song filtered through the night told me I was a natural.

The apartment was a blend of man cave and love nest; a huge flat screen TV dominated a room carefully decorated with handmade soft furnishings. Destiny sat on a small couch next to a potted fern straining towards the window. The bookshelf on the other side was stacked with self-help books and flickering candles scenting the room with lavender.

I heard Drake shut the door behind me, turning what sounded like a dozen locks. Destiny gestured towards a chair opposite the couch. Drake sat next to her, dwarfing her small frame, making the couch sink to one side. He picked up a couple of cheap glasses and a bottle of Jim Beam from a bronze-topped end table.

"Destiny has a problem with your hometown," he said. "She needs your help."

"I'm listening," I said, sitting besides him, accepting a my drink.

"Destiny had a friend at the Cheetah. Marie Dupree. A kitchen worker from the Dominican Republic."

I heard the words "had' and "was" and prepared myself for a sad tale of loss, one of hundreds I'd seen and heard over many years.

"Marie had a daughter named Yanira back in the DR. Marie paid to have Yanira smuggled to her cousin in —"

"Rhode Island," I finished.

"Yanira was six," Destiny said, her voice flat.

"Marie's cousin," Drake continued, "the guy who was supposed to pick her up? Said the daughter never made it. The men had the kid and they wanted more money. So Destiny writes a check, clears out her savings, and Marie sends the money."

"Marie wanted to see her baby girl," Destiny said, tearfully.

"Yanira disappears," Drake said, leaning forwards. "The men stop answering the phone. They're gone too. Marie takes a bus up to Rhode Island to look for her kid. Next thing you know, *she* disappears. Destiny waits a couple of weeks, then heads north to find 'em. No trace. She decides to stop in on the Providence police, file a report."

"What did they do?" Destiny asked desperately.

"Destiny," Drake said, his voice wrapping around her like the blanket given to house fire victims. "You're safe."

"They raped me," Destiny said, leaning forward, gasping, the words choking in her throat. "Two of them."

I waited. We all waited.

"They should have killed me like they killed Yanira and Marie," Destiny decided, maybe for the first time. "They should have killed *me*."

Destiny collapsed back onto the sofa, spent, exhausted, inconsolable.

I thought about saying something to ease her pain. I knew what Destiny wanted to hear: I'd find out what had happened to her friend and her daughter. That I'd expose the Providence Police officers who'd raped her. I also knew my hometown didn't give up its secrets easily. And that revealing corruption isn't the same as ending it.

Even so, something inside me was deeply offended. Providence was bad enough on its own, for its own, for people who considered its rampant amorality and graft nothing more than background noise. The idea that the City sucked innocent lives into a black hole of crime from thousands of miles away made me want to right Destiny's wrong.

Yes but . . .

Watching Destiny's expression change from helplessness to bitterness, I had to acknowledge the truth: she didn't want justice or change. Like so many people I'd known throughout my life, maybe even all of them, she wanted revenge.

"So now you know," Drake said, later, holding open the door to my Uber, staring at me intently, waiting for a reply.

"So now I know," I said.

Drake nodded his massive head. His expression wasn't encouraging. It was the face of a man sending a soldier off to a battle both of them know will be bloody, with little to no chance of success. Which is pretty much how things turned out.

Chapter Five

I'm not a party animal, but I love a good get-together. My favorite: a shindig thrown by the whip-smart Rhode Island School of Design grad student who'd kept me entertained one long hot summer.

Mary Beth Rogers assembled a quirky cast of characters for her beach blanket bingo: classmates, artists, professors, a couple of well-known restauranteurs, a rabbi and his wife, a local fisherman, a professional motorcycle racer, several members of the Narragansett Indian tribe and a Providence Police officer.

We partied on a private beach, a few houses down from a pop star's Newport mansion. Dogs romping along the shore, kites flying in the salty breeze, swimmers body surfing, the sound of the ocean pounding the sand, the sun sinking into the sea, the smoke and smell of a New England clambake. Laughter. Dancing to reggae by the bonfire.

Mary Beth's supply of Hawaiian grass had something to do with the party's success. The Maui Wowee supercharged my libido, Mary Beth was more than obliging and I never laughed so hard in my life. It was one of those perfect days when all that matters is what's right in front of you.

As I stepped out of my sedan at an East Side fundraiser for "undocumented Americans," memories of that mid-summer romp came flooding back, thanks to the faint aroma of marijuana tickling my nostrils.

"Be careful with her," I warned the valet, surveying the parade of high priced vehicles across from the drop-off area.

The Gen Z kid glanced at my Honda and laughed. I gave him a serious look and a five dollar bill. Neither impressed him. But then I was out of uniform. I was wearing clothes Mia deemed suitable for a high end New England charity event: a charcoal grey suit, dark blue dress shirt, silk tie and slipper soft Bruno Maglis. Just to push the fashion envelope, Mia inserted a white pocket square.

I caught another whiff of weed in the frigid night air. Even if I were a hypocrite, even if I could have ID'ed the pot smoker in the dark, I wasn't going to bust someone for toking-up behind a bush on the legendary Herndon estate. It would have ruined the tone of the evening. And my shoes.

I entered the Spanish Revival-style main house through an enormous oak and wrought iron door and surrendered my coat to a cheerful twenty-something. I inhaled a heady mix of expensive perfume and spiced food, reminding me of Mia's last minute bailout and my empty stomach.

Party planners positioned pre-Colombian masks around the tiled foyer, adding a creepy vibe to the house's subdued splendor. Lest I make it more than four steps into the reception hall without a drink, a tuxedo-clad waiter confronted me with a silver tray of champagne. I leaned against a marble column and sipped bubbly from a crystal coupe — a glass modeled after a woman's breast. Helen of Troy? Marie Antoinette? Madame Pompadour? Someone sporty.

Small groups of bejeweled East Side matrons knocked back the yellowish orange beverage with practiced grace, lubricating themselves for the evening, swapping gossip under the not-so-watchful eyes of overfed, equally hard-drinking captains of commerce.

Mother was amongst them. Elizabeth Canali's regal bearing, Armani dress, single-stone diamond earrings, Tiffany pearl necklace, Cartier "crash" watch and Jimmy Choo shoes identified her as a well-heeled top tier socialite: a formidable force who knew everyone "worth knowing."

Mother was standing next to Chief Lamar, weighed down by his medal-heavy dress blues. The Chief didn't see me. Mother did. I raised my glass, toasting her existence, such as it was. Mother didn't react, not even blessing me with her trademark scowl. She stood there like a statue: a haunting and forbidding image of maternal power that sent a shiver down my spine.

It gradually dawned on me that Mother wasn't looking at me. I turned to see the victim of her attention. She was staring at Luke Herndon, the teenage first son of the Herndon clan. Dressed in an ill-fitting sports jacket and dark trousers, Luke was talking quietly to a pretty young thing, trying his best to look casual.

I wouldn't have felt a greater jolt of fear and panic if I'd been facing a firing squad. Deep in my bones, I knew what was going to happen.

Mother shifted her gaze to look straight at me. The contempt in her eyes was literally stunning; I was rooted to the spot. She returned her attention to Luke, then back to me, regarding me with undisguised disgust.

She knew.

The prospect of spending a boring evening watching once-percenters shell-out the equivalent of my monthly salary for luxury goods and services suddenly became a mad dash through an enormous minefield. I had to find Veronica Herndon Luke's mother, fast.

She was standing by the entrance to the ballroom, dressed in a black off-the-shoulder evening gown with a red sash and a sweetheart neckline. She'd pulled back her silky blond hair in a French knot, leaving a clear view of a dazzling diamond and ruby necklace.

Age had been kind to my high school sweetheart, the quintessential girl-next-door. Despite a few lines in her face, Veronica was the same girl I'd met in ninth grade: a kindred spirit who'd read my poetry, only laughing at the intentionally funny bits. The same beautiful woman who met me at a seaside motel one fateful summer afternoon when her husband Max was away on business.

Veronica didn't see me. She was busy greeting guests making their way into the ballroom, greasing the wheels for the charity auction with an appreciative smile.

"She's out of your league Johnny. Always has been."

Mother hovered over my shoulder, sharing my view of the procession.

"Mother," I said warily.

"And yet she spread her legs for you," Mother said. "Imagine that. Which you were just doing."

"*Mother . . .*"

"You should've told me," she said with less sympathy than a desk sergeant.

"Told you what?" I asked, stalling.

"Oh please," Mother said, waving her champagne glass dismissively. "I suppose I have to give you *some* credit for hiding him from me all this time."

"What?" I said, continuing to play dumb.

"Luke Herndon is your son."

I said nothing, draining my glass.

"He looks just like you did at that age," Mother said. "That's a shame, but there it is. You know when I knew? When I saw him staring at that girl's tits. All you Canalis are pigs."

"Listen to me," I said. "Fuck with me all you like. I'm used to it. But do *not* fuck with an innocent child."

"You should have thought of that before you stuck your dick in another man's wife."

"You're going to use this, aren't you? I don't know how, but you will."

"You should have been a detective. Or *something*. Anyway Johnny, I'm thinking I should groom my grandson," she teased. "Take him under my wing. A second chance if you will."

"Everything you touch turns to shit," I observed, praying she'd keep her mouth shut to protect her vaunted reputation.

"You should know," Mother said.

"Why do you hate me so much?" I asked.

"Don't be silly John," she cautioned. "I hate everyone."

A waiter replaced my empty glass with a fresh one. I watched Mother enter the line for the ballroom.

"Veronica, *darling*," she said flashing her most gracious smile, air kissing the hostess. "We simply *must* get together. We have *so much* to talk about. I just saw your son. Luke is it? I have to say he reminds me of someone. I'm not sure who."

Veronica caught on in a second, but didn't give Mother a moment's satisfaction. She held her smile firmly in place, then looked over Mother's shoulders and stared at me accusingly. Mother didn't even have to glance in my direction; she knew *exactly* what was happening.

As soon as Mother broke eye contact with Veronica, The Lady of the Manor cruise-missiled straight for me.

"*Holy shit Johnny,*" she half-whispered, enveloping me in Dolce & Gabbana Light Blue. "Your mother knows. How does she know? Did you tell her? How long has she known?"

"About two minutes," I replied, answering the easiest question.

"I'm amazed she hasn't told anyone," Veronica said, looking around at her guests as her color rose alarmingly.

"The night is young" I said, watching Mother exchange pleasantries with the wife of a prominent banker who'd narrowly avoided prison during the credit union mortgage scandal.

"Jesus Christ Johnny," Veronica said. "Jesus fucking Christ. What the hell are we going to do?"

"Someone's got to tell your husband. We can't keep this a secret any longer."

"*Fuck,*" Veronica swore. "Max is going to kill me."

"He's going to kill both of us. Or pay someone else to do it."

"That's my Johnny," Veronica said. "Always looking on the bright side of life."

"Who's going to tell him?" I asked.

"I'll do it. Break it to him as gently as possibly. You can be the bad cop."

"Nothing new there."

"Once more unto the breach, dear friends, once more."

Veronica grabbed my champagne, downed the bubbly in a single gulp, handed me the empty glass and headed for the ballroom. Not knowing what else to do, I entered the line at the bar, hoping a drink or three would tamp down the adrenaline coursing through my veins. As I waited my turn, I mentally rehearsed my conversation with Max Herndon. I couldn't think of a single way it would go well. I could think of a dozen ways it wouldn't.

"Heck of a party," a boozy voice said as a distant gavel came down on a spa day at the Boston Ritz.

"Well if it isn't Mark Mingle," I said more nastily than I'd intended. "Mingle by name, mingle by nature," I added, repeating his catchphrase.

I didn't expect to see the Porsche salesman to Rhode Island's rich and famous at the Herndon fundraiser. Mingle may have ditched his leather jacket and porcupine quill hairdo for a Brioni blazer and a buzz cut, but he was still a tradesman.

"I'm a married man," Mingle announced, pointing at a dark-skinned teenager sitting at a nearby table. "That's Roseline Mingle."

Mrs. Mingle's natural beauty was hidden by a thick layer of foundation. Blue-tinted eyelids supported enormous fake eyelashes. She'd poured her skinny, child-like body into a slinky dress, cut high at the leg and low at the neck. I'd seen shish kabob skewers shorter than her heels. Judging from her age, attire, makeup and bored attitude, I got the distinct feeling Mingle's new wife had something of a history.

"Why don't you introduce me to your bride?" I asked.

"Introduce yourself," Mingle replied, determined to keep his place in line.

"John Canali," I said, offering my hand to the teen as I slipped into the empty chair next to Mingle's better half.

"Roseline," she said tendering a hand adorned with French nails.

I couldn't quite place her accent. French? German? Polish? Something. Before I could ask the young lady to say "the rain in Spain falls mainly on the plain" Mingle handed me a bourbon on the rocks, having remembered, guessed or heard about my drinking habits. I got up from my chair and tried to ignore the cloying cloud of Cacharel surrounding the car salesman.

"So Johnny, how's it hanging?" Mingle enquired.

"Sir dresses left," I replied.

"Huh?"

"I'm good," I said, feeling anything but.

"I hear you're banging Mia Sporcatello," he said. "You're out-kicking your coverage there."

I laughed. It was true in so many ways.

"You ever pass geometry?" I countered.

"Oh, I'm real good with numbers now," he boasted.

"Here's one for you," I said. "Zero. The odds that I'll buy a car from you."

"The same odds that you could ever afford one."

He got me there. Not that I cared. I'd pulled over enough horrible people in expensive cars to know that wheels don't maketh the man. Or something like that.

I let Mingle get the last word, bid his wife *adieu, Auf Wiedersehen and do widzenia*, covering all the bases, and entered the ballroom. Not having paid $1000 for a place ringside seat, I slid into an abandoned seat near the back of the room. I positioned myself out of Mother's eye line, within sight of the evening's host and hostess.

Max Herndon was a short, barrel-chested man, dressed in a tux tailored to hide his bulk. He sat next to his wife, smiling at the MC's jokes, making sure his guests recognized the *real* Master of Ceremonies. Herndon consulted his Apple watch from time-to-time, as an industrialist with factories churning out cheap luggage at home and abroad.

Veronica sat next to him, a woman who'd add glamor and class to a New York City Met Gala, never mind a room full of swamp Yankees in a state whose golden age passed in the late 1800's. I could tell she was stressed. Maybe it was the way she couldn't focus on anything in particular, her eyes roving the room. Maybe it was her smile when Max looked over at her: an empty expression hiding inner turmoil.

Veronica knew I was watching her. I was about to bail, to step out of the line of fire, when the unctuous auctioneer offered the assembled throng a chance to bid on a cedar wood humidor filled with 75 Montecristo Linda 1935 Corona-sized cigars. "Legally imported," of course.

Bidding started at $1700 dollars. Herndon's hand shot up, triggering a wave of laughter from a crowd familiar with their host's habit. I raised my hand for $2000. The guests turned to see who dared challenge Max Herndon about anything, ever. I ignored Mother's stare and looked straight at Veronica. She regarded me with astonishment, then, as the bidding crested $2600, amusement. Max, not so much.

The price soared to $3500. I don't know why I decided to antagonize the man I'd wronged for so long. What point was I making? That I was as good as Max Herndon? Was I throwing down the gauntlet for the conflict to come? Trying to prove something to my mother? All of that and more, I suppose.

When the bidding suddenly stopped at $8000, when Max's arms-crossed posture told me he was done, suck on that government employee, I came to my senses. The silence in the room was deafening. I'd violated social norms, made an ass out of myself, been outwitted by Max Herndon and was on the hook I didn't have. I was seconds away from paying the piper some serious coin.

"Ten thousand dollars."

Veronica's bid arrived at the last possible moment, bringing a gasp from the audience, then cheers and clapping.

I shook my head, relieved and thankful. Max mimed getting his wallet out of his trousers, triggering a wave of laughter. Veronica's delighted smile wasn't for her husband, though. It was for me. A smile that took me back to high school.

Back in the day, one of my classmates drove a heavily modified Nissan. He raced his Z-car against anyone and everyone, all the time. He blew through lights, took corners at absurd speeds, did whatever it took to win. We all knew Dwight was going to die behind the wheel.

When that day arrived, he collided head-on with a Mack truck. Rumor had it Dwight hadn't slowed before meeting his maker. No skid marks. He *accelerated* to his doom.

That's how I felt that night. And it felt good.

Chapter Six

I'd been off Providence's mean streets for a couple of weeks. I'd been through a lot: a decapitated head rattling around a plastic garbage bin, the killer's cranium exploding next to my face, a bomb blast at the FBI that left four people dead and twice as many wounded and a red-headed dancer seeking revenge. Not to mention the possibility of an encounter with my son, who'd never met me.

In case I didn't know, Dr. Helen Kilroy told me I had a lot to "assimilate." Even so, the Police Department's designated shrink cleared me for duty after a 50-minute discussion in an interrogation room. Sorry, "therapeutic safe space" designed to make hardened cops spill their guts. I mean, "enable their emotional journey."

Our conversation focused on my lack of sleep, disorganized eating patterns, antagonistic relationship with fellow officers, hatred of authority and something called feelings. I somehow neglected to mention that I'd been "outed" as Luke's father, or the fact that I was doing the horizontal mambo with a mafia boss' daughter.

At some point, I steered the conversation towards Sigmund Freud. Dr. Kilroy let me ridicule the cocaine-sniffing father of psychoanalysis uninterrupted, until I heard myself talking about the Oedipus' occupational hazards and realized I sounded like a total nutcase.

The only good thing I can say about my chat with Dr. Kilroy: I liked the 50-something's fashion sense — I know a Hermès scarf when I see one — and the quote she'd put on her wall. "Life turns out best for people who make the best out of how life turns out."

According to Dr. Kilroy, life wasn't turning out well for Officer Swanson. My most recent partner had been off duty since he'd shot and killed the decapitator. Swanson was having difficulty "coming to terms with the emotional consequences of his actions."

"I don't want to violate patient confidentiality," Dr. Kilroy said, violating patient confidentiality. "But I'd appreciate it if you could stop by Officer Swanson's house. I'm worried he might do something rash."

I left Dr. Kilroy's office, thanking her for looking after my fragile mental health, promising to look in on Officer Swanson.

After calling in a 10-8 — officer in service — I spent the day corralling a couple of homeless people fighting over a bottle of rotgut, directing traffic around a fender bender, writing up a shoplifter at a Thayer Street boutique, hassling a fit woman with a handicapped sticker and cruising the city for trouble. I wasn't exactly fulfilling my desire to make the world a better place. But the routine gave me chance to analyze my situation and mull over the options. Make some calls. Do some digging.

I wanted to see Luke. Had Veronica told him I was his father? She'd gone radio silent. I suspected I was *persona non grata* amongst the Herndon clan. A fancy way of saying permanently unwelcome.

As my shift came to a close, the weather took a turn for the worse. An April Nor'Easter was barreling towards the Ocean State, promising fierce winds and six inches of snow. I wasn't looking forward to the late snowstorm or checking-up out on Officer Swanson. The brooding sky and dropping temperature did nothing to increase my enthusiasm.

I rolled up on a small single-family house in Elmwood: a vinyl-sided 1920s build with a bay window out front and a dormer on top. A short woman with gray hair and Swanson's facial features opened the door. She took a look at my uniform and moved aside deferentially. I introduced myself as her son's commanding officer. The house's sparse but tidy interior that told me money was in short supply, though cleaning products were not.

"Darren's out back," she said, leading the way to a sun room tacked onto the back of the property.

I was happy Mrs. Swanson used the rookie's first name; I'd been racking my brains trying to remember it. I was less happy with her hushed tone, affirming Dr. Kilroy's opinion that Swanson — Darren — was in a bad way.

The unshaven officer sat in a ratty plaid recliner dressed in a faded blue-and-gold sweatshirt emblazoned with his high school's mascot. Swanson was holding a football, staring at a flat screen TV at the other end of the room, the sound muted, distant. Empty vodka bottles flanked the chair.

Bruce Springsteen's song *Glory Days* played in my head. I took off my coat and looked for a window; the semi-sweet smell of sweat, booze and misery assaulted my nostrils.

"Officer Swanson," I said, hoping it wouldn't be long before I went nose-blind.

It took Swanson a second to get his bearings. A small smile crossed his youthful features — then disappeared.

"Lieutenant," he said, like I was a coach from his increasingly distant past. "What are you doing here?"

"I came to see you," I replied, clearing a space on the coffee table in front of his chair.

"I don't think I'm ready for duty," he said, continuing his habit of making piercing glimpses into the obvious.

"No rush Darren," I said sitting down next to a well-worn high school football program. "Take your time."

"What day is it?" Swanson asked, looking at his watch, a gigantic G-Shock I'd reprogrammed when he was in the station house shower.

"Tuesday," I answered, ignoring the confusion on his face. "We need to talk."

"I don't think that's a good idea," he said shaking his head. "I really don't."

"What's going on?"

Not getting a reply or a change in his expression, I pulled rank.

"Officer Swanson, I'm your commanding officer. Talk to me."

I could see Swanson struggle to say something. And then struggle *not* to say something.

"You know what's strange?" Swanson asked, finally.

"Tell me."

"How easy it was. I thought it would be a lot harder, you know? You ever shot anyone Lieutenant?"

"You know I have."

"How many?"

"In total or at one time?" I half-joked.

"Total."

"A few."

Swanson laughed abruptly.

"Did you know you were going to do it?" he asked. "Before you pulled the trigger?"

"Who knows? Everything happened pretty quick."

"I didn't know if I could do it. But I did it alright. I shot him twice. I shot him twice In the head. Oh my God . . ."

If crying is therapeutic, Swanson should've been cured; his sobs went on for an eternity. I thought about getting up and hugging him. I dismissed the idea almost as quickly as it occurred. Maybe it was my policy of keeping an emotional distance between myself and rookies to maintain my authority. Maybe it was something deeper.

"I had to do it," Swanson announced. "I didn't have a choice. *You* wouldn't have done it."

I couldn't tell if Swanson meant the remark as an accusation or a compliment.

"We all make mistakes Darren. But we get better with experience. Live and learn. That's about as good as it gets."

Swanson nodded, then looked around wildly, his right leg starting to bounce up and down.

"Hey Darren, I want to take you to Butler. They can help calm you down. Get some sleep. When was the last time you got some sleep?"

"It's been a while," Swanson admitted, looking out the window. "But I'm good Lieutenant. I swear."

"Are you thinking about killing yourself?" I asked as casually as possible.

"What? Why do you say that?"

"Dr. Kilroy is worried that you might accidentally shoot yourself while cleaning your gun."

"Is that what they tell the insurance company?"

"C'mon Darren," I urged, noting that he hadn't give me a yes or no on the suicide front. "Let's take a ride to Butler before the weather gets worse."

"It sure is starting to blow," he observed.

I stood up, hoping my movement would motivate the rookie.

"Put the ball down" I instructed, picking up my coat and gesturing towards the door. "Let's go,"

"No way Lieutenant," Swanson said, hugging the ball tight to his chest, visibly alarmed by the idea. "They'll think I'm gonna talk."

"You *need* to talk Darren."

Swanson laughed. In a flash, his expression turned from amusement to anger.

"I think it's time you left," Swanson growled. "Ma! Lieutenant Canali is leaving. *Ma!*"

Mrs. Swanson darted into the room, grabbed my arm and pulled me towards the door.

"You leave my boy alone!" she hissed. "You and those men better not come 'round here again. I won't have it. You hear me? Leave."

Outside, snowflakes swirled in a stiff breeze. I warmed up the Honda and switched on the wipers. Something wasn't right. What "men" had visited Swanson? Union reps? Internal affairs? What did they say that upset him and his mother? Common sense told me I'd be well advised to heed Mia's warning not to pull up rocks. Make waves? Cause trouble? Whatever . . .

"A decision's only as good as the information it's based on."

Solid advice, courtesy Lyndon B. Johnson, the Texas-born President who knew a thing or two about corruption. My father used that quote on a regular basis, as you might expect from a mob lawyer trying to keep intellectually-challenged crooks and murderers out of prison.

My father's connection to the *Cosa Nostra* was a matter of public record; Franco Canali's name was attached to many a media story on high-profile criminal cases. A fact that raised a question few Rhode Islanders and none of my superiors bothered to ask: how can a mob lawyer's son be a cop?

The same way a mob boss' son could become Mayor of Providence, and then a Congressman, while *his* son became a mob lawyer. Standard stuff in a state nicknamed "Rogue's Island" in the early part of the 18th century. The Sewer of New England. The Licentious Republic. Etc.

By the time I arrived at my father's office, the snow was coming down hard. Father's Lincoln was disappearing under a white blanket. Any sensible person would've been home, listening to the weatherman tell them to sit tight and ride out the storm.

Then again, my father's office was his home. He'd converted a run down North Providence house into a run down suite of offices; the cheap plywood paneling barely clinging to the walls being a particularly nasty addition. The only sign of prosperity: a collection of vintage guitars resting on metal stands surrounding my father's desk and a bottle of Jefferson's Presidential Select 25-Year-Old Straight Bourbon next to his phone.

"I hear you got news for me," my father said as I shook off the snow and hung my coat on an oversized hook by the door.

The grey-haired dentally challenged overweight version of myself poured us both a drink. He tilted his desk chair backwards and held a sip on his tongue. He swallowed, grimaced in pleasure and bounced on the chair slowly, rhythmically.

"Damn that's good stuff," I observed, feeling the liquid burn its way down my throat. "How much did that bottle cost?"

"Don't ask. You can't afford it. So when do I get to meet my grandson?"

"So you heard."

"I heard."

"Mother?"

"Couldn't wait to tell me. Knew I wouldn't spill the beans. I get the feeling she didn't tell me out of the goodness of her heart."

"I wasn't aware she had one," I observed.

"Why didn't *you* tell me?" Father asked. "Back in the day."

"I don't know," I said, taking an immoderate swallow of bourbon. "Veronica wanted it that way."

"Well I give you credit for keeping it secret for what?"

"Fifteen years."

"That's gotta be a record around here. When do I get to meet him?"

"After me."

"When will that be?"

"I don't know."

"I heard about your new job," Father said. "Congratulations."

"It's not official."

"Not much is 'round here. Negotiator huh?"

"Copy that," I said, toasting my good fortune. "I'm not sure I have skill set to talk people out of doing stupid things. I'm usually the one doing them."

"You're a troublemaker Johnny. Just like your old man."

"Just like my Mother you mean. You're the problem solver, right Dad?"

"Back in the day, I was on the other side of all this," my father said, firing-up Salem and waving at his office. "Now, yes, I'm a problem solver."

"And a damn good one. God knows how you kept *me* out of jail."

"And God isn't saying."

"*Omerta.*"

"Very funny," Father smiled, sucking on his menthol cigarette.

"Right?"

"As much as you love your dear old *padre*, I'm thinking this isn't a social call. What brings my only son to my place of business on a night like this?"

"The headless guy," I said. "The news says he was a Venezuelan. What do do you know?"

"What do *you* know?"

"I know the guy who got busy with the knife was set to testify to a grand jury. My rook and I were supposed to keep an eye on him. That didn't go as planned."

Father exhaled a plume of foul-smelling smoke, then tapped his cigarette ash into a plastic ashtray full of spent butts.

"I have no idea who your headless guy is," he said. "The other guy. The skinny one your partner shot? It's no secret, or won't be for long. Rico Nardelli."

Father tapped his cigarette again, then stood up and raised a reluctant window. A bitterly cold wind and flakes of snow came racing into the room. My father worked the handle until the window was open a sliver, sending a stream of cold air into the stuffy office.

"Rico was no saint," my father said, returning to his chair.

"That's a bit of an understatement considering he cut off someone's head. You'd think Mr. Nardelli would have wanted keep a slightly lower profile."

"Maybe he thought killing the Venezuelan would reassure certain people he'd refuse to testify. Or maybe it just happened. Rico was an animal."

"Client?"

"I had Rico pegged as a stand up guy," my father said, stubbing out his cigarette. "What do I know? Other than the fact that a friend of ours figured Rico was better off dead."

"Wait. Are you saying my partner was *paid* to shoot Rico Nardelli?"

"I wouldn't say 'paid'," my father said, shaking out a fresh death stick. "More like convinced. A distinction without a difference but there it is."

"I stopped in on my partner today. Turns out I wasn't his first visitor. His mother said a couple of guys talked to Swanson before I got there. I don't think she liked them."

"You get a look at them?"

"Nope."

"Good."

"Jesus," I swore before pouring myself a refill. "Swanson. What an idiot."

"You're assuming your partner had a choice."

"That's what *he* said. He didn't have a choice."

"Did he?" Father asked pointedly.

"Everyone has a choice."

"That's a dangerous thought Johnny. Lose it."

"What was Rico's thing?" I asked.

Father wrote an address on a slip of paper, folded it and shoved it across the desk. I opened the note and read it silently: 32 Molton Lane.

"Go easy on that bourbon willya?" my father said, his brows furrowing. "Cost me a fortune. Well, someone. You better get out of here while you can. Do me a favor willya? Set up a meet with my grandson. Me, a grandfather. About fucking time."

Father beamed at me as we set our empty glasses down, stood up and headed for the door.

"For God's sake, Johnny," Father advised, putting a hand around my shoulder. "Break it off with Mia Sporcatello. The sooner the better."

"She's hot," I said sheepishly.

"So was your mother. Look where *that* got me."

I know where my testosterone got *me* that night: Mia's apartment. What can I say? My father's son? Moth to a flame? Something like that . . .

"*Benvenuto a casa*," Mia said, dressed in a black silk nightgown that clung to her curves like a Ferrari to a winding road.

"Sorry I caught you in the middle of house cleaning," I said, taking off my shoes and coat.

"Don't stop," she said, watching me disrobe.

I didn't.

"Looks like you missed me," she said, dropping her nightgown, then sinking to her knees.

It was a prelude to another frantic sex session. When I was finally spent, Mia changed pace, lavishing me with slow, loving attention. Not that I'm complaining. There's nothing quite like a beautiful woman's hands on your body when you have nothing left to give. Or *think* you have nothing left to give.

"*Tesoro*," she said. "Are you angry I didn't go the Herndon party?"

"Do I look angry?" I asked, arranging a pillow under my head.

"You look *stanco*," Mia answered, placing my hand on her breast.

"Tired? I wonder why that is," I said, squeezing her nipple.

"Don't get me started," she said with a slow moan, putting her hand on top of mine.

"There's something I want to ask you," I said.

"*Non farmi una domanda se non vuoi sentire la risposta*," she said, staring into my eyes.

"I take that as a no."

"It depends."

"What do you know about 32 Molton Lane?"

"*Niente*."

Mia may not have been aware of all her father's "interests" but she knew every street in Providence. If a house was home to investment bankers, crack dealers or some other criminal enterprise, she was clued-in — if only to judge house values. Mia propped herself up on an arm and started stroking my chest.

"You're a dangerous man, John Canali."

"And you're a dangerous woman, Mia Sporcatello."

Mia smiled. I smiled back. We stayed like that for a while, calculating the risks and benefits of our relationship, such as it was.

"I want to tell you a story," she began.

"Rosebud is the sled," I joked.

"*Che?*"

"*Citizen Kane*. Never mind. Go on."

"You are making fun with me."

"*Tutto il tempo. Andiamo.*"

"When I was a *piccola ragazza* my father took to me my grandmother's garden," Mia said slowly. "He picked a *limon* for me. Is it sweet he asked. No, I said, it is sour. His knife cut it open. He squeezed the, how do you say?"

"Juice."

"Yes juice. Into his mouth. Like this," she pantomimed. "'The juice of your own lemons always tastes sweet,' he said."

I slid a hand between her legs.

"Your juice tastes sweet."

"Oh Johnny this will not go right," Mia said, thrusting her hips into my hand, grabbing my baby maker.

"Tell me that in ten minutes."

"Make it fifteen," she replied, leaning back and picking up her phone.

"No video," I warned, shifting into position, taking the phone from her hand and throwing it across the room.

"*Amore* you always spoil my fun."

Phone or no phone, I don't think I spoiled her fun that night. Far from it. But I did soon enough, and for a long time thereafter.

Chapter Seven

There's an old saying Rhode Islanders use when mother nature throws a curve ball: if you don't like the weather, wait a minute. Less than a week after a Nor'Easter hammered the Ocean State I was admiring a Porsche 911 Targa on a balmy spring day.

Mark Mingle emerged from the dealership aiming a fat key at the sports car. Metal, plastic and glass parts performed a mechanical ballet, turning and flipping until the Porsche's glass roof disappeared into the beast's back end.

"Come to see how the other half lives?" Mingle asked, stroking the German vehicle's curvaceous flanks.

"That man is richest whose pleasures are cheapest," I answered, throwing down Thoreau.

"Yeah whatever," Mingle agreed. "What can I do you for?"

"I need some advice."

The appeal to Mingle's ego found fertile ground; he nodded like he'd been expecting me to seek his counsel. He led me through the Porsche showroom, a glass-fronted ballroom for box fresh vehicles promising luxury weekend getaways and parking lot prestige. It looked like a hospital and smelled like money.

"Official business," Mingle told a tall executive dressed in a finely tailored suit as we passed, in case he thought the uniformed officer violating his domain was about to bust an employee. Or accept a padded envelope.

We entered a glassed-in office. Mingle motioned me to sit across from a desk with a computer screen and a black Porsche mug.

"Welcome to the room where small pens sign big checks," Mingle said, looking at his screen before giving me a smile devoid of both welcome and warmth.

"So Mark," I said, declining a breath mint that ended life in the salesman's mouth. "I'm the Providence Police Department's SWAT Team negotiator."

"And?"

"No congratulations? No 'What makes *you* qualified to get a bad guy to lay down his weapon and coming out with his hands up?' Just 'and?'"

"And what can I do for you?"

Mingle was always a guy in a hurry, first as a schoolyard drug dealer, then as a car salesman to people who loved German engineering almost as much as they loved themselves.

"How do I sell someone on the idea of giving up?" I asked. "You know, surrendering."

"Let me get this straight. For the record. John Canali — the captain of the soccer team who got straight A's — is asking Mark Mingle how to do his job."

"How about that? The guy who went to college is asking advice from the guy who graduated from selling drugs to selling cars."

"Rhode Island's number one Porsche salesman," Mingle boasted. "You always *were* a smart ass Canali."

"And you will always always be a Guido, Mark."

"O.K. that's done," Mingle said pleasantly. "You want to know how to sell something? Qualify, present, close. Thank you and goodnight."

"That's it?"

"That's it," he repeated, raising his right hand and lowering his head. "What do you want? Here it is! Do you want to buy it?"

"What's the trick?"

Mingle looked around as if he was plotting to overthrow a dictator.

"Ask for the sale. Most salesman never do. Can you believe it? Pussies."

"Always?" I asked.

"This never happened, at least not officially. But just for the sake of argument, let's say I'm with a customer test driving a one-hundred-and-fifty-thousand dollar automobile — plus tax, title, color-matched seat belts and a few other tasty options. The engine stops. Just like that. *Basta.* You know what I do while I'm sitting there waiting for the tow truck?"

"Give the guy a blow job?"

"I ask for the sale, " Mingle said, refusing to rise to the bait. "'You wanna buy the car?' Just like that. Can you believe it? Guess what he said?"

"Let me think. Wait. I got it. Yes?"

"Yes," he repeated, waiting for Mark Mingle's magnificence to sink in. "You gotta have balls Canali. *Cojones.*"

"You don't ask you don't get. What about qualification. What's the trick there?"

"Simple. Remember one thing: people don't know what they want or why they want it. They *think* they know but they're clueless. They just make up some bullshit in their head."

"The unexamined life is not worth living."

"Huh?"

"Socrates," I said, flashing back to failed tutoring sessions with the flunking freshman. "Continue."

"People are creatures of habit," Mingle said, shamelessly glancing at his gold-banded Rolex Submariner.

He stood up without so much as a "we're done here" and led me back through the showroom, out to my Honda.

"Tell me three things you like about your car," Mingle asked.

"It's reliable, it handles well and . . . "

"And what? You gotta have three. It's the holy fucking trinity."

"It's comfortable. Great seats."

"Ba-Bam! You've been qualified. *That's* what you want in a car. *That*. In that order. Done."

"Past behavior is the best predictor of future behavior," I said, impressed by the simplicity of Mingle's method.

"When I show a customer a new car, I don't talk about price or luggage space or how it's gonna get him laid. I just sell them on what they want to hear. For you, reliability, handling and comfort."

"Nice," I said with genuine admiration. "Let me try a variation on you. Tell me three things you're going to like about prison."

"What?"

"Some people *like* prison Mark. It's the first time in their life they get into a routine. Not a very nice routine, but it gives them a sense of stability. What else? Some people *really* enjoy the company of other men."

"That's two," Mingle said, curious where I was going with my rant. "You need three."

"O.K., they get three square meals a day. Changes their whole outlook on life."

"What's this got to do with me?" Mingle said, mentally reviewing things he did on a regular basis that could send to jail.

"I've got a friend who works for the Immigration and Naturalization Service," I answered. "You don't know him. But he knows your wife. He says Roseline Aristede came into the country from the Dominican Republic on a student visa, just before her 18th birthday. I gotta say it Mark: your wife doesn't look like the academic type. And here's the really strange thing: a little bird told me he saw Roseline *before* she entered the Land of the Free on an F-1 visa. Saw her as in fucked her."

It was an educated guess, but you don't accuse, you don't trap. Or something like that.

"Screw you," Mingle said, his eyes daggers. "*And* the piece of shit you rode in on."

"That's no way to talk about a Honda, Mark. They're reliable, they handle well and they're *very* comfortable."

"What do you want outta me?" Mingle asked, his accent returning to his roots as he squared his shoulders, ready for a fight.

"I'm looking for a couple of Dominicans. Marie and Yanira Dupree. Mother and daughter. Now that you're a member of the community, I figure you've got connections."

I handed him a snap of mother and child taken on a city porch somewhere in midtown Atlanta. They looked happy. Normal.

"Ask your lovely wife where I can find them."

"You don't know who you're messing with," Mingle warned, pocketing the picture furtively.

"Let me guess. A happily married man?" I asked, opening my car door.

"Hey Mamma's boy," he called over the sound of a Boxster S revving its flat six. "You forgot something."

"Yeah? What's that?" I said, pausing for his parting shot.

"You forgot to close," Mingle said, a crooked smile crawling across his face.

"Call me," I directed. "This week."

It took Mingle three days to respond. I was about to listen to his voice mail when I got a call.

"Lieutenant Canali."

"Yes?"

"This is Max Herndon."

The reality of the situation was even more awkward, more uncomfortable than I thought it would be. It was like the bad old days, when Mother was about to drop the hammer on her little boy. I felt a suffocating sense of shame.

"I want a word with you," Herndon said ominously. "Meet me at the house at three."

The Lord of the Manor greeted me at the door, giving me what Italians call *malocchio,* the evil eye.

"Officer Canali," Herndon announced, practically singing the executioner's song.

He led me through the darkened interior of his East Side fortress. Our echoing footsteps ended in a study larger than my apartment. High walls of leather-bound books surrounded a desk as big as a ping pong table. The door shut behind us like a bank vault.

"Time to face the music," a familiar voice called out.

I nearly jumped out of my skin. Mother was hiding behind the door, waiting to ambush me.

"I know about Luke," Herndon said, opening a liquor cabinet shaped like a globe, retrieving a bottle of something brown and expensive, pouring a drink into a cut glass tumbler. "You little *shit.*"

Mother circled around to stand next to Herndon, her arms crossed, her expression smug.

"What kind of man are you Canali?" Herndon demanded, taking a long pull on his drink. "What kind of man lets another man raise his own son? I'll *tell* you what kind. A selfish bastard. An evil little *fuck.*

The shoe fit, so I wore it.

"You know what I've got to do now?" Herndon asked rhetorically. "I've got to tell Luke the truth. What do you think *that's* going to do to him? You didn't think of *that* did you? You only thought of yourself."

Not true. I loved Veronica. Loved her enough to protect her marriage, her reputation. By staying away. By keeping quiet about our boy. But it was hardly the time to profess my love for another man's wife.

"How can I ever look at Veronica the same way again?" Max asked. "She's been lying to me every single day since Luke was born. Since he was *conceived.*

"Actions have consequences," Mother added, her eyes ablaze.

"They sure do," Herndon agreed.

Herndon reached over to his desk, pulled out a ledger and a Mont Blanc pen. He wrote on a check, ripped it from the book and thrust it at me. I read my name and the words "one hundred thousand dollars."

"Leave town Canali. And don't you *dare* contact Luke. Your mother and I will handle it from here."

Herndon opened the study's massive door. Not one to abandon protocol, mother walked ahead of me.

"Go ahead Liz," Herndon said, Mother wincing at the shortened version of her name. "I have some things to say to your son no lady should hear."

Mother exited the room, smirking, leaving the door open behind her. I waited until I was sure she was out of earshot.

"I'm not leaving town," I said defiantly, staring at Herndon's check. "And you know what? Despite everything that's happened, despite everything that's *going* to happen, I think you got the better part of the deal."

"Do you?" Max Herndon said. "Do you *really?*"

We glared at each other. And then, unexpectedly, miraculously, Herndon smiled.

"So do I," he said.

"What?" I asked, bewildered.

"Luke's a great boy," Herndon said, shutting the door to his study and hitting a switch on the wall.

A gentle hum filled the room.

"Smoke extractor," he explained, pointing at the ceiling. "Veronica isn't the only one with secrets," he added, putting the check on the desk and retrieving a couple of cigars from a mahogany humidor perched on his desk.

"Recognize these?" he asked. "Cost me a *fortune.*"

"Tax deductible," I said.

Herndon smiled, then clipped the Cubans with a silver cutter, aiming the severed tops at a metal wastebasket flanking his desk.

"I've known Luke wasn't mine since he was two," Herndon admitted. "I mean, c'mon, look at him. Look at me. You'd have to be an idiot not to see it."

Herndon handed me a Montecristo. He retrieved a silver lighter from a drawer, put the flame to the check and used it to light his cigar. He handed me the lighter and dropped the last of the check into the trash can.

"I love all my kids" Herndon said, sending a plume of smoke skywards, leaning against the desk, pointing at a huge leather chair. "Your boy — our boy — is, how do I put this? Full of piss, shit and corruption."

"You're not angry?" I asked, taking my assigned place, accepting the lighter and firing-up my cigar.

"I was, once. But I kept it to myself. Here," he said handing me a Herndon Industries coffee mug. "Use this for an ash tray."

We puffed our cigars, Max behind his desk, me sitting opposite. The tension left the air as the smoke filled it — only to be sucked away by the humming extractors.

"Do you still love her?" Max asked examining the ash growing on the end of his cigar.

"What's not to love?" I shrugged.

"You shrug like a Jewish lawyer," he said.

"You throw a party like a Roman emperor."

I savored my stogie and studied the label.

"Closest thing to a second coming," Herndon said, squinting at the Montecristo cigar band encircling his cigar.

"Mr. Herndon—" I began.

"Max."

"Max. Why did you put on that song and dance just now?"

"Your mother . . ." he said.

Wistfully? Regrettably? I couldn't tell.

"You did it for *her*?" I asked.

"I know you think the worst of your mother John. But whatever you think, you don't know the half of it."

"Do I *want* to know?"

"No," Herndon said, grim faced. "You don't. Which is why we have to proceed carefully."

Which we did. Just not carefully enough.

Chapter Eight

The Providence Police SWAT team was called to a standoff. One hostage taker, male; two hostages, a woman and a child.

I was halfway to the crime scene when it hit me: I was responding to the same address where I'd first met Mia. I felt a sudden urge to detour to a church for confession. I'd had the chance to arrest one or both of the warring Goodrichs for domestic violence. I gave them a pass in exchange for a date with Mia. Whatever did or didn't happen was my fault, on some level.

Setting aside my unease and code three safety protocol, I speed-dialed MBD — Mob Boss' Daughter.

"You're in *such* a hurry to see me *Caro*," Mia joked over the sound of the siren.

"You remember where we met?" I yelled. "Divorced couple? Big fight? Power Street."

"Rich folks live on Power. Most people live off Hope. Hope Street. I seen it on a poster."

"This is kinda important."

I paused to bleep and creep past a driver who couldn't figure out what to do when a police car with lights flashing and siren blaring crawls up his ass.

"Tell me something about Mr. Goodrich," I said.

"*Banchiere.*"

"Banker."

"No molto importante," she said. *"Straight arrow. Always wears a tie. Maybe in the shower."*

"Tie guy. Good to know. Got to go," I said, swerving to avoid a UPS truck that couldn't quite get out of its lane.

"Solo dop," she promised.

"Later," I repeated.

The SWAT team — a politically correct cohort representing all of Rhode Island's ethnic groups — assembled down the street from the crime scene. Despite the fact that I'd only trained with the team a couple of times since my promotion, the officers greeted me as a rifle-less comrade in arms.

"Where's the Mobile Command Center?" I asked Officer Alvarez.

"Engine trouble."

Captain Douglas gave me the 411 from behind a phalanx of squad cars parked down the street from the Goodrich residence.

A neighbor called it in. Charles Goodrich told arriving officers he didn't want to discuss family matters with the police, mentioning the fact that he was holding his wife and child at gunpoint. The officers withdrew and called SWAT. No demands. No further communication.

"We've got his cell," Captain Douglas told me.

I punched in Mr. Goodrichs' number, touched the little red phone icon and stared at the house.

"Charles Goodrich," a voice announced, as if his secretary had put through a call from a client.

"Mr. Goodrich, my name is Lieutenant John Canali, from the Providence Police Department. You may remember me from a previous visit."

"I do," he said simply.

"I understand you've had some trouble today."

"You could say that."

"I'm here to help sort this out. Do you mind if I call you Charles?"

"Not at all, if I can call you John."

"Of course. Charles, please put the gun down and come out so we can talk. Do you think you could do that?"

"I could. But I won't," he replied, rebuffing my attempt to close the deal. "And don't bother sending anyone in. We're in a safe room."

I mouthed the words "safe room" to Captain Douglas.

"No one's coming in," I told Goodrich. "What's the problem Charles?"

"My wife can't see sense on the custody front."

"You're an ass," a woman's voice declared.

Mr. Goodrich responded ballistically. I flinched at the sound of a single gunshot, accompanied by a piercing scream, followed by a small child's high-pitched wailing. The SWAT team hunkered down and looked at the Captain expectantly. He held them off with an downturned palm.

"What's going on?" I demanded.

"I shot her," Goodrich said over the din.

"Open the safe room door Charles," I said, sounding like an astronaut denied access to the mothership.

"No. I won't."

"*Mommy's bleeding!*" a child's voice screamed.

"What part of her body did you shoot?" I asked, dry mouthed.

"Her leg," Goodrich said. "Her thigh I think. For Christ's sake shut up Elaine! You're scaring David."

"Open the door Charles," I repeated.

"No."

"Then take off your tie. Do it. Do it now."

"What?"

"Take off your tie and put me on speaker."

"I'm sorry, I don't see the point."

"Either you're going to open that door or you're going to put a tourniquet on her leg," I said, as if those were his only choices. "We don't have much time."

"Very well then," Goodrich said, sighing. "You're on speaker and my tie's off. I suppose you want me tie it around her leg."

"Not yet. Listen carefully. Do you have a flashlight in there?"

"Why wouldn't I?" he asked, annoyed.

"Tie one end around the flashlight. Tight."

I waited, listening to Mrs. Goodrich and her son's sobs and crying, hoping the former man of the house was busy following my instructions.

"Done," he said, finally.

"*Now* put the tie around her leg. Up high, Charles. High as you can. Quick as you can."

"Don't hurt her!" young David protested as her mother's screams suddenly grew louder.

"Wrap the other end around the flashlight. Make it tight. Got it?"

"Yes yes," he said impatiently.

"Twist it clockwise. Keep twisting it until she screams. And then twist it some more. Hard as you can. All the way to the bone."

"Don't worry, David," Charles said in what he probably thought was a soothing voice. "Daddy's helping Mommy."

"You shot her!" his son protested.

"She's going to thrash around Charles," I said. "Hold her down. Sit on her."

Mrs. Goodrich screamed; I could hear it coming from both the house and the phone. Right until she went quiet.

"She's dead!" David said. "You killed Mommy!"

"Did the bleeding stop?" I asked urgently.

"Yes. It's stopped."

"Now open the door so we can get her to a hospital."

"David, come here."

Goodrich hung up.

"Fuck!" I said, looking at the phone.

I tapped the call button. Twice. Three times? A bunch.

"What?" Goodrich snapped.

"Charles, I need you to bring Elaine and David out. *Right now.*"

"I don't want to go to prison," Goodrich protested, a hint of desperation in his voice. "I want to be with my son."

I paused, thinking.

"Charles, tell me three things you like about your life."

"What?"

"Three things you like. Just three."

"Well I like to read."

"What else?"

"Exercise. I've always stayed in shape. Unlike *some* people I know."

Mrs. Goodrich moaned, whether from the insult or her physical injuries I couldn't tell.

"One more. One more thing you like."

"I like talking to my son. He's excellent company. Normally."

"I'm not going to lie to you, Charles. You're right. You might going to jail for this. Not forever but for a while."

"That's the *best case* scenario."

"It's not that bad," I said, as if Mr. Goodrich was destined for a Holiday Inn rather than one of Rhode Island's convict-filled hellholes. "You can read in prison, you've got lots of time to exercise and you can see your son on visiting day."

"She won't bring him."

"What if she agrees to bring David to see you every week? Will you come out then?"

"Elaine can't be trusted," Goodrich said.

"What if she puts it in writing?"

"She'll never sign."

"Hang on, her lawyer's here," I lied outrageously "What his name?" I asked, leaving the question hanging, hoping Charles would answer.

"Kileen," Goodrich said. "Duncan Kileen. A name that will live in infamy."

"What?" I yelled with mock exasperation. "Oh come *on*. My boss won't let him talk to you. But he says he'll *make* her sign."

The odds that Goodrich would believe his wife's lawyer just happened to be at the crime scene were perishingly small. But then I'd met hardened criminals who believed me when I told them God wanted them to confess.

"I can read anything I like?" Goodrich asked.

"No porn."

Goodrich chortled, an obnoxious sound I'd heard in my mother's living room more times than I cared to recall.

"Why not?" he asked. "It can't be any worse than that studio apartment. And I need a break from work."

"Sure you do Charles. Time to recharge. Let's do this."

The SWAT team fractured Goodrich's nose when they tackled him, splattering his dress shirt with blood. The EMTs whisked Mrs. Goodrich — lucky to have life and limb — to Rhode Island Hospital.

The crime scene resembled a block party. There were police officers everywhere, gossiping neighbors behind crime scene tape, TV crews interviewing everyone but themselves and two helicopters jockeying for position.

"I should have arrested them," I said to no one in particular.

I spied a matte silver Mercedes G Wagon parked a little ways down the street. I tuned-in to the sound of its V8 rumbling through coffee can-sized side pipes. I tried to see inside its blacked out windows.

Something told me it belonged to one of Leo Sporcatello's men. Checking-up on me, or worse? The moment I started walking towards the G-Wagon it eased away from the curb, turned on a side street and disappeared.

"Just because you're paranoid doesn't mean the world's not out to get you," I said, continuing my conversation with myself.

"Hey Canali," Captain Douglas said, walking up to offer his congratulations. "You know what? You're actually a nice guy."

"*La troppa bonezza finisce nella monnezza*," I said. "Nice guys finish last."

How right I was.

Chapter Nine

"Luke, I am your father."

As I cruised Wickenden Street looking for a parking space, the *Star Wars* movie line ran through my head. The other bit of dialogue too: "If only you knew the power of the Dark Side."

I did. My work had taught me what happens when bad people take total control: no one's safe. Not at the top, where people in power play an endless no-holds-barred game of King of the Hill. And not at the bottom, where little guys constantly fight for scraps from the master's table — when they're not escaping the grim reality of their non-existent prospects with drugs, gambling or prostitution.

Sure, Rhode Island has a number of good, honest, gainfully employed people. One out of every four residents pulling down a paycheck works for the government — many in no-show jobs, more than a few double-dipping their way to a huge pension the State hasn't funded in decades. Most of the rest get a paycheck from universities and hospitals, institutions that rival the government for inefficiency and unaccountability.

Bottom line? You can't have a healthy animal when it's home to so many leeches. Not even Luke Skywalker could sort *that* out.

Speaking of improbable events, the parking gods delivered unto me a space right near Cafe Z. As I parallel parked, I silently prayed Veronica and Max Herndon had sheltered young Luke from Rhode Island's cancerous culture of crime and corruption. I hoped my son would grow up to be a straight shooter in a crooked town. Or leave Providence for greener, safer, more prosperous pastures.

My dreams were dashed before Luke opened his mouth.

My once-secret son was sitting at a small table in Z's garden, his back to the entrance. The woman across from the teenager looked in her mid-twenties. Silky blond hair cascaded onto a skin-tight button down red sweater open to her breast bone. Bright, amber-colored eyes and a come-hither smile sang a siren song few men could resist — never mind a high school sophomore.

Luke's lunch companion held a sheaf of papers, pointing at a page approvingly. She was listening to him, looking back and forth at the paper. I tapped my son on his shoulder. He turned around and smiled. It wasn't like looking a mirror. Luke's face was softer than mine; he seemed more wide-eyed, open and trusting. He had his mother's pale Irish skin, with a few freckles gathered around his nose.

Still, there was no mistaking my genetics. Even though Luke was seated I could tell he was tall and broad shouldered, starting to fill out. He wasn't destined to be a bruiser, but he wouldn't be a push-over either. But it was the mischievous glint in Luke's hazel eyes that reminded me most of myself. A younger self, before life had beaten me down.

"Dad," Luke said cheerfully as I approached the table.

My heart jumped. It wasn't a feeling of pride. Nor, I admit, love. It was a sense of belonging. Not Luke to me. Me to Luke. Somewhere in heart of hearts, I realized my actions would be held to account here, on Earth, even if Luke never knew what they were. I couldn't tell what Luke was feeling; he was playing it cool in front of his lady friend.

"Diana's my history teacher. We were just going over my term paper. Diana, this is my biological father, John Canali," Luke announced, as if we'd known each other since birth.

I shook the woman's delicate hand as she rose from the table, taking note of her wedding and engagement rings. She collected the papers and gave Luke a discreet smile.

"Nice to meet you Officer Canali."

I sat down and waved off the waiter.

"What should I call you?" Luke asked.

"John will do."

"Tell me a little about yourself John-will-do," Luke said, sipping his iced tea.

"You first."

"I'm a housewife," Luke joked. "Mother of three. I enjoy tennis, swimming, sailing and macramé."

I laughed. Luke's eyes lit up with delight. Mine followed suit.

"Now you," he said.

"I'm a 42-year-old Lieutenant and SWAT team negotiator for the Providence Police Department. My backhand sucks, I swim and I don't know how to sail. I'm an excellent ceramicist."

"Really?"

"No. I just like the sound of the word."

"I love words," Luke said.

"Callipygian," I said.

"Use it in a sentence."

"Your teacher is callipygian."

"I don't think I'll touch that," Luke said.

"I suspect it's too late," I said pointedly. "I suppose you have a lot of questions for me—"

"You carrying a gun?"

I looked around the room, seeing nothing but ladies who lunch and a few men who drink, heavily. I returned to meet Luke's gaze. We locked eyes, taking stock of each other.

"I'm carrying," I said. "Goes with the job."

"I'm going to carry a gun when I'm twenty-one."

"That's no easy thing. At least not legally. Do you have a criminal record?"

It was supposed to be a rhetorical question; the clean-cut kid in khakis sitting in front of me looked as innocent as baby Bambi. When Luke's eyes darted right, I knew the truth, and prepared for his lie.

"The charges were dismissed," he admitted, daring me to take him to task. "Lack of evidence."

My heart sank. Sleeping with a married woman and at least one arrest. Our reconciliation wasn't going to be as easy as I thought, and I'd thought it would be difficult. But at least we had rapport. I liked my son.

"What charge?" I asked.

"Possession with intent to distribute," Luke revealed with a sense of relief — and no remorse. "The evidence disappeared."

"Max Herndon pulled some strings," I concluded, trying to decide if I should be thankful. "You want to talk about your mother and me?"

"That's none of my business," Luke said, crossing his arms.

"That's not what I expected you to say."

"What *did* you expect?" Luke asked.

"The third degree."

"Yeah, well, now what?"

"I don't know," I said with a heavy sigh. "I honestly don't."

"We could hang out," Luke suggested.

"I'd like that. But I have to ask you a question first," I said, leaning forward.

"Shoot. So to speak."

"Do you still deal?"

"No," Luke answered. shaking his head vigorously, his eyes darting right.

I pretended I believed him.

"Would you bust me?" Luke asked, playing with a fork absent-mindedly. "You know, if I was?"

"I would."

"Would you? I feel like you're just saying that. I mean, you *would* say that."

I nodded slowly.

"How about you take me shooting?" Luke asked. "I've never shot a gun. Mom's one of those anti-gun nuts. Thinks only cops should have guns."

"Lucky me. When are you free?"

"Next Thursday. After crew."

"Crew? As in rowing? That's not a sport, that's work."

"Tell me about it," Luke said, rolling his eyes. "I feel like a galley slave. Still, it's a great work out."

We both smiled.

"Mom says you used to be captain of the soccer team," Luke said. "Played in college."

"True story. You play?"

"I can barely row a boat. Pick me up at the river at five-thirty."

"I'll check the roster. I should be free. Call me so I can text you confirmation."

"I'll send you my vCard."

Luke texted me his details. Entering Luke Herndon into my iPhone felt strange.

"Well it's been nice meeting you," Luke said, slapping a crisp twenty on the table. "I've got stuff to do."

Luke caught sight of my raised eyebrow.

"School work," Luke said, the Devil-make-care glint returning to his eyes, increasing my worry tenfold.

Walking back to my car I realized I had a new job: steering my son away from a life of crime. I didn't have the slightest idea how; I was a cop, not a counsellor. Or an experienced father. Or a shining example of an honest, upright citizen.

Luke needed something to give him a sense of purpose. Something that could lift him out of the snake pit that was my home town. Something legal. I had no clue what that something could be. Worse, I suspected I was too late. But I wasn't late for my Mother's post-Luke-reveal "come to Jesus" meeting.

I parked my car a block away from mother's Congdon Street lair and lingered in the shadow of Roger Williams' statue in Prospect Park. Puffy white clouds cast moving shadows on the city. The muted hum of rush hour traffic rose up from the city below. The smell of fresh cut grass was practically dizzying.

"Lieutenant Canali," a small man called from a respectful distance. "FBI Special Agent Pistone. Got a minute?"

Pistone was the least FBI-looking FBI Agent I'd ever seen. The scrawny fed wore dirty jeans and a T-shirt sporting a faded image of the *Roomful of Blues* first album. His pock-marked face was scarred across his right eye.

"What can I do for you Agent Pistone?"

"Help me nail the mob," he replied in a thick New Jersey accent.

"That's *way* above my pay grade," I said, walking away.

"Marie and Yanira Dupree."

I stopped. I checked my Timex and walked to the railing keeping tourists from tumbling off a 50-foot cliff. Agent Pistone joined me. He pulled a crumpled pack of Camels from his front pocket and lit one. We gazed silently at the capitol city, waiting for the conversation to start.

"That building," I said, pointing at a tall office block with about as much style as loaf of white bread. "My father calls it Gifford's last erection."

"Architect?" Pistone asked, exhaling blue smoke though his nose.

"Banker. The guy who had it built."

"Why do that call that one the Superman building?" Pistone asked, pointing to the City's tallest structure, a 26-floor stepped skyscraper.

"Everyone thought they used it in the old back-and-white Superman TV show. 'Able to leap tall buildings in a single bound!'" I intoned in my best narrator voice.

"Not true?"

"Nope. Great building though. Art Deco. Empty. The City's thinking about tearing it down, of course. So Agent Pistone," I said, waving away his second hand smoke, "what you know about the Duprees?"

"I think you got that backwards," he said. "What do *you* know?"

"I think you ain't got nothin'," I said, imitating his Jersey accent. "A couple 'a names."

"We know you're looking for them."

"That and two dollars will get you downtown."

Pistone looked confused.

"My father's expression. Bus fare. He used to say 'that and fifty cents gets you downtown. Inflation.'"

"You want the Duprees. We want Leo Sporcatello. Apparently you and his daughter have a quite a thing going."

"I'm not going all Donny Brasco. Not for all the tea in China."

"The Agency hasn't forgotten what you did down in Quantico," Pistone said his tone softening. "Taking on that Hogan's Alley psycho? You showed some serious balls."

"Or, to quote the official report, 'irresponsible and reckless behavior'."

"We're prepared to offer you a job. Salary, benefits, pension, the works. Get you out of this shit hole."

"This shit hole is my home," I said, nodding towards the City. "Besides, what difference would it make? If Sporcatello goes away someone else will take his place."

"So much for serve and protect."

"You judge me you make *yourself* look bad. All you feds want is a scalp. Bust some bad guy, make headlines and leave. What changes? Nothing."

"What's it going to take to get you on board Canali?"

"No sale."

"The only thing necessary for the triumph of evil is for good men to do nothing," Pistone said.

I'd seen a lot of law enforcement officers in my time. I can count on one finger the number who could quote Edmund Burke. I had to give the feds credit for finding someone who looked like Joe Sixpack familiar with 18th century European political philosophy.

"You're assuming there are good men in this state," I said, sizing Pistone up again.

"I *am* assuming. You."

"The jury's out."

"Let's hope it doesn't come to that," Pistone warned, grinding out his cigarette on the railing and putting the butt in his pocket. "You love her?"

"Jesus Christ. You guys."

Pistone shrugged.

"O.K. let's hear it," I said.

"What?"

"The threat. You were about to threaten me."

"Oh right," Pistone said, as if I'd reminded him of a doctor's appointment. "Cocaine's a federal crime. Five hundred grams gets you five to forty at Club Fed. If you're lucky."

"Never touch the stuff. Makes me even more of an asshole."

"You don't, but someone you know does."

"I know lots of people who do."

"Someone close."

I tried to think of a coke head the Federal Bureau of Investigation could use against me. It hit me like a ton of bricks.

"Luke's a good boy," Pistone said sadly. "I'm sure you can straighten him out."

"What's the penalty for punching an FBI Agent?"

"Simple assault, no weapon, not part of an ongoing felony? A big fine and a year inside. But don't forget: I punch back."

I left without a word, denying FBI Agent Pistone the chance to close the deal.

It was a short stroll to Mother's house, past a series of lovingly restored colonial cottages backing onto the City. To the west, Congdon Street dead ended onto Angel, past a Baptist Church built by the state's African American community, exiled by gentrification.

I knew how that felt; my mother couldn't wait for me to pack my bags for college. And neither could I. I pushed the memory from my mind, hesitating at Mother's heavily lacquered door. She opened it for me.

The view at the end of her living room was spectacular, a vista of a river city that had once eclipsed Boston for wealth and sophistication. My mother's mood was equally impressive, but not in a good way.

"Why did you refuse Max Herndon's check?" she demanded.

"I'm staying Mother. This is my town too."

"Is it?" my mother asked, lowering herself on a Windsor chair that belonged in a museum. "You don't belong here John. You're a square peg in a round hole. I should've sent you to boarding school."

"Regrets, you've had a few. But then again too few to mention."

"How *dare* you judge me," she practically barked. "You have no idea what I've sacrificed to get where I am."

"Love?"

"Enough with the psychobabble," she snapped. "There's a check on the counter. If I were you I'd take it."

"If you were me you wouldn't be you."

Talking to the woman who gave me birth was like a tennis match where both participants held razor-sharp swords. I was used to the vicious back and forth, but that doesn't mean I liked it.

"How did you find young Luke?" Mother asked, opening the second set. "And don't give me driving directions."

"He's troubled."

"Interesting."

"Jesus Mother. Do you ever stop scheming?"

"I wouldn't call it that."

"*You* wouldn't."

I went to her Sub Zero and retrieved a can of blackberry Clean, a caffeinated herbal drink that donates part of its revenue to drug rehabilitation, ironically enough.

"Do me a favor," I said, almost laughing at the words coming out of my mouth.

"What?" Mother asked without enthusiasm.

"Stay away from Luke. For a while."

"I don't see where you have a say about it," Mother said dismissively.

"How do I put this diplomatically?" I asked, for no real reason. "This isn't a good time to add to his stress."

"Nonsense," Mother said, rising from her throne. "My grandson needs a guiding hand. I will steer him straight."

"Straight to hell you mean."

"Speaking of going to hell, why don't you? If there's one thing I don't need it's a dim-witted child giving me advice."

I walked over and picked up her check from the counter. Two-hundred-thousand-dollars. Double Max's offer. That's now much Mother wanted me out of town. Out of her life. I folded the paper and put it in my wallet.

"You're leaving?" she asked, not even trying to hide her satisfaction.

"Sure. Why not?" I asked, the idea finding fertile ground in my weary soul. "Once I get Luke sorted."

"It's for the best," my mother said solemnly, following me to the door. "For all of us. I do love you, you know," she added without a hint of kindness.

"I'm sure you think you do."

My mother smiled condescendingly, waiting.

"Love you too," I said pecking her cheek.

Stepping onto the street, I scanned Mother's 'hood for my FBI friend. A woman tending a technicolor flower box next door nodded a greeting. I tipped an imaginary hat and made my way back to the car. A black Porsche sat idling behind it, gleaming ominously in the fading light.

Chapter Ten

Mark Mingle peered out from the driver's seat of the black-on-black Targa S I'd seen at his dealership. The Porsche salesman's trademark tan practically illuminated the car's dark interior.

"Grüß Gott," I said, hitting him with the greeting I'd learned from a German tourist who'd had his rental car stolen.

"I got some information," Mingle said. "About those missing women."

"I'm listening."

"What are you, Frasier Crane? Get in the car."

"Hey Mark, you gonna take me for a ride?" I said doing my best mobster impersonation as I dropped down into the Porsche's loving embrace.

"Yeah sure," he said, scanning the road. "Let's go for a ride."

"Excellent! I'm in the market for one of these. Although I've got to say I really like the AMG. The engine's where it should be. Not like this ass-engined Nazi slot car you got here."

Mingle said nothing. He blasted down Jenkes' hill, glanced left at the intersection with Benefit Street, spun the wheel and floored it, giving me the full lateral G-force experience. He slapped the Porker's paddle shift and gunned the beast down to North Main, the water-cooled six wailing obediently.

While I enjoyed breaking the speed limit as much as the next guy, especially in a vehicle that made my Honda look like a pedal car, Mingle's steering inputs lacked finesse. Either he was nervous or a shit driver. Or both.

"So Mark," I said as we flew through a freshly red light. "How'd you know where I was gonna be? You following me?"

"I saw your car on my way to an appointment."

"With whom?"

"My customers are private people," he said.

"And I'm a nosy guy. Spill."

"You want to hear about those Dominicans or not?" Mingle asked, his jaw set, his eyes focused on the road ahead.

"Where are we?" I asked as he turned right towards Hope Street.

"I'm taking us down by the river so we can find a quiet place to talk."

"My son does crew on the Seekonk."

"What?"

"Rowing. It's a sport, apparently. You know I have a son, right?"

"Yeah sure," Mingle replied, glancing at the clock in the center of the Porsche's dash.

"Did you know I have a gun?"

Drawing my GLOCK was a clumsy business; the Porsche's seats hugged me like a python. Transferring the gun to my left hand without pointing the muzzle at my legs was also a bit awkward. But I got there eventually.

"Hey c'mon," Mingle said, spying the business end of my pistol pointed at his chest, panic raising his voice a full octave. "What's that for?"

"It's a gun Mark. For shooting people. In this case, you. The guy who never misses a buying signal. Except when he does."

"C'mon," Mingle said again, swerving to avoid a minivan parked by the side of the road, his gift of gab gone.

"Pull over," I commanded, traffic cop style. "Do it."

Mingle hit the brakes hard, slamming the Porsche to a stop at the top of a hill over-looking the Seekonk river. There was a mansion on one side, Blackstone Park on the other. I could see the empty boathouse in the distance.

"Get out," I said. "Slowly."

"What the fuck," Mingle protested, forgetting to unbuckle his seatbelt, then figuring it out and extricating himself from the car.

I slipped out the passenger door with a ballerina's grace, or so I'd like to think. I re-aimed the nine mil at Mingle's center mass, keeping the Porsche between us.

"You lack empathy, Mark. Did you give one thought to how *I'd* feel about being rubbed out? No it's all about you. You're a selfish prick."

Mingle looked around, ready to bolt.

"Hey Mark, can you run 1200 feet per second?"

Mingle shelved his escape plan and glanced at his Rolex.

"You late for something?" I asked pointedly.

I pulled my knife from my pants with my left hand; the blade opened as I extracted it. Keeping the gun trained on Mingle, I bent down and stabbed the Porker's front tire. The car salesman winced. Just to be sure, and because I enjoyed the feeling, I yanked out the knife and plunged it in again.

"Tell your friends you had tire trouble," I advised.

I folded the blade with one hand and clipped the knife back into my pocket.

"Good news," I said. "I've come into some money. I'm in the market for a sports car. Bad news: I'm going to have to buy it from someone else."

"You'll never get away with this Canali," Mingle swore. "You're a cop."

"Jesus Mark, if a cop can't get away with murder in this town who can?"

Mingle looked down the empty street. As if on cue, the lamps lining the curving road flickered to life. Nearby trees swayed in a gentle breeze. A seagull called from somewhere.

"Quick question," I said. "Who put you up to this?"

"What are you, retarded?"

"I guess that answers *that* question. I've got one more. Why? You owe them? They paying you? Someone put a gun to your head?"

"I didn't have a choice," Mingle said, shrugging his expensive blazer.

"Why does everyone keep saying that?" I sighed, raising the pistol. "Well, the show's over Mark Mingle."

"You're a dead man Canali."

"You first."

I considered pulling the trigger. Mingle had tried to kill me. Well, to deliver me to people to kill me — no doubt after conducting their own, more unpleasant interrogation. Shooting the car salesman would be self defense. Maybe even legally. I'd have to make up a story about the slashed tire and convince someone that a Lieutenant pulling down $96,580 per year was in the market for a $90,000-plus sports car. Internal Affairs were real ball busters, but I was sure I'd think of something.

More philosophically, would the world would be any worse without Mark Mingle? What had the Italian-American sleaze ball contributed to society? Dollars to donuts he cheated on his taxes. Shooting Mingle would send a message to the hit man or men waiting for me down the road. Not that it would stop them, but it would ruin their day. Then again, maybe not.

"In this town a man's gotta do what he's gotta do," Nicky "The Fish" Carducci famously declared on the witness stand before going down for a triple homicide. "*Or else.*"

Defending that piece of shit in court was my father's job. Mine? At that moment? I couldn't say. But I was reasonably confident putting a bullet into a mobbed-up car salesman wasn't part of my official job description

"You're not gonna do it," Mingle said, sensing my lack of resolve.

"You're right," I said, slowly lowering the gun. "I guess I've reached my reservation point."

"Your what?"

A black SUV thundered up the road. It was my turn to look for a way out. Given the SUV's speed and the complete lack of cover or concealment within sprinting distance, I was shit out of luck.

Mingle smiled triumphantly. I aimed the gun at the approaching truck's front window, determined to go down fighting. Something made me hang fire. Which was just as well; FBI Special Agent Pistone called to me through the open passenger window.

"Car trouble?" he asked.

"*Some* kind of trouble," I said holstering my gun.

I couldn't tell if Mingle was happy or unhappy at the sudden turn of events. He certainly looked relieved that I wasn't going to shoot him. He also knew the men waiting for my arrival were not, as my father used to say, the most understanding of people.

"Need a lift?" Pistone offered.

As I walked around the rear of the sports car towards the SUV, Mingle made a move to follow. I waved him back.

"You don't want to leave a nice car like this out here this time of night. Who knows what might happen to it?" I asked.

I clambered into the Tahoe.

"Nice timing," I said, shaking slightly.

Pistone smiled to himself and put the truck in gear. We hadn't made it more than a couple of blocks before I felt sick to my stomach.

"Pull over," I gasped.

I didn't puke my guts out; that's physically impossible. But it sure felt that way.

"Sorry," I said, slumping back into my seat, wiping my mouth with my sleeve.

"Normal post-combat reaction. Me? I go off somewhere and have a good cry. After that, I'm all better."

A second later a police cruiser lit us up, flashing its lights, hitting us with the pull-the-hell-over air horn.

"I hope you've got a box of Kleenex in here somewhere," I said.

Agent Pistone knew there was one reason Providence's finest "happened" to pull us over a few blocks away from Mingle's stricken car, and it had nothing to do with a busted taillight. Pistone tensed and looked ahead, left and right.

"I wouldn't," I said, placing a hand on his arm. "They'll have the whole force after us. You strapped?"

Pistone nodded, relaxed his grip on the steering wheel and lowered his window. For the second time that night, I unholstered my GLOCK. I held it tight to my right leg, next to the car door.

I recognized the officer approaching the vehicle from the passenger side, his huge frame growing larger in the side view mirror: Officer Victor Tressa. A veritable mountain of a man, Tressa was one of the most violent and corrupt law enforcement officials who'd ever worked for the City of Providence. And that's saying something. Tressa's flashlight blinded me, then lit up Agent Pistone. I lowered my window.

"Who's your friend Johnny?" Tressa asked without so much as a hihowareya.

Tressa had to bend down to go eye-to-eye. I couldn't see his hands but I had a sneaking suspicion one of them wasn't empty.

"FBI Special Agent Joey Pistone," I said as officially as I could, guessing my new best friend's first name.

"Huh, how about that," Tressa said, shining his light into Pistone's eyes. "A fed?"

I could almost see the gears whirring in Tressa's head. If the scruffy-looking man behind the wheel *was* employed by Uncle Sam, opening up on him would be a bad career move. If the driver *wasn't* a fed and Tressa *failed* to take me out, his reputation for getting things done would take a serious hit. So to speak.

"Credentials?" Tressa demanded.

"I'm undercover *asshole.*"

Pistone practically spat the expletive, figuring a good offense was the best defense. Either that or betraying pre-combat anxiety.

"So what brings you to town Agent Pistone?" Tressa asked.

"None of your God damn business."

"I'm *making* it my business," Tressa insisted.

I had no clue where to go from there. Neither did anyone else.

"Why don't you ask him something only an FBI Agent would know," I suggested. "Like how much he gets *per diem.*"

I silently cursed myself. Tressa had no more idea what a *per diem* was than he knew what *carpe diem* meant — assuming he hadn't seen *Dead Poets Society.*

Officer Caldwell — a smaller example of a corrupt cop who considered the law to be less than a rough guideline — appeared in the driver's window behind Pistone. A stupid move by a stupid cop; Caldwell placed himself and his partner directly in the line of fire, should either of them start shooting. Pistone saw me looking over his shoulder and guessed what was I was thinking. I swear I saw his right foot twitch.

"Speaking of business," I said, quickly. "Does you old man still run that barber shop over on Atwells?"

"He's retired," Tressa said.

"Well it won't be long before I am too," I said, retroactively aware of the potential irony.

Tressa tried to stare a hole into Agent Pistone. After an extremely tense ten seconds, he gave up. Just like that.

"The sooner you're off the force the better," he said, before retreating.

"Right?" I responded, reaching over with my left hand to hit the window switch and end our *schmooze*. Pistone wasted no time leaving the potential scene of the crime.

"I thought that went pretty well," Pistone said his voice cracking ever-so-slightly.

"I need a drink."

"Hungry?" Pistone teased.

"You want a moment alone?"

We celebrated our continued existence at Legal Sea Foods. As the designated drinker, I made my way through a couple of low carb bourbons. Doubles.

"This place is worse than New Jersey," Pistone said, rattling the ice cubes in his unsweetened ice tea.

"Only hell is worse than New Jersey," I said, putting my recently recovered digestive system to the test, slurping a cherrystone.

"New Jersey *is* hell," he countered.

"So now that we've faced death together how about you tell me about what happened to the Duprees?"

"That's on a need to know basis. And my first name is Lawrence not Joey."

"Larry? That's funny. Where's Moe and Curly?"

"How can you eat those things?" Pistone asked as I squirted lemon juice onto my third raw clam.

"That's on a need to know basis. Listen Larry, if anyone needs to know what happened to those two females, it's me.

Agent Pistone played with his rice pilaf, pushing it back and forth across his plate, piling it on one side, then the other.

"They're gone," he said. "I doubt we'll ever find them. If we do there won't be much left."

"For the crime of?"

"Marie made the same mistake you did. She asked too many questions. Understandable, but there it is."

"Yanira?"

"She got too old to work."

"Are you saying what I think you're saying?"

"I am."

"How old is too old?"

"Eight. Maybe eight-and-a-half."

"Jesus."

"She was six when she started turning tricks. Jesus I hate saying that."

I can't say I was surprised. Or even shocked. But angry? Oh yeah I was
angry. When people like Mingle or Tressa turn to crime, when they give in
to their base instincts and prey on adults, that's one thing. Turning kids into
sex slaves? Raping them? Destroying their lives before they've even begun?
That's a whole 'nother level of evil.

"You know that guy your partner shot?" Pistone asked.

"Rico Nardelli. The Decapitator."

"You make it sound like a Schwarzenegger movie," Pistone said.

"Been there, seen that," I said, trying to dismiss the image of the Nardelli
holding the bleeding head by his side. "But I think I missed the plot."

"Mr. Nardelli kept tabs on the house where they kept little Yanira. We
thought we had a good chance of turning him."

"Why didn't you put him in protective custody?"

"That was *your* job," Agent Pistone said accusingly.

"What was the decapitated guy's story?" I asked, ignoring the dig.

"The one whose head ended up in the trash can?"

"Yeah that one."

"At first we thought he was a customer who didn't appreciate being blackmailed. Turns out the vic was Jorge Gonzales. An 'undocumented immigrant' up from Venezuela."

"And?"

"He was a little boy's father. I don't think he was very happy with his son's care."

I drained my bourbon and put my hand over the glass to hold off the waiter swooping in for a refill.

"Now what?" I asked.

"I can't tell you any more," Pistone said, handing the waiter his plate.

"Alright. When?"

"When what?"

"When are you going to shut them down?"

"Tell me something," Pistone said, leaning across the table. "What's *your* angle in all this? What do *you* care? And what are you doing with that mobster's daughter?"

"None of your business," I said, knowing that I was completely, utterly wrong.

"Mia Sporcatello's a good looking woman Johnny," he said. "But maybe it's time you thought with the big head."

"Maybe so," I demurred.

We ordered coffee. Pistone destroyed some bread pudding.

"We need your help," he said cautiously.

"With?"

"Sporcatello."

"Again with Sporcatello. In case you hadn't noticed, he doesn't like me."

"That could change."

"That it could."

A waitress refilled my coffee.

"We're watching you Johnny," Pistone said, leaning back in his chair.

"You're either with us or against us?"

"Something like that."

"Here's the thing, Larry. I like you. But I don't trust you. Like I said, you feds swoop in and swoop out."

"We've got a program."

"Good for you. But I don't feel like changing my name and opening a flower shop in Kansas, looking over my shoulder for the rest of my life."

"You don't trust anyone."

"The problem being? Anyway, that's not entirely true."

"Good," Pistone said, summoning the check. "You're going to need all the friends you can get. I'll text you my number"

Pistone pulled out his phone.

"Store it under Red Carpet Smoke Shop."

"That place went out of business years ago," I said, remembering a collection of beautifully carved meerschaum pipes.

"Exactly. When you've got something to tell us, call. Sooner rather than later. Later may be too late."

I entered the contact.

"Can I give you a ride home?" Pistone asked, signing the check and pocketing the receipt.

"I think I'll stay here and cogitate for a while."

"Sounds painful," he joked.

"It usually is," I said "Thanks for dinner."

"Your tax money hard at work. Just remember: there's no such thing as a free lunch."

"Tell me something I *don't* know."

"I already did," he said.

But not nearly enough, as it turned out.

Chapter Eleven

Mia Sporcatello lay on her stomach, breathing quietly. I ran my fingers up and down her back, exploring the exquisite geography of her athletic physique. We were both spent after a long, sweaty bout of the most frantic sex of my life.

Maybe it was the thought that kept running through my head: at any second a killer's going to burst through the door, pull me off the mob boss' daughter and take me out.

Mia shifted positions, putting her head on my chest, wrapping her body around mine. She sighed contentedly. I kissed the top of her head. Her hair smelled of jasmine.

"Mia, I need your help," I whispered in her ear. "I need you to get your father to call off his dogs."

"*Cave cane,*" she murmured drowsily. Beware of the dog.

"I'm serious. Leo wants me dead."

Mia sprang up.

"What you have done?" she demanded.

"You really want to know?"

"Don't answer a question with a question," she said, narrowing her eyes.

"Remember the decapitated guy?" I asked, as if it might have slipped her mind. "His killer was named Rico Nardelli. Nardelli ran a house on Molton Street with sex slaves. Children. The guy Nardelli murdered? He was the father of one of the children."

"And?" Mia said, although I'm sure she was way ahead of me.

"Nardelli works for your father," I said, making sure it didn't sound like a coincidence.

I watched Mia carefully, looking for signs of prior knowledge. Nothing.

"And this is your problem because?" she asked, tilting her head like a curious Schnauzer.

"I've been asking around," I said, waiting for her reproach.

"*Acqua in bocca.*"

"I don't understand."

"Pulling up rocks. *Why are you doing this Gianni?*" she pleaded.

Mia's question was a good one. What chance did I have to stop a child sex slavery ring? I wasn't a detective. I was a street cop working for a police department with its hand out. A law enforcement agency that saw organized child rape as just another day in the big city.

Nosing around had made me the target of a mob contract. The hit would only end — *might* only end — if I agreed to turn a blind eye to the child sex ring. Why not just step aside and let the FBI do its job? They had the resources to get it done, and they were already on the case. It was only a matter of time. Or so I wanted to believe.

It sounds terrible, but I concluded that the child sex slavery ring wasn't a hill to die on. What good would it do to take on Sporcatello — especially if I failed? If I was dead? So I nodded. Yes. Yes, I'd back off.

Mia slipped into her silk nightgown and disappeared into the living room. I could hear her on the phone, speaking rapidly in Italian. Her voice grew louder and more insistent, until I could only catch a few words. Struggling to translate on the fly, exhausted by the day's events, I found myself drifting off to sleep.

"*Non si preoccupi*," Mia said later as she scratched my head. "It's finished now."

"Is it?"

"It is," she repeated, her hand moving down my chest.

Mia's face held the same look of fierce determination that captivated me the first time we met. Only the light in her dark eyes wasn't sexy. It was sinister.

"I've got to go," I said, pushing her hand away, reaching for my underwear.

"You don't want me anymore," she declared.

I didn't answer, continuing to dress.

"You think you are so better than everyone," Mia said crossing her arms over her barely covered breasts. "I told you: you are not that special."

"Correct," I said, hoping to appease Leo Sporcatello's daughter long enough to make a clean getaway.

"My father owns your father," she said with no small measure of satisfaction. "And now he owns you."

Monstrous anger — self-loathing? — welled up inside me. I could hardly tie my shoes.

"You are a whore now John Canali. Just like your father. Like those *bambini*. You are *my* whore."

I never hit a woman in my life — until Mia said those words. I didn't mean to. I couldn't help myself. I just did it. I slapped her.

Mia raised her hand to the corner of her mouth, tracing a trickle of blood. She examined her finger and smiled. She wore a look that told me she'd always known there was darkness inside me. That she'd won a battle I didn't even know I was fighting.

"Again," she whispered, her voice thick with excitement.

I turned my back on her and left. I felt as dirty as I'd ever felt in my life . . .

The following week's weather was glorious. Daytime temperatures hovered in the mid-'70s. Cotton clouds drifted through clear blue skies. Trees burst back to life. Flowers assaulted the senses with improbable riots of color. The smell of renewed life was everywhere.

And yet I felt as cold and bleak as Second Beach in the dead of winter. Nothing held any pleasure; not my job, not my favorite music, not the passing of each picture perfect day.

I went about my work like a robot, not caring about anything or anyone. I ignored my mother's calls. My father's calls. Luke's texts. Veronica's calls. I ate and watched TV between shifts. I wasn't sleeping much, haunted by multiple nightmares. Nothing made the slightest dent on my bone-deep fatigue or suffocating depression. Alcohol didn't help. Marijuana didn't help. I was distraught.

After a few days zombieing around, I deposited my mother's check and searched job availability in Austin, Seattle, Sioux City — places thousands of miles and a lifetime away from Rhode Island.

One day, after my shift, I found myself sitting on a curb about a half block away from 32 Molton Lane, the address my father had scrawled on a piece of paper that snowy night. I had to see the house of horrors for myself.

I was sitting on the curb for God knows how long, thinking God knows what, when I felt a tap on my shoulder. A small boy smiled at me. He was no more than eight. He looked carefree. Happy.

"Whatcha doin' Señor?"

"Enjoying the beautiful morning," I lied.

"You want a blow job?"

The world stopped.

"You off duty?"

I was speechless.

"Police get it free."

I couldn't breathe. I looked at the boy's face. I'd been wrong. He wasn't happy. He was drugged.

I stood up and started walking to the house, oblivious to everything except the forlorn structure ahead of me. A mangy German shepherd chained to a fence growled and bared its teeth. I ignored it.

I mounted the rotting stairs. I looked down and saw a gun in my hand. A Hispanic-looking man opened the door.

"You're early," he leered.

I shot him twice in the chest. He screamed and fell by the wayside. I entered the house.

Two children stood outside bedroom doors on either side of the hallway, staring at me with dead eyes. One was a little girl, wearing a "school uniform." The other was a little boy, dressed in an extra small Harley Davidson muscle shirt. I smiled at them. They didn't smile back.

A gray-haired woman in her 70's emerged from the door at the end of the hallway. She held a shotgun at her hip, unaware or unconcerned that a blast at that range would hit one if not both of the children.

I shot her. Three, four, maybe five times. It wasn't a particularly tight shot group, but all the bullets found their target before she could open fire.

Another woman — younger but clearly an adult — ran from a room to my right. Deafened by my own gunfire, I could see but not hear her yelling. She bolted straight past me towards the front door. I aimed my GLOCK at her as she passed.

Peering into the room she'd left behind, I saw a video camera on a tripod pointing at an unmade bed. Leather restraints lay on top of the sheets. Empty. Waiting.

"Go!" I yelled at the children, waving my GLOCK at the door.

They didn't move. Nor did I. We stood there looking at each other.

I thought I heard a prayer in the distance: "By the power of God, cast into hell Satan and all the evil spirits who prowl about the world seeking the ruin of souls." It took me a moment to realize I was having a *Pulp Fiction*-style auditory hallucination, courtesy Father Flavio of the St. Joseph Church.

The next thing I knew, I heard approaching sirens. I was about to holster my gun when I saw a teenage boy stick his head out from what I guessed to be the bathroom.

He looked straight at me. His eyes weren't blank but they sure as Hell weren't friendly. A fact he confirmed when he stepped into the hallway aiming a revolver at me. It was too late to stop him; I'd hesitated long enough for the shooter to finalize his aim.

Even so, I was going to fire my weapon. My finger found the trigger a second after he pulled his. I didn't get the chance to squeeze. Somehow, my gun fired itself. A damn good shot too, right into his sternum. It took me a moment to realize someone *else* had opened fire on the sex slavery worker. Someone behind me.

A searing pain pierced my right side. It felt like an elephant was standing on my shoulder. A heart attack? How could *that* be? I was in good shape. The elephant pressed me into the floor. Slowly, the scene faded to black . . .

"He's got nothing to say," my father's voice insisted from far away.

In my drug-addled mind, I was back in high school. My father was standing in front of principal Jakes, taking the fifth on my behalf. I was accused — rightly — of punching a bully named George. My classmate had only landed a couple of blows; one to my head, the other to my chest. So why did I feel like I'd been run over by a truck?

I slowly realized where I was — in a hospital bed — and what I'd done — murdered two people in a house used for child sex slavery.

Opening my eyes was a struggle. I couldn't tell how much time went by before I managed it, blinking, wincing at the afternoon light filtering through cheap window slats. They reminded me of the slat curtains at the bank in Hogan's Alley; the ones with the bomber's blood and brain matter splattered on their shiny surface. It was not a pleasant memory.

My father stood by the window, staring into the distance.

"I bet you're dying for a smoke," I said.

"Like you read about," he said, turning to face me.

The look on his face killed any thought of a quick recovery.

"What happened?"

"You were shot."

"That would explain it," I replied, noting that my right arm was dead to the world, my mouth dry as David Sedaris.

"Congratulations," he said, walking over and tousling my hair. "You're a hero."

"I lost it."

"Don't say anything Johnny. Things are bad enough as it is."

"For me," I croaked. "What about the kids?"

"They're in care."

I spent a few minutes assessing my ability to breathe and move body parts. Everything hurt.

"There's a federal Marshal outside your door," my father said. "Friends of yours?"

"I don't have friends."

I closed my eyes. When I opened them again Father was gone. A middle-aged nurse was in his place. She hovered above me, insisting that I listen to a list of injuries before she doled out pain meds: a gunshot wound, concussion, two cracked ribs and a cracked tooth.

Two days later, getting more sleep than I'd had in years, Luke walked through the door dressed for school in pressed jeans, a white polo shirt and sneakers.

"Hey Dad," he said casually to the father he'd met once before. "How's your shoulder?"

"Doc says I won't be tossing you a ball for three months."

"Six," the nurse corrected, checking my chart before leaving the room.

Luke plopped himself down in the visitor's chair and grabbed my untouched bran muffin.

"Ugh," he said, his voice muffled, returning the pastry to the plate. "This is like eating sawdust."

"You'll survive."

"What about you?" he asked. "It must have been pretty rough in that whorehouse."

"Don't call it that," I protested weakly.

"Is it true you took out three people?"

"Talk to my lawyer."

"Grandpa? We get on like a house on fire. That's one of his expressions. He's got a million of 'em."

"Is your mother here?"

"She's downstairs getting coffee."

"Listen to me," I said slowly, licking dry lips. "The FBI knows about your extracurricular activities. They're using it as leverage on me."

"For what?"

"You need to stop, before it's too late."

"You ratted me out?"

"It's not like that," I protested, suddenly feeling sleep stealing over me.

"So what *is* it like?"

"You're dealing. It attracts the wrong kind of attention."

"As opposed to what? What *you* did? I bet a lot of people aren't too happy with you right about now."

"You included?"

"I don't know anything about you, *Dad.* But yeah, me included. You're bad for business."

"That I am," I said, closing my eyes, surrendering to my fatigue.

Veronica knocked on the door some time later.

"Hey," I said, smiling as best I could.

"Hello Johnny," Veronica said, sitting on my bed. "How are you?"

"Alive," I replied.

"You're a cockroach. You can't be killed."

I laughed. causing one of my damaged ribs to say hello, and not very cheerfully.

I stared at the Veronica and Luke: a perfectly preserved East Side matron in the making and a 15-year-old boy on the brink of manhood. I wondered about the family I'd never have. The life I'd missed. A little voice inside my head said *fuhgeddaboutit*. Somehow, the realization didn't depress me. Quite the opposite.

Luke and Veronica's presence in the hospital room made me want more time. Time to be *some* part of Luke's life. To do the right thing for and by him, no matter how small, no matter how effective or ineffective. I knew I was guilty of neglect. I promised myself I'd do something good for the kid even if I died trying, which, given my injuries and the close call with mob hit men, seemed a distinct possibility.

Mia walked into the room.

The mob boss' daughter stood just inside the door, hands on hips, dressed in stylishly ripped jeans and a form-fitting sweat shirt that told the world that "happiness is expensive."

I'm not sure what alerted Luke and Veronica first: the scent of Coco Chanel wafting into the room or the look in my eyes as I stared at my lover. Former lover? Bruised and battered, I wasn't sure where we stood.

Luke was impressed in the way you'd expect a 15-year-old boy to be impressed. Veronica regarded Mia as if the twenty-something Italian immigrant was a beetle about to chow down on prize-winning roses.

I felt a surge of energy, relatively speaking. Maybe it was the drugs or maybe it was Mia. Either way, my mind started sending me warning signals. Putting the two women together struck me as a bad idea, on all sorts of levels.

"We'll see you when you get out," Veronica called, nudging Luke out of his hormonal trance and heading for the exit. "When will that be?"

"I don't know," I said.

Mia stood aside, smiled enigmatically and watched them go.

"My father wants to meet you," Mia said, sitting in the chair Luke had vacated.

"You sure you've got the right verb?"

Mia took a second to figure it out.

"*Può essere.*"

"Perhaps? Oh great."

"*Tesoro*, I'm sorry for what I have said to you," Mia whispered, putting my hand in both of hers. "I was bad."

"*Multo*," I croaked.

"I was missing my regular *distrazione,*" Mia said, looking down, pretending to be embarrassed. "But I'm all better now!" she announced, looking up, smiling and leaning back. "Sweet as cake."

"Pie," I corrected gently. "*Torta.*"

"You have so much to teach me Johnny. And I want to make you all better. But first I think you must meet *Babbo*."

"I don't think I'll call your father that. This meeting, do I have a choice?"

Mia shrugged.

"What could we possibly talk about?"

"Me!" Mia said happily.

"*Ovviamente.* I'll do it on one condition."

"*Dimmi.*"

"Bring me a Wimpy Skippy pie from Casserta's. The food here sucks."

Mia pretended to consider the deal before nodding yes. She got up slowly and closed the curtains.

"Time for a rest."

The harder I fought the urge to sleep the drowsier I got. As I drifted off, Mia whispered in my ear.

"*Io e te mai soli.*" You and me, never alone.

Chapter Twelve

I expected to meet Leonardo Sporcatello on Federal Hill, breaking bread with the mob boss in a corner booth of a family-style Italian restaurant, negotiating for my life with an overweight goomba slurping spaghetti. That's not how it happened.

Mia arranged our little *faccia a faccia* for the Fishbein wing of the Rhode Island School of Design museum: a glass fronted gallery for people who consider representational art so two thousand years ago. She helped me remove my sling and put on a dress shirt befitting a meet-and-greet with the head of a homicidal criminal conspiracy.

"How is it?" Mia asked, watching me try to ignore the pain.

"It heals a lot faster in the movies," I said.

To help me identify her camera shy father, Mia showed me a photo of a trim, grey-haired fifty-three-year-old. Leo Sporcatello looked like an Olympic gymnast who'd never stopped training. And there he was, sitting on a bench, staring at a piece of white fabric.

"Lieutenant Canali," Sporcatello said in a thick southern Italian accent, rising to shake my hand gingerly. "*Sta bene?*"

"*No che male,*" I replied, deciding not to praise the effects of pain medication.

Sporcatello gestured for me to join him on the bench. We took a moment to get comfortable with each other's presence.

"No bodyguards?" I asked, looking around the mostly deserted space.

"Says who?"

I glanced at the young couple contemplating a giant doorknob. Mushroom? Something. I remembered the handsome art student having trouble focusing on his reading, leaning against the wall outside the Fishbein's front entrance.

"I don't like modern art," Sporcatello announced, gesturing at the gauzy material that seemed to float in front of the wall opposite.

"Neither did Hitler," I pointed out.

"It's important to understand things you do not like."

"Is that why we're looking at leftover curtain material?"

Sporcatello nodded.

"Do you collect art?" I asked.

"A little. But not like this. I have a weakness for hyper-realistic paintings. Art without technique, without execution, is *vuoto*. Worthless."

"'Execution' being the operative word."

Sporcatello flashed a smile that wouldn't have seemed out of place on a crocodile.

"Do you know why you're alive John Canali?" the mob boss asked, turning to look me straight in the eyes.

"Because I'm banging your daughter?"

It wasn't the smartest thing I'd ever said. If Sporcatello had been a traditional Italian mobster, maybe even a traditional Italian man, he would've pulled a knife and slit my throat right then and there. God knows how I would have stopped him with my right arm out of the game.

Sporcatello's underlying assumption — that I lived or died at his pleasure — rubbed me the wrong way. The Ocean State was a morass of moral, political and financial corruption, but it wasn't a dictatorship. At least in theory. In reality, the homicidal fury in the mobster's dark eyes told me that the law of the jungle was the only law that applied to Leonardo Sporcatello.

"Mia has strange tastes," he said, his anger passing like an errant thundercloud.

"What about her father?" I asked, doubling down. "Was Molton Lane business or pleasure?"

"I like real men," Sporcatello replied, placing his hand on my thigh and leaving it there. "Like you."

"Now there's a threesome I hadn't considered."

Sporcatello seemed genuinely amused. He removed his hand from my leg and resumed contemplating the fabric in front of us.

"Enough *chiacchiere*," he said. "You're alive because you're useful to me. You have done me a favor."

"Everyone makes mistakes."

"Uncle Sam has been *indagando su*. How do you say? Sniffing around. Thanks to you, they have to sniff somewhere else. I want to know where. What."

"You want me to spy on the FBI."

"Your friend Pistone, he likes you very much."

"And you not at all."

"You can't please everyone."

"And if I don't please you?"

"Then you will have problems."

"You mean I'll have no more problems."

We spent a moment watching the white material wave in a breeze let in by a panhandler looking for a bathroom.

"Do you believe in free will?" I asked.

"Muslims think our fate is written on our forehead," Sporcatello replied. "Only Allah can read it."

"Can you read mine?" I asked.

"I'm not God."

"No you're not. And He's going to send you straight to hell for what you did to those children."

"You think they had somewhere else to go?"

I laughed; a short, sharp sound that betrayed my disbelief. What do you say to someone who sees child prostitution as a compassionate act? How do you not put a bullet in their head?

"Do you love my daughter *Ufficiale* Canali?"

The question caught me off-guard. I needed a second to switch from thinking about killing Leonardo Sporcatello to declaring my feelings for his daughter.

Did I love Mia? I could no more resist her charms than I could say no to a Dell's frozen lemonade on a hot summer's day. But something wasn't right about our relationship — something to do with the fact that Mia was amoral, a woman who'd do *anything* to get her way. Which wasn't a comfortable thought for someone whose mother answered to the same description.

"Yes I love her," I said as convincingly as I could, unsure if I was lying or admitting something to myself.

Sporcatello stood up, satisfied.

"I've enjoyed our little talk. We have a deal?"

"Pinky swear promise," I declared, putting every part of my body on the chopping block.

"I want you to come for dinner," he said shaking my hand with a firm grip.

"How do I get in touch with you?" I asked.

"You don't."

As Sporcatello left the gallery he removed a wad of cash from his jeans' pocket, peeled off a twenty and pressed it in the bum's palm.

"*In bocca al lupo*" he said.

"In the mouth of the wolf." Italian performers use the expression to wish someone good luck before they go on stage. As Sporcatello made himself scarce, I whispered the proper response. *Crepi*. May the wolf die . . .

It's a 45 minute drive from Providence to the Tiverton Rod and Gun Club. Luke spent the time tapping his iPhone and flipping between radio stations devoted to forgettable songs based on unforgettable hooks. I survived the musical assault all the way to Fish Road.

"You remember the four safety rules?" I asked, switching off the radio.

"Copy that Blue Falcon."

"Barney."

"What?"

"We call a useless partner a Barney, after Barney Fife. A small town deputy sheriff in a '60s sitcom. His boss trusted him with one bullet."

"How many do we have?"

"Lots."

We drove down the dirt road to the club's cabin, a small structure requiring constant attention from its blue collar members. I signed the ledger on the porch and drove down the dirt access road to the range.

"Here's a safety rule the NRA doesn't teach," I said retrieving my pistol case from the trunk. "Always carry a loaded gun at a gun range."

"Why's that?" Luke asked, playing with the volume control on his active ear protection.

"Criminals love three things: drugs, cash and guns. They come to the range because that's where the guns are."

"What about pussy?"

"Four things. Assuming we're talking about gay women or straight men."

"I'd rather talk about pussy."

I set four handguns on the beat up wooden table facing the target stands: a Ruger .22 revolver, a Smith & Wesson .38 revolver, a Walther 9mm semi-automatic pistol and a .45 caliber Ruger 1911.

"Keep your gun pointed downrange and nothing bad will happen," I assured my flesh-and-blood.

"I'm not nervous," Luke said nervously.

I taught him the proper shooting stance, adjusted his grip and had him dry fire until the Ruger didn't move when he pulled the trigger.

"Bullets face forwards," I joked as he fed a single .22 cartridge into the revolver's cylinder.

Luke took aim at the target and fired his first shot. Bullseye at 10 yards.

"Nice shooting Tex."

A proud smile lit up Luke's young features. He wasn't the only one who was proud. I suddenly understood how my father must have felt the first time he took me shooting. I suddenly knew what it meant to *be* a father. To have a legacy of flesh and blood. The realization stunned me into silence.

"More bullets please," Luke said, keeping the revolver pointed downrange.

Luke was a natural. As we switched calibers and handguns, pausing to suck down some Coke Zeros as the morning warmed, he mastered each firearm with growing confidence.

"Youth is wasted on the young," I sighed as Luke peppered the center of a target from 25 yards with the Walther.

"O.K. old man, show me how it's done."

I picked up the polymer pistol and loaded it with a fresh magazine.

"Keep in mind I'm shooting with my left hand," I cautioned.

I aimed the pistol's sights at an unmolested silhouette target we'd posted some 15 yards away.

"This is called the failure to stop drill. More colorfully, the Mozambique."

"Why's that?"

"Mercenary territory."

"Wish I knew the story," Luke said.

"Two to the chest, rapid fire, then one to the head, slow fire."

I shot two rounds to the silhouette's center mass as fast as I could, then took my time and fired a single shot the head, missing by a good two inches.

"For shooting someone with body armor?" Luke asked, smirking at the hole to the right of the targets head.

"Exactly," I replied, firing my three shots twice more, managing to get the third shot of each series in the pretend perp's brain box. "Your turn."

Luke's rounds were sloppy — it was his first time rapid firing the nine. He quickly dialed it in, making short, accurate work of the target. I clapped him on the back. He set the hot gun down, muzzle pointed downrange.

"I need to take a leak," Luke said.

"Over by the bushes. Look out for poison ivy. Leaves of three let it be. They're pointed at the tip."

"So am I."

Luke came back to the shooting line, sniffing. He replaced his ear protection and picked up the Walther.

"Watch this."

He unloaded an entire magazine at the target, turning the middle of the paper into a reasonable facsimile of Swiss cheese

"Center mass baby!" Luke shouted triumphantly.

I slowly took the gun from his hands, removed the magazine, racked the slide and set the pistol down on the table.

"Now try doing it when someone's shooting at you," I said. "When there's no place to hide, when bullets are whizzing by your ears and your nervous system's lit up like a Christmas tree."

"Copy that," Luke said with a cocky grin.

I didn't say a word about Luke's dilated pupils and sudden case of sniffles all the way to Evelyn's drive-in restaurant. We rode in a comfortable silence, giving me time to think of a way to set Luke straight. To *get* him straight, before worst came to worst.

None of my schemes seemed likely to succeed — especially given my own history of teenage lawlessness and my parents' inability to keep *me* on the straight and narrow. Until I somehow discovered it for myself.

Luke and I sat at a picnic table by the harbor, eating lobster rolls and clam cakes, basking in a warm sun tempered by a cool sea breeze. We watched a gull-stained fishing boat pass a small sailboat heading downriver.

"How long have you been using?" I asked casually.

"Using what?" he asked, pretending not to understand.

"That little bathroom break back there? I'm thinking you powdered your nose. I assume you're dealing to support your habit."

"That's ridiculous."

"Where does a 15-year-old *get* cocaine?"

"Don't go there," Luke said, staring across the waves at stately summer houses waiting for their owners.

"You're not smarter than the cops Luke. O.K., you're smarter than ninety percent of cops. Maybe more. But a cop doesn't have to be a genius to put an addict's balls in a vise, proverbial or otherwise."

"Fuck," Luke said, leaning back and looking around.

"'Fuck' I'm going to get help and stop, or 'fuck' I'm going to keep dealing so I don't run out of Bolivian marching powder?"

"Just fuck."

"Does you mother know?"

"Did you tell her?"

"No."

"Then no. She's got her own problems. I don't think you need to add to them."

"That's my decision, not yours . . . What kind of problems?"

"Max."

"What about him?"

Luke shook his head.

"Luke you're in a world of trouble. You need to go into rehab."

"What for? I'm an honors student, I'm in the number one boat *and* I'm getting laid."

"The word you're looking for is statutory rape," I corrected. "Luke, I want you to know —"

"With all due respect," Luke interrupted. "Butt the fuck out. Just like you did for the last, what was it? Oh, yeah. *Fifteen years.*"

We both knew that wasn't going to happen. Now that we'd connected, there was no way I was going to stand by as my son went down for felony drug trafficking. At least not without a fight.

We watched a pair of seagulls wheeling overhead, riding a stiffening breeze blowing in from the ocean.

"What was mom like back in the day?" Luke asked.

"Smart," I said. "Funny. And pretty. *Very* pretty."

"Why'd you do it? Why'd you sleep with her after she was married?"

"It just sort of happened," I said, adjusting my sling. "No. That's not right. I've always felt like a drowning man. Your mother saved me so many times. From myself mostly. But also from the feeling that I could never win. When I was with her all was right with the world. I thought I'd be O.K. when I left for college. I'd come back different. I didn't. I still needed her. And it turns out she still needed me."

"She was married," Luke said.

"People grow up Luke. Make decisions. Get married to the wrong people for the wrong reasons. They have to live with that. One way or another."

"Do you wish you'd worn a condom?"

"Time will tell. Just kidding," I added after a dramatic pause. "I'm glad you're alive Luke. I was happy from the moment your mother told me she was pregnant."

"Why didn't you tell me you were my father before?"

"Your mother wanted to protect her marriage. Your brothers. I agreed."

"And?"

"And the years just kinda rolled by. I won't say I thought about you every day, but you were always on my mind."

"What time is it?" Luke asked, throwing the gulls a cold fry.

"Luke, there are a lot of good treatment programs —"

Luke started to interrupt. I held him off with a raised hand.

"Whatever comes next, I'm ready to help."

"What if I don't *need* any help?"

"No man is an island."

"I think we're done here," Luke said.

We dumped our trash and headed back to the car.

I should have been angry. How could I be? Luke was hardly the first kid to get hooked on drugs, or the first drug addict to live in denial. Equally, I hadn't been there for Luke's childhood, when I could have shaped him into a different person, a different man. Isn't that what fathers are supposed to do?

"Going with the flow" wasn't an option, what with Luke poised on the edge of arrest and the FBI, the mob and Mia wanting to own me. And me not wanting to be owned. I needed a plan. But first I needed coffee . . .

Two teenagers sat on the bench outside the coffee shop perched on the river by Route 44. They gave us the hairy eyeball as I opened the screen door. I glanced back down the street as I held the door open, eyeing a beat up Reagan-era Chevy parked nearby.

The not-at-all dynamic duo's leader was inside the coffee shop, loitering at the counter. A steaming cup of Joe sat on the counter. The kid pretended to contemplate the few remaining treats in the pastry case. He was no actor, but he was straight out of central casting. Send me an armed robber in a dark hoodie. Make sure he knows how to act shifty. Tell him to keep his hands in his pockets.

"This is my son," I told hoodie boy, making sure to keep arms' length away from his wiry frame, despite the store's crowded confines. "He doesn't want to take my advice. If I were you I wouldn't make the same mistake."

Hoodie boy looked at Luke. My son rolled his eyes, failing to see that his fellow "customer" was sizing up Luke's ability to take a punch. Kick to the groin? Knife to the stomach? Bullet to the chest? Something . . .

"I advise you to re-join your friends outside," I said menacingly. "Don't worry about paying for the coffee."

"You a cop?" the kid demanded, squaring up to me ominously. "A one-armed cop?"

"Yup."

"You gonna *make* me leave?"

Tough talk, and I didn't like those hands in his pockets one bit.

"Maybe. But I'm betting you're going to leave of your own free will."

Hoodie boy looked confused.

"Your choice," I clarified. "And you're not coming back. Do you know why?"

"Why?"

"Because it's not worth it."

The aspiring robber looked at me with expressionless eyes: the stare that tells me a man — or a woman — has nothing to lose. It was decision time, for both of us.

Hoodie Boy removed a hand from his hoodie, fast. I should have attacked, grabbed his arm and kneed him in the balls. I didn't. If I went hands-on with the thug Luke would never see me the same way again. He'd think of *me* as a thug. Just another vicious cop in from a City known for the breed.

If hoodie boy had had a weapon, I'd have been screwed. Luke too. Luckily, he was unarmed.

The frustrated robber grabbed the coffee off the counter, spilling scalding liquid onto his hand. He toughed it out and left, throwing me a surly "I'll be back" expression as he slammed open the screen door. I followed behind, watching the gruesome threesome get in their piece of shit and leave.

"You're such a bully," Luke said, shaking his head.

The barista stepped back from the counter. His shaking hands held a small shotgun — known as a "coach gun" for its service in the Wild West — in shaking hands. He replaced the weapon in its hidey hole under the counter and nodded his thanks. Distracted by the drinks menu on the chalkboard overhead, Luke missed the exchange.

"I'm not a bully," I said, ordering a black coffee. "I'm a cop."

"No, you're a 'negotiator,'" Luke said dramatically.

"Damn straight. And we need to negotiate."

Truer words were never spoken. But not many were said on the ride home; none about the crisis to come. I dropped off Luke at the Herndon estate, sighing as enormous wrought iron gates silently swung closed behind me. I made my way to East Side Liquors . . .

"Hello officer," the salesman said, reminding me that I'd never make it undercover. "Can I be of assistance?"

"Australian?" I asked.

"South African," he replied. "You're not the first to make that mistake."

"I need a bottle of something special for a dinner party. The host is Italian, from Sicily."

"Wine, liqueur or digestif?"

"Yes."

"Something dignified and refined or wild and crazy?"

"Yes."

"I've got just the thing," he said, gesturing at a bottle on the shelf above my head. "Let me get that for you," he added, retrieving a rounded bottle with a thin neck and silver-plated top that looked like it belonged in a chemistry lab.

"Grappa," he said reverentially. "Are you familiar?"

"Can't say that I am."

"It's made from leftover grape skins, pulp, seeds and stems."

"Taste?"

"Depends on the vineyard. It's either sublime or like a grenade going off in your mouth. This one's from the Nonino, made from a single varietal grown especially for the purpose. It packs quite a punch but I've never met anyone who didn't like going a few rounds."

"Expensive?"

He turned the bottle to show me the price tag.

"Struth!" I declared, forgetting that the salesman wasn't an Aussie. "Sorry. What do South Africans say?"

"Ongelooflike," he said. "Unbelievable. It's dear but it *is* a *riserva*."

"Goes with what?"

"Best served after dinner, chilled. Ideally? Ten degrees celsius."

"Fifty degrees Fahrenheit."

"I'm impressed. Will it do?"

"We'll see," I said, breaking out my credit card.

"My treat," he said, sliding the bottle in a brown paper bag and holding the package towards me.

"That's not necessary."

"Happiness is a necessity," he said, placing the package in my hand. "Let me know if your host enjoys it."

Uniformed officers aren't allowed to accept freebies from local businessmen. Nor is walking to a squad car carrying a bottle in a brown bag a great image for taxpayers. But if Rhode Island has one rule, it's that rules are meant to be broken.

I was sure Leo Sporcatello would agree with the sentiment. The question was, what game were we playing and who held the cards?

Chapter Thirteen

I spent the weekend readying myself for active duty: practicing my one-handed draw, chatting with my physical therapist, reading to relax and second guessing myself. Was I really going to leave Leo Sporcatello's sex trafficking operation alone, assuming, as I had to, that it hadn't ended at Molton Lane? Less urgently, was a bottle of grappa an appropriate house gift for a mob boss?

Mia wasn't much help on the *mafiosi* fealty front. When I asked for an alternative present she yelled out random nouns in broken English, knowing full well I wasn't going to show up at her father's doorstep with a snow cone, helicopter or leisure suit. When the time came to rejoin the rat race I headed to PPD HQ.

The Providence Public Safety Complex is a bland blend of traditional and modern architecture perched on the edge of I-95. I entered its three-story interior atrium wishing its designer had paid more attention to acoustics; the hubbub sounded as muddy as the first classical music recordings. I made a mental note to refuse to perform Vladigerov's *Piano Concerto #3* in its cavernous space, should someone ask.

An overcast sky loomed above the empty space, darkening the lobby, threatening thunderstorms. Going back to The Job reminded me of unfinished business. A little voice inside my head told me I was complicit in the world's worst crime. It wasn't wrong.

I signed for my badge and gun, my left hand scrawl a poor match for my usual signature. Chief Lamar intercepted me before I could hit the streets.

"Disability payment," he said, pointing at my sling.

"For life," I said, unnecessarily.

"We need to have a little heart-to-heart," Lamar said, leading me into his office.

"You *have* a heart?"

"If you prick me do I not bleed?" Lamar joked, a smile inching across his face as he settled in behind his desk.

"I dunno," I said, sitting in the chair facing him. "Let's find out."

Chief Lamar's smile disappeared to the sound of distant thunder.

"Actually, there's only one prick in this room and I'm looking right at him."

"Is there a mirror behind me?"

Chief Lamar lacked the ability to stand in someone else's shoes and understand how they feel. But he wasn't without emotion.

"*God damn it!*" Lamar barked, slamming his fist on his desk, sending a pair of pens two inches into the air. "I will *not* stand for your insubordination!"

I resisted the urge to point out that the Chief was sitting. Instead I watched Providence's top cop carefully repositioning his pens, trying to control his temper.

"You don't like me, do you Canali?"

"No more than I like rhetorical questions."

"I'm not going to lie," Lamar said, making a promise neither of us expected him to keep. "You're not very popular downstairs. Your whorehouse heroics blew a six-month investigation. There's only one reason the DA doesn't charge you with murder: no jury in this state would convict you. Still you never know. He might want to send a message about killer cops."

Lamar paused to make sure I understood that I wasn't in the clear for discharging my weapon at Molton Lane, three homicides resulting.

"I don't think anyone at the Attorney General's office is about to join the John Canali fan club," he added, in case I missed his point.

"That's O.K. Membership is limited to law enforcement officials who don't stand around while an eight-year-old girl has a dick shoved in her mouth."

'That's not how I'd put it."

I almost said "so to speak."

"Justice delayed is justice denied," I said, instead. "Especially when you're a child getting raped day in and day out."

"We had them in our crosshairs," Lamar insisted. "Right until our main witness lost his life. The witness *you* were supposed to protect."

"The decapitator who ran the house? Yeah that was a real shame."

"Did you ever hear about the college graduate who applied to the New London Police Department with an IQ of 125?" Lamar asked. "They rejected his application. You know why?"

"He was too smart for the job."

"Do you know *your* IQ Lieutenant Canali?"

"If I'm so smart how come I'm not rich?" I asked.

"Because you don't care about money. The question is, what *do* you care about? You want me to guess?"

"Sure."

"Being a Boy Scout. Consequences be damned."

I couldn't argue with the Chief's analysis. So I didn't.

"That makes you a dangerous man around here. To the department. To me."

"Sorry about that Chief."

Lamar nodded, as if my apology was sincere. In some ways it was.Chief Lamar was a political appointee, serving at the Mayor's pleasure. Like all elected officials, Lamar's boss held onto power by protecting and rewarding his friends. A circle of supporters that included some of the world's worst low-lifes, fancy cars and big houses be damned.

If Lamar rattled the wrong cages, the Mayor would have relieved him of command in a New York minute. Despite the Chief's obvious need to "go along to get along," despite his lack of empathy, for better or worse, we were on the same team.

Lamar unfolded a small cleaning cloth and rubbed a pair of reading glasses with the silky material. Our meeting was drawing to a close. Before I went back on duty, I had a question of my own.

"Hey Chief, why haven't you fired me?"

"Union," Lamar answered, not missing a beat. "Besides, you're useful."

"If I had a dime for everyone who said that . . ."

The Chief took a moment to register my comment.

"The Goodrich incident," he said. "It turns out you're pretty good at negotiating."

"One for one."

"Defusing dangerous situations is a rare skill. And not just on the streets."

Lamar left that one hanging. So did I. The idea of helping the Chief negotiate Providence's criminal and political garbage dump made me distinctly queasy.

"I don't think I have to say it, but I will," Lamar said. "Keep digging into this Molton Lane thing. Report directly to me."

"In writing?" I asked, knowing full well that Lamar wanted a paper trail like he wanted another hole in his head.

"My door is always open," Lamar answered, putting on his glasses, turning his attention to a file and gesturing at the closed door behind me. "This isn't my first rodeo, Canali," he added as I got up, keeping his eyes on the paperwork. "Just make sure it isn't your last."

Forewarned, I made my way to the parking lot. I opened the cruiser door and found Officer Swanson in the passenger seat.

"You're shitting me," I said.

The mob *and* the FBI considered me an informant. The Chief of Police was watching my every move. The AG was holding homicide charges over my head. The feds had my drug dealing son on their radar. I was romantically involved with a mob boss' daughter. And there he was: a mentally unstable dirty cop riding shotgun.

"When are you going to thank me for saving your life?" Swanson asked later, interrupting a half an hour of blissful silence.

I pulled into Riverside Park, just as the storm hit.

"I know you think we're square," I said. "I didn't rat you out for double tapping Rico Nardelli and you almost stopped a scumbag from shooting me. But there's an important difference. You're a hired gun. A hit man for the mob."

Swanson looked at me, his face blank.

"That would be fine if it was *your* problem," I said. "The thing is it's my problem too. We try to bust someone connected — maybe someone with a gun pointed at me — and I'm going to wonder whose side you're on. Whose side *are* you on Darren?"

Swanson looked a long way from remorseful.

"I'm not proud of what I did," I said. "But I did it for the right reasons. Whether you like it or not you're working for the mob now, now and for the rest of your life."

That was a bit rich, given my arrangement with Leo Sporcatello. But there's a difference between talking to the mob and killing for the mob.

"It's not like that," Swanson protested.

"KBISFB."

"What?"

"Keep believing it shit for brains. I'm never going to trust you. I don't even trust you to hand me a cup of coffee."

"C'mon Lieutenant."

"C'mon? That's it? That's the best you've got? Jesus."

The rain hammered the cruiser's roof; the windshield wipers barely kept up with the downpour. I don't know how long we sat there in silence, but it was a while. And then the call came in: a hostage situation in Elmwood.

I drove way too fast, and not well. Trying to scare Swanson? Probably. Putting the pedal to the metal on the rain slicked streets, dodging potholes and slow moving traffic, relieved some of my tension.

This time the mobile command center made it to the scene — a much-appreciated shelter from the downpour. I left Swanson in the car without instructions, without looking back.

Commander Jimenez brought me up to speed. A small time drug dealer named Jaylen Jones imprisoned a woman in his apartment in a converted textile mill.

"A neighbor said she heard a woman yelling she was being held hostile," Jimenez told me.

"You mean hostage?"

Jimenez looked as if I'd pissed in his cornflakes. I punched-in Jones' cell number, provided by his parole officer.

"What?" a voice demanded, sounding more annoyed than angry.

"This is John Canali with the Providence Police Department," I said, using my best late night DJ voice. "I understand you're keeping a young woman company. Your girlfriend?"

"Nah she ain't my girlfriend," the voice on the other end laughed. "She's with some other guy."

"Who would that be?"

"What are you soft?" Jones asked. "I'm not telling you."

"Are you from Massachusetts?"

"How'd you know that?"

"Your accent. Also, Rhode Islanders use the word 'retarded.'"

"They teach you that in cop school?"

"Sure. And they teach us that people from Taxachusetts don't know what a bubbler is."

"What is it?"

"A water fountain. Speaking of which, do you need a drink?"

"I got Mountain Dew."

"Be careful with that shit. It's got more sugar than most third world countries."

"That's OK I'm planning on using the Twinkie defense."

"How'd you know about the Twinkie defense?" I asked, recognizing the legal ploy used by a California killer who claimed that his withdrawal from a sugary diet accounted for his mental instability.

"I read about it in when I was inside," Jones said.

"Hey Jaylen, do you mind if I have a word with the young lady?"

"She ain't no lady. Here."

"What the fuck is wrong with you people?" the hostage yelled. "Get off your fucking ass come in here and cap this motherfucker!"

Jones pulled the phone from the girl.

"She's a real charmer," Jones said.

"So Jaylen, what's it going to take for you to come out of there?"

"An all expenses paid vacation to Hawaii."

"How am I going to arrange that?"

"I like kayak.com," Jones said.

"You're a funny guy."

"That's what people say. Only most of the time they don't get it."

"Tell me about it. So who's the girl?"

"Let's just say she belongs to a friend of mine."

"Friend?"

"Business associate."

"Is she local?"

"What difference does that make?"

"You tell me and I'll tell you."

"Cranston. You heard that accent. Like nails on a blackboard."

"So you didn't take her out of state?"

"Nah she just dropped by. Brought some blow that was all kinds of stepped on. How my supposed to move *that*?"

Jones had admitted that he was a dealer. A good sign? Maybe, maybe not.

"Baby laxative?" I asked.

"Yeah no shit."

"Lots of shit."

It was an easy joke but Jones laughed pretty hard, increasing my suspicion that he was high as a kite.

"What were we talking about?" he asked.

"The girl you're visiting with. She's local. That's good news. You kidnap someone across state lines and it's a federal beef. And then I got to let the FBI take over."

"So good news for *you*."

"That depends on what you do next."

"I'm going to Hawaii."

"They do have some killer weed."

"That's some seriously expensive stuff."

"It's pretty cheap over there. Hang on a second willya? Be right back."

Hostage negotiation protocol says always keep the bad guy talking. My father had a different take: "he who controls the silence controls the conversation."

Jones didn't seem about to kill anyone. And I needed a moment to review his record. The 23-year-old perp had racked up three drug busts, a simple assault and grand theft auto. He'd been in for a year about two years previous.

"I've got an idea," I said, returning to our conversation. "How about I get my associates to pay your friend a little visit. Show him a good time down at headquarters."

"Kill two birds with one stone?" Jones asked. "That's what my mother always says."

"Smart woman."

"Well I ain't no bird and I ain't no rat."

"Don't look at it that way. Think of it as payback with no strings attached. A way to make sure I don't have to tell your mother Jaylen Jones died in a hail of bullets."

"Yeah," Jones admitted, inhaling something. "He gonna know I told you where to find him?"

"Nope. It'll be a courtesy call. Tell him what's happened to his girlfriend."

"I already told him."

"Then he'll be expecting us. You know where he keeps his stash?"

"In a shed behind his apartment," Jones revealed, his reluctance to rat out his friend gone in a puff of smoke. "There's a Rottweiler tied up there. He's not real friendly."

"The guys love dogs. What's his address?"

"I don't know about this . . ."

"Yeah you do. You know this is what's going to happen."

Jones paused.

"You bust him and I'll come out," he agreed.

We did and Jones came out quietly. The girlfriend not so much. She was shouting at the top of her lungs, threatening to sue the cops, the city, the President of the United States.

Thirty seconds after one of the Commander's minions read Jones his Miranda rights and popped him into a squad car, my phone rang.

"Hello John, this is Destiny calling."

And so it was.

Chapter Fourteen

Destiny's phone call interrupted wrong-handed handshakes, high fives and congratulatory head nods. I knew the good vibes wouldn't last. Not that I cared. The PPD was staffed by a farrago of narcissists, sycophants, sociopaths, psychopaths, nymphomaniacs, alcoholics, drug addicts, idiots and fools. An incomplete list that cried out for a Venn diagram.

"I'm just callin' to let you know I will be in Providence Friday," Destiny said, hitting me with her best Blanche DuBois. "Where would you like to meet?"

I leaned against a lamppost, rubbed my shoulder and watched Detectives Cruse and LaValle heave themselves up the metal stairs to Jones' fourth floor apartment, no doubt cursing a broken elevator. The sun made a sudden appearance on the dark horizon, bathing the scene in golden light. I inhaled the post-rain scent, a heady combination of bacteria, plant oils and ozone.

"Don't you mean y'all?" I asked Destiny, watching the detectives. "To tell y'all?"

"Y'all is a collective noun," Destiny corrected. "I'm coming to see you."

"Friday's not good," I said, chastened.

"I am *sure* you have more important things on your mind than the murder of a mother and child," Destiny said, swaddling her words in honeyed condescension.

I didn't feel like sharing the fact that Friday was the day I was having dinner with the head of the criminal organization responsible for the disappearance of her Dominican friend and her friend's child.

"I am *waiting* for your answer," Destiny said.

"Make it Saturday afternoon. Prospect Park. I'll meet at you the pedestrian bridge over the highway. Do you think you can find it?" I asked, the resulting sigh and silence making me wish I hadn't.

As the week wore on, my anxiety levels rose faster than Providence's public debt. Work was like Marty Ray's cover of *Ice Ice Baby*: same shit, different wrapper. I felt like a pilot of a small plane dodging bad weather. Without knowing its exact location or severity. With nowhere to land.

That Wednesday, I got a call for a welfare check at an East Side residence. A relative hadn't heard from her brother in a week. Swanson was off, so I handled it solo.

FBI Agent Pistone answered the door.

"My name is Lieutenant John Canali." I said. "I'm here to perform a welfare check on behalf of a concerned relative. Do you mind if I come in?"

"Not at all."

There they were: three members of the fed's organized crime task force. Two Fibbies I hadn't met rose from the couch and introduced themselves as Agents Schneider and Othello.

"What is it with you guys as 'Agent This' and "Agent That'?" I asked as they shook my left hand. "Can I be Agent K?"

Schneider looked to be in the tail end of his thirties. The tall, dark-haired agent was suited and booted, wearing a belt buckle bigger than my badge. His smile was professional and warm.

"Call me Bud," Agent Schneider said in an accent straight-out of Compton Texas. "Sorry about Quantico Lieutenant. We owe you one."

"Call me Kevin," Agent Othello advised.

Othello wasn't Schneider's total opposite, but close. Dressed in perfectly pressed tan slacks and a dark blue Ralph Lauren polo shirt, Othello wouldn't have been out of place at the Warwick Country Club. He was small, like Pistone, but young, unmarked, clean-cut.

The four of us sat down in the living room, a cluttered space that hadn't been updated since Hawaii joined the United States.

"We understand you had a meeting with Leo Sporcatello," Schneider said carefully. "Do you mind telling us what y'all discussed?"

"Hyper-realism," I replied. "Mr. Sporcatello has a thing for paintings that look like photographs," I added, in case the FBI didn't train its agents in art history.

"That makes a change," Othello said. "Most of our targets have terrible taste."

"John Gotti wore Brioni suits," I reminded him.

"Lieutenant," Pistone said, ignoring the opportunity to discuss Dapper Don's fashion sense.

"You gonna make me an offer I can't refuse?" I interrupted, figuring there was nothing like a quote from *The Godfather* to break the ice with the FBI.

The three agents laughed.

"Seriously," I said. "What does Uncle Sam want from me?"

"Whatever we can get," Othello said.

"At the moment I've got a dinner invitation from the Sporcatellos."

That got their attention.

"I am *not* wearing a wire," I protested preemptively.

Othello looked disappointed. Pistone and Schneider nodded grimly, a gesture that did nothing to make me believe I'd make it to desert at the Sporcatello household.

"We realize that meeting with us could put you in an uncomfortable position," Othello said.

"Having my dick cut off and shoved in my mouth certainly qualifies as 'uncomfortable'."

"I'm not going to lie to you Lieutenant," Schneider began.

"If I had a dime every time someone said that . . ."

"Hear me out. Agent Pistone — Larry — told me about your concerns. You're right. We're here to nail Sporcatello, not clean up your city. But I'd like you to think about something. There are bad guys and there are bad guys. Leo Sporcatello is one of the worst. I know: we take him down and someone will replace him. Maybe someone better, maybe someone worse."

"But definitely *someone*," I said.

"As my pastor used to say, doing nothing accomplishes nothing. We take our victories where we can and hope for the best."

Schneider paused, pretending to think about what he was about to say.

"What do you know about kudzu?" he asked.

"Somewhere between absolutely nothing and nothing," I said, wishing I was sitting on a porch sipping a mint julep.

"It's a vine. Loves the heat. Back in the '30s and '40s the government told farmers to plant kudzu to stop erosion. They planted over a million acres. Bad idea. Kudzu grows like wildfire. It covers native plants, steals their sunlight and kills them dead. It's damn near everywhere in the South now. There's only one way to kill it: cut it off at the root. Even then you have to keep an eye on it for ten years.

"Truth is, you're never going to get rid of kudzu. But that doesn't mean you shouldn't try. You can't kill evil, Lieutenant Canali. The best you can do is cut it back. Do you understand what I'm saying?"

Damn these southerners and their down home metaphors. I knew *exactly* what he was saying.

"OK Agent Schneider, I get it. So let me ask you something. What will busting Sporcatello do about child sex slavery in my state?"

All three men looked at each other.

"I'd like to say it will have a big impact . . ." Othello said.

"But you can't," I finished.

"No sir, I can't," Othello admitted. "I've worked in that area. Let me explain."

"Please."

"First, there's no organized child slavery distribution channel, not as such. No kingpin. Coyotes are freelancers. Sometimes they'll use a child to create a fake family for immigration. Sometimes they'll hold the child for ransom.

Sometimes they'll sell them to a private buyer, who may or may not prostitute the child."

"Children," I said.

"Children," he agreed. "If they put them into prostitution, they'll use only a few per location. They rent a house for a few months or so, then move on. Strange men coming and going at strange hours tends to attract the wrong kind of attention. Concerned citizens. Journalists."

"Cops," I added.

"Leo Sporcatello's people don't run the house.," Schneider said. "His organization just makes sure child protective services and law enforcement turn a blind eye. Leo takes a cut of the revenue — and there's a *lot* of revenue."

"It's a protection racket," I said. "With a side of blackmail."

Othello nodded.

"How many children are we talking about?" I asked. "In total."

"Rhode Island's a small place," Pistone said, indisputably. "We've heard rumors of a couple of other house, location unknown."

"Nationally, we estimate between ten and twenty thousand children are victims of human trafficking," Schneider said.

"What happens when they get too old?" I asked, not really wanting to hear the answer.

"Mostly? They're killed," Briggs said. "In rare cases they're sold back to their relatives. In many cases, they go to private buyers. When *they're* done they make a call."

I'm not a huge fan of humanity. But the idea that someone would murder children to order was the most sickening thing I'd ever heard. Sicker than the men whose perversion fueled the trade, leading to the abused children's death in some lonely, God-forsaken spot? Hard to say.

Equally hard to say: it was a safe bet that my father knew about the heinous crimes committed at Molton Lane. Not the only terrible crime he had to keep secret, but by far the worst.

And then there was Yanira Dupree, the Dominican six-year-old who left a life of poverty to fall straight into a worse hell, discarded like a piece of trash. And her mother, Marie. Killed for trying to save her child from monsters. Victims whose fate weighed even more heavily on my conscience, confronted as I was with the scope of the crime that claimed them.

"If I inform on Sporcatello," I asked, "will you drop the charges against my son?"

"We will," Pistone said, staring straight at Othello, who returned the look with a blank stare.

"There's something else you should know," Schneider announced. "We have reason to believe that your boy's stepfather — Max Herndon — is laundering money for Mr. Sporcatello."

"His Rhode Island factories are a front," Othello said. "None of them make any real money."

"Now there's a surprise," I said.

"He inflates expenses and shuffles in cash from Sporcatello," Othello added. "And that's only one of his schemes."

"And you're telling me this because . . . " I asked.

The agents' silence spoke volumes. If the feds wanted me to keep Herndon's money laundering for Sporcatello on the down-low, they wouldn't have told me. They had to figure I'd share news of their investigation into Herndon's finances with Leo Sporcatello — either on a friendly basis or the business end of an ice pick.

Was the FBI using me to rattle Sporcatello's cage, to get Herndon to flip? Provided they had their ducks in a row it was a sensible play. For them. For me, my son, his mother and his brothers, not so much. Or Max Herndon, obviously.

"Well gentlemen," I said, standing up and heading for the door. "It's been fun. But then I like root canal surgery."

I had a lot of work to do, including my actual job. Which I blew off the next day, telling the duty Sergeant that my shoulder was playing up, which it was, constantly. I arranged to meet Veronica in Newport for a stroll down Cliff Walk.

It was a cloudless day. A bracing wind blowing off the Bay put a distinct chill in the air. Veronica met me at the parking lot, a vision of middle-aged beauty in a brown cashmere sweater and black jeans.

"John," she, leaning in for a polite hug, careful not to squeeze me too hard.

"Veronica," I replied, laying my hand on the soft fabric on her back for a moment, kissing her cheek.

She walked on my left side and threaded her arm through mine as we made our way down the Forty Steps to the cliff's edge.

"I enjoy long walks," she said as we headed down the path. "Especially by people who annoy me."

"Oscar Wilde?"

"Fred Allen," she said, reminding of the time we'd smoked a bone, listened to radio's Golden Age ad libber and made out.

We were both quiet for a while, lost in our thoughts. We passed in front of the Breakers — a massive relic of the days when robber barons built palatial summer homes for the four-week summer season. Veronica stopped and turned towards me.

"Trouble?" she asked, as if there was any doubt.

"Lots."

Veronica waited for me to continue, brushing aside a strand of blond hair blowing into her face.

"Luke's dealing drugs," I said. "Again. Still."

I studied Veronica, trying to see if she was surprised by her son's continuing illegal activities. If she did, she didn't show it. I added unflappability to Veronica's long list of qualities.

"What drugs?" Veronica asked.

"Cocaine. I don't know if there's anything else. There could be."

"Is he using?" she asked.

"Yes."

"That explains a few things. What else?"

I avoided her gaze.

"You said 'lots of trouble'," Veronica pointed out, her expression letting me know there was no chance of ignoring the question.

I started moving again. We walked side-by-side, a small space between us.

"What do you know about Max's business?" I asked.

"Not enough, apparently."

I watched the waves hitting the rocks, thinking about what I was going to say, committing myself to saying it.

"You were always terrible at giving me bad news," Veronica said with a small, nervous laugh. "Just tell me."

"Max is involved with some bad people."

"How bad?"

"Bad."

Veronica lowered her head into the wind and pulled her sweater tighter around her slim frame.

"What's he do with them?"

"Money laundering," I replied, not knowing how to sugarcoat her husband's involvement in the wrong kind of high finance.

"When?" she asked, not even breaking stride.

"When what?"

"When's the shit going to hit the fan?"

"Soon."

"Max is a good man," Veronica insisted. "A good father. A good provider. I don't want to see him hurt. I don't want to see *any* of us hurt."

"It's out of my hands," I said wearily.

"Is it?"

"It is."

"What should *I* do?" Veronica asked.

"Batten down the hatches. Make sure you have a good lawyer."

"Will that help?"

"It won't hurt."

"Tell me," Veronica demanded, stopping to face me again. "Tell me *everything*."

"I can't."

"You mean you *won't*. You *owe* me John Canali. You owe our son."

"We both made our choices Veronica. You made yours, I made mine. Max made his."

"Oh bullshit," she snapped, her eyes boring into me. "What world do *you* live in? Here in the real world you do whatever it takes to survive. To protect the people you love."

"Don't bullshit *me* Veronica," I countered. "You live in a mansion. You take luxury vacations all over the world. Throw huge parties. Shop in New

York, Paris and God knows where else. Your kids are in private school. All that comes at a price. Max paid it, you lived it. Now the bill's coming due. *That's* the real world. You're not stupid. Don't tell me some part of you didn't know Max got his hands dirty."

"You live in the *gutter* John," she snapped. "You, your father *and* your mother. I loved you once. More than I loved anyone. More than I ever thought I could love anyone. We have a son together."

"We need to talk about Luke."

"No *we* don't. *I* raised that boy. I'm the one who's got to save him. *Me*. Not you."

Veronica strode away, leaving me looking out to sea, wondering if I'd done the right thing. My revelation — if that's what it was — set yet another wheel in motion. Veronica would confront Max with the fact that the feds were onto him. Max would report to Leo. Leo would want to know the source of the information. I'd be back in hot water — an analogy that didn't begin to cover the punishment his soldiers could mete out at a moment's notice.

Veronica would also confront Luke with his dealing and using. That wouldn't go down well, for him or me. For us.

I comforted myself with the thought that I owed Veronica a chance to get her house in order before she was hit with a FBI raid and/or a Sporcatello-shaped wrecking ball. She'd been there when the pain of being me seemed too much to bear. She'd been my life preserver. I could at least try to be hers.

I didn't expect to see Veronica standing by her BMW in the parking lot, but there she was. Nor did I expect her to hug me. But she did. Tight, and for a long time. When she pulled back, tears streamed down her face.

"I'm sorry," she said. "I know you're trying to help. It's just that I have so much to lose. I'm afraid. I really am."

I couldn't think of anything to say. So I hugged her again.

"John," she said, staring into my eyes. "Do me a favor."

"What?"

"Don't speed," she said, smiling hopefully.

I was confused by her parting words. Veronica knew cops get a free pass when they're pulled over for speeding. She was also aware that my speeding days were over.

As I passed over the Newport Bridge, I put on *The Talking Heads '77,* a debut album released the year I was born. *Psycho Killer* was one of my favorite sing-a-longs — until the lyrics summoned images of Rico Nardelli carrying Jorge Gonzales' severed head.

I quickly instructed Siri to play *Gurf Morlix*. Another mistake. Morlix's ode to lost love, *She's a River*, fired-up the waterworks. The mournful ballad reminded me of moments spent with Veronica, including the stolen ones that created our son Luke. The way the sun set on the motel room that had been our sanctuary.

I switched songs again, opting for R.E.M.'s *What's The Frequency Kenneth*. It brought back a memory from my Senior year in High School, when a bottle of Mingle-supplied speed spilled out of my backpack. Mr. Hanson, my math teacher, was not amused. Neither was Principal Otto. I was looking at suspension. My college career was on the line.

Veronica had been my rock, making fun of the bleak future looming on the horizon, giving me hope, sustaining my spirits with the love and support my mother couldn't provide.

My father got me out of trouble, again. Veronica congratulated me on my fourth second chance. As I hugged her, I caught a glimpse of something plastic catching the light in the corner of her locker. A bottle just like the one I'd fumbled in front of Mr. Hanson.

"Your mistake Johnny?" Veronica said with the same smile she'd given me in the Newport parking lot. "You got caught."

Veronica's strange warning, advising me not to "speed," made sense. It was her way of telling me that she wasn't as naive as I thought she was. I smiled. My sense of foreboding faded, if only a little bit.

I was nowhere near as optimistic about Luke. I'd met enough addicts to know that beating addiction is just this side of impossible. I was Catholic enough to believe in miracles. If I couldn't arrange some divine intervention, at least Luke wouldn't be alone. Well, not as alone as he had been.

Chapter Fifteen

The next day, the FBI busted Luke.

The Fibbies must have teed-it-up the week previous, before my meeting with the Organized Crime Task Force. Operation Fuck with Canali — or whatever they called it — started by arresting a college freshman for possession.

After a little talk with the feds, Ms. Susan Alexander "happened" to bump into Luke on Thayer Street. They went for coffee, then snorted lines in the Brown University freshman's dorm room. She asked Luke to supply some weight for her Ivy League *amigos*.

The second money and drugs changed hands between the jammed-up college kid and my teenage son half-a-dozen FBI agents swooped. They cuffed Luke, read him his rights and hauled him off — right in front of his classmates and their parents, just outside his private school's Victorian gates.

The feds found 215 grams of coke in Luke's backpack. They charged him with felony possession of a Schedule II substance with intent to deliver. If tried as an adult — highly unlikely but not impossible — Luke was facing five to forty and a five million dollar fine. A fact I didn't reveal to Luke's mother. Veronica was angry enough as it was.

"This is *your* fault!" she screamed down the phone. "*You* did this! To your own son.*"

I caught myself before I could say it wasn't my fault. Because it was. Not directly. But I'd brought the attention that led to Luke's arrest.

"No one forced him to deal," I said in my defense.

It was a stupid thing to say. Cocaine users can easily get to the point where they need the stimulant to feel normal. Once they're on *that* train, once want becomes need, dealing coke is one of the best ways to ensure a regular supply. Right until it isn't.

My father's advice — to stop believing people always had a choice — rang in my ears. But I didn't back down. Luke was the victim of my "friendship" with the FBI, but his dealing was never going to end well. The *way* his arrest went down may have been avoidable, but the probability of an arrest had been hanging over his head since he sold his first gram.

I promised Veronica I'd do whatever I could to help.

"I'm doing my best," I said, not quite understanding what that was, could or would be.

When Veronica disconnected, I made a few calls. Judge Andrew Matthias ordered Luke held pending a full bail hearing. Normally, judges only deny minors an immediate bail hearing if they have a history of violent offenses, don't have a safe place to stay or posed a flight risk. None of which applied to Luke.

It got worse.

Matthias sent Luke to the Adult Correctional Institution — a prison complex about as child friendly as the Russian front during World War II. The whole thing smelled vindictive, coercive and a bunch of other big words meaning the FBI had screwed me but good.

I clocked out and headed for the ACI. I left a message for my father and another on the Red Carpet Smoke Shop's old number, as per my FBI handler's instruction. A minute later, Agent Pistone returned my call.

"What do you have for me?" Pistone asked before I could get a word in.

"Why?" I demanded, unleashing F-bombs, hitting Pistone with the "c" word and sharing some ideas for inserting inanimate objects into his digestive system's end point. *"Why'd you do it?"* I yelled, running out of expletives.

"They don't trust you," Pistone said with aggravating calm.

"Trust *me*?" I asked incredulously.

"They want you to know we mean business."

"Who the fuck is 'they'? Othello? Schneider? You? Someone else? Who is this 'they' who thought it was a good idea to fuck with *my son?*"

I pressed disconnect before I threatened a government agent with a slow, painful death. Or maybe after, I'm not sure.

The State of Rhode Island and Providence Plantations was detaining Luke at Moran. The medium security prison wasn't the Ritz, but it wasn't the ACI's worst hell: the 19th century edifice known as "steel city." Moran's Visitor Center was officially closed. I called in a marker with the prison's detective — a man who owed me for letting his son skate on a street racing beef — and high-tailed it down 95 to Cranston.

The visiting room consisted of a row of twenty evenly spaced black stools cemented to the linoleum floor facing tall plexiglass windows. The spaces between the windows held a pair of telephones attached to the wall by a steel cable. The guard watched me from behind a thick plastic window at the end of the row, trying to see the cop who had enough juice to visit a prisoner outside of official hours.

"Hello *Dad*," Luke said, his voice dripping with sarcasm.

Luke was bent slightly forward, rocking gently on his stool, holding his free arm across his chest protectively. His hair was disheveled. A multi-colored bruise sat beneath his right eye.

"The FBI do that?" I asked, nodding towards his injury.

"I'm in protective custody. Nothing could *possibly* happen to me, right?"

"You'll be out of here soon," I promised.

"Really?" Luke laughed. "Ya think?"

"I didn't do this," I said slowly.

"*Then who did?*" Luke yelled, drawing a warning stare from the guard behind the window.

"The FBI."

"Sure. The FBI. Nothing to do with *you.*"

"It's complicated," I said, not wanting to lie.

"No it's not," Luke hissed, running a hand through his greasy hair. "I'm in this hole because *you* put me here."

"You're in this 'hole' because you sold cocaine to an FBI informant."

"*You* fucked me," he swore.

"You fucked *yourself.* Keep using and your life will *stay* fucked, no matter *what* I do."

Luke slammed down the phone and got up, waiting impatiently for the guard to take him back to his cell. I should have told Luke I loved him. That I would move heaven and earth to get him out, get him straight, help him to be the man he could be. I said the three words to his empty stool and headed home . . .

The next day I rolled up to my dinner party at Leo Sporcatello's "summer house." The clam shell driveway crunched under my tires until I reached the Sporcatello residence. Long rectangular windows ran across its length, a few feet from the flat roofline.

"Here goes something," I said to myself, retrieving the bottle of grappa from the Honda's passenger seat and checking my smile in the rear view mirror.

The front door opened before I made it ten feet from my car. A gently glowing afternoon sun framed a solitary man standing with his hands by his sides. His outline revealed him as something of an athlete, confounding my expectations of the usual mafia man mountain enforcers.

The closer I got, the more Leo's hired muscle looked like he belonged in a Times Square underwear ad. The black-haired bodyguard's tight polo shirt and chinos clothed a physique without about as much body fat as a leopard. His dark eyes did nothing to dispel the impression that I was facing a supremely capable and practiced predator.

The bodyguard retreated inside the house and waited for me to complete my journey. Before I entered, he opened his hands, silently instructing me to prepare to be frisked. And frisk he did, leaving no inch of my body unmolested.

"Are you this thorough with Mr. Sporcatello?" I asked.

The bodyguard put his face inches from mine and grabbed my balls, hard.

"I'm thinking yes," I said through gritted teeth, waiting for him to relieve the pressure on the boys.

The bodyguard placed my iPhone, wallet, keys, GLOCK 19, spare ammunition and backup Smith & Wesson .38 on the foyer table. As he scanned me with a bug detector, my host walked up, dressed in a loose-fitting Tommy Bahama button-down short-sleeved shirt, khaki shorts and sandals.

The Silver Fox picked up the smaller of the two guns.

"Don't put your finger on the trigger until your sights are on target," I advised.

The bodyguard and I waited to see if he'd go there. Sporcatello slowly lowered the gun onto the table. He picked up the bottle of grappa sweating in the afternoon heat, examined it respectfully and handed it to his man.

"Please," he said gesturing towards the back of the house.

Sporcatello's summer place lacked flow — there were rooms off of rooms off of rooms — but they all offered spectacular views of Narragansett Bay and the mainland beyond. We walked onto a deck high above a kidney-shaped pool, a half acre of manicured lawn and low scrub.

"It's good to be king," I said.

"You know what's missing?" Sporcatello asked, leaning on the balcony, looking out to sea.

"Children," I answered.

His nod told me right answer. Was it? I could imagine myself sitting on Leo's deck, soaking-up the rays and sipping iced tea as laughing children sprinted up the path from the beach, calling for their father to get off his ass and play Marco Polo.

What I couldn't imagine: being tied to Leo Sporcatello by a bond of blood. I'd have to toss my moral compass into the sea and watch it sink to the bottom. Then again, Mia . . .

My *piccola tigra* emerged from the swimming pool like Aphrodite from the sea. Leo's daughter gathered her jet black water-slicked hair and tied it in a knot behind her head, removing any distraction from her flawless face and perfectly toned bikini-clad body. Did Mia *know* we were watching? Had she timed her entrance? Probably. But at that moment, her love of showing off wasn't a major concern. Concealing my desire was.

"*Bella donna*," Mia's father said.

"She is beautiful," I agreed as Mia wrapped a white towel around her tanned torso, looked up at us and smiled.

"*Andiamo*," Sporcatello said, turning back towards the house. "Ignazia has prepared us a special meal. Light but full of flavor."

The dinner table was perfectly arranged with white linen, silver cutlery and crystal glasses. Mia sat across from me, with Leo at the head of the table, of course.

Somewhere back in Providence a small grill turned green with envy. The meal was as delicious as anything I'd eaten at any of Providence's upmarket Italian restaurants, I was especially impressed with the Sicilian olive chicken and the *pesce spada:* swordfish rolls filled with raisins and pine nuts. As we sipped a fine Fiano, Sporcatello held forth on art, history, culture, literature, science, space exploration, international relations, food, opera, literature — everything except organized crime, severed heads and mob hits.

"Your mother is a bit of my hero," Sporcatello revealed as we ate almond pudding flavored with orange blossom water. "Her collections are superb."

Sporcatello paused, suddenly aware that dinner was coming to an end.

"And you are a clever man, getting me to do all the talking," he said.

Clever or selfish? Encouraging Sporcatello to monologue gave me time to steal glances at my lover. Her low-cut black dress and seductive smiles made it difficult to get the food from my plate to my mouth — never mind comment on the connection between African tribal art and Freudian psychology.

Mia hadn't contributed much to the conversation. She was busy doing something I'd never seen her do before: listen. Outside of her father's company, Mia was the center of attention. Here, at his table, she was a student, soaking up every word coming from Leo Sporcatello's restless intellect.

I never thought Mia was stupid. But I hadn't known that her mind was as sharp as the knife Sporcatello used to carve up the *Tarocco* blood oranges that ended our meal. Mia's questions and observations were few and far between, sometimes asked in her native Italian, translated by her father. They were always relevant, insightful and challenging.

We sipped espresso for a short while. Mia excused herself. The mob boss and I strolled to a small gazebo facing the Bay. A Viking yacht bobbed at a dock protruding into the ocean, waves slapping gently against its towering hull.

The entire scene was ripped from the pages of a fashion magazine; the kind of idyllic backdrop that makes followers yearn to swap places with social media influencers. I'd watched classmates ascend to these financial heights, assembling a portfolio of houses, cars, children and ex-wives. I'd never been tempted. As my father used to say *al povero mancano tante cose, all'avaro tutte*. The poor man is lacking many things, the greedy man all.

Sporcatello set the bottle of grappa and a pair of chilled glasses on a table between two Adirondack chairs. We settled into the wooden seats like old friends, which we definitely weren't.

"We can talk freely here," Sporcatello said, pouring the grappa. "*Â saluti!*"

My first taste of grappa confirmed both parts of the South African salesman's prediction: it was like a sublime grenade going off in my mouth.

"The house," Sporcatello said quietly, holding his glass up to the setting sun, then sipping the clear liquid.

"A jewel," I said, trying to think of the Italian word. "*Gioiello.*"

"Not this house. Molton Lane."

"Oh," I said, taking a few seconds to recover my wits. "You mean the one where I shot two people pimping little children?"

"Yes, that one."

"What about it?" I said, arming myself with a hit of grappa.

"What you did was *smoderato*. I think the English word is rash."

"Yes it is. Was."

"Some people think you should not have gotten away with it."

"You?"

"Sometimes a man can't control himself," Sporcatello said, shaking his head. "It happens."

"Yes it does."

"We are not so different I think," Sporcatello said, eyeing me carefully.

"We *are* different. For you it's always business."

"Yes, for me business comes first."

Sporcatello paused to look into his drink.

"How is your son?" he asked.

A different sort of grenade went off — in my head.

"It's terrible when a child is in trouble," Sporcatello pronounced sadly. "A father would do anything to help."

"What are you saying?" I asked, knowing full well what the mob boss was saying.

"This problem can go away," Sporcatello said, snapping his fingers. "Like that."

I remembered Luke's confession; Max Herndon had disappeared my son's previous possession charge. No doubt the industrialist had depended on Leo's connections to make the evidence disappear. Could Leo Sporcatello get Luke out of legal trouble a second time with a quiet word in someone's ear?

For the *mafiosi*, it would be just another day in the office. Luke could finish his education and get on with life, probably at another school. Someplace a lot better than jail — after detox, rehab and whatever else it took for him to get clean. But at what cost? What was my reservation point? What was Leo's?

We sat in silence for a full minute.

"The FBI," Sporcatello said. "Tell me. What do you know?"

"I know they're lying bastards."

"What else?"

Something about Sporcatello's expression told me he already knew the feds were looking at Max Herndon for money laundering. The Silver Fox was testing me, to see if I'd hold out on him. If I did, there'd be hell to pay. For me *and* my son.

I had to give Sporcatello *something* to free Luke from the prospect of jail and a permanent criminal record. And save my own neck. I'd already figured the FBI expected me to tell Sporcatello they had Herndon in their sights, to get Max Herndon to flip. And what did I owe Max, a criminal enabling the sexual exploitation of children?

"The FBI's interested in Herndon," I said, throwing Veronica's husband under a mafia-shaped bus.

"Interested how?" Sporcatello asked, his face revealing nothing.

"Money laundering," I said, leaving out "for you."

"They told you this," he said, not pressing the point. "Just like that."

"Yes. Just like that."

Sporcatello sipped his grappa and nodded. I downed my remaining drink.

"O.K." Sporcatello said softly, pouring himself a fresh glass of grappa, l leaving my glass empty. "We will talk again when this unfortunate situation is, how do you say? *Risoluto.*"

"Resolved," I said taking the hint to end our audience. "*Grazie per la cena.* It was delicious."

"*Conosco I miei polli*," Sporcatello said, bidding me farewell.

Literally translated, the expression means "I know my chickens." Spoken by Italians, it means "I know what you're like, what you're likely to do." At that moment, that made one of us.

I paused below the house and turned to the sea, contemplating the lights shining from across the Bay. They seemed to come from another world. As did Mia, waiting for me by the patio doors. She looked as beautiful as ever. And just as lethal.

"How did it go?" Mia asked, raising a dark eyebrow.

I didn't know how much Mia knew about my situation. About her father's plan to use Luke's arrest to trap me in his web of crime and corruption. I wanted to believe she knew nothing. I grabbed Mia and kissed her, deeply and passionately, like a drowning man clinging to a piece of wreckage.

"Not so good then," she announced when we stopped.

As I said, Mia's was no one's fool. But was I hers? That remained to be seen.

Chapter Sixteen

Destiny emerged from the mist shrouding the pedestrian bridge to India Point Park. She was hard to miss. Not just because of her flaming red hair; Sergeant Moses Drake walked by her side, a giant of a man next to a slip of a girl.

"Welcome to Rhode Island," I said, gesturing at the mist with my left hand.

"I sure am glad this isn't the 1700s," Drake said.

Destiny looked perplexed.

"Rhode Island ran America's slave trade for nearly a hundred years," I explained. "Mostly out of Bristol and Newport."

"Well that explains a lot," Destiny said, her southern accent as thick as the fog rolling off the water.

"I'm sorry about what happened to the Duprees," I said as the three of us walked along the water's edge.

"It wasn't entirely unexpected," Drake said.

"Who killed them?" Destiny demanded, her voice tight with anger.

"I don't know," I answered.

It wasn't what Destiny wanted to hear.

"Do you know how old Yanira was when she was murdered?" Destiny asked. "Eight. Eight-years-old. Do you have any kids?"

"A son."

"Imagine your eight-year-old son being raped by strangers day every day for two *years*."

"I can't."

"Sure you can. You just don't *want* to," Destiny said. "And that's understandable," she continued, suddenly adopting a conciliatory tone. "Thank you for shooting those people at that house."

What could I say? You're welcome? I wasn't proud of what I'd done. But I wasn't ashamed of it either.

"I want to see the place for myself," Destiny said to Drake. "I want to see where those sick fucks abused her."

"We don't know she was there," I said.

"What about Yanira's mother?" Destiny asked. "Who made *her* disappear?"

"That case is still open," I said. "The truth is — "

"Sporcatello," Destiny said, pronouncing the name like an ancient curse.

I stopped. A jungle gym, a pyramid of steel bars shrouded in the fog, loomed ahead of us.

"Don't even think it," I said urgently. "Is that why you're here? Drake, what the fuck?"

The Georgia State Police negotiator put his arm around Destiny and shrugged his shoulders.

"Someone's got to pay," Destiny announced, stiff inside Drake's arms.

"Sporcatello *will* pay," I insisted. "The wheels of justice are slow but they grind exceedingly fine," I added.

"I want him dead," Destiny said, unimpressed with ancient Greek philosophy. "You hear me? I want that piece of shit dead."

"The FBI is closing in," I said, trying to talk Destiny off the ledge. "It's only a matter of time before Sporcatello's behind bars."

"Not good enough," Destiny said.

"Drake," I pleaded. "You know better than that. That's insane."

"You can get us close," he answered. "That's all we want."

"I understand your desire to remove Sporcatello from the land of the living," I said slowly. "*Believe me* I get it."

"But?" Drake asked.

"Sporcatello has bodyguards. Pros. You'll be killed and Sporcatello will laugh. Nothing will change. Nothing."

"That's a risk we're willing to take," Drake said.

"*We? Drake, what's the matter with you?*"

Drake's stoic expression confirmed what I suspected: the soon-to-be-retired cop was ready to die in a hail of gunfire, to be the hero his lover never had.

"How about this?" I asked, trying to think of a way to derail their murderous mission. "I'll find out who killed Marie and Yanira Dupree. The actual guy. If you take out Leo Sporcatello you'll never know who pulled the trigger on the Duprees."

I stopped myself from considering other ways mother and daughter might have died. I had a hard enough time getting my head around the idea that I was offering the Drake and Destiny the scalps of one, maybe two or three men in exchange for Leo Sporcatello's life. Assuming that delivering the Dupree's killers would satisfy their need for revenge.

"I'm need more time," I pleaded. "Blow town until I get some names. You'll just draw attention to yourselves."

Destiny left her lover's arms and stood in front of me.

"If you don't tell us who did this thing, I swear I'll jerk a knot in your tail," she warned.

"Destiny," Drake cautioned the redhead, turning towards me. "Promise me John. Promise me you'll find out who killed them."

"I promise. If *you* promise to leave Providence and let me handle this."

Drake and Destiny had a silent conference. Their body language told me who was leading the discussion. She sighed heavily and nodded.

"We're not waiting forever," Destiny said. "One way or another, someone's got to pay."

When it come to violence, someone *always* pays. It was only a question of who, when, where and how. Two days later, I got a terrifying reminder of that fact, when dispatch ordered me to a stand-off in Onleyville.

I parked my cruiser down the street from a grey triple-decker, a better version of the house *mafiosi* Rico Nardelli had called home. Dozens of cops surrounded the structure, aiming rifles, shotguns and handguns at the house from behind squad cars, trees and telephone poles.

"Commander," I said breathlessly, stepping into the vehicle. "The effective range of an AR-15 is 600 yards. We're *way* too close."

"We've got her boxed in," Commander Jimenez said with Custer-like confidence.

Jimenez's face told me that arguing the point would be fighting a losing battle. I pushed the sense of impending doom to the back of my mind and listened to the briefing . . .

The court issued an "extreme risk protection order" against Mary Bennet, a 27-year-old former Army sergeant who'd made threats against her neighbors and talked about suicide. Two officers arrived at Bennett's house to confiscate her firearms. Bennett shot both of them at the door with a handgun. Officer Cortez was dead. Officer Smith was clinging to life in intensive care.

I sat at a desk facing the monitors and inserted an earpiece. The radio chatter was chaotic. Angry voices exchanged random bits of information, stepping all over each other.

"Permission to contact the shooter," I asked.

Jimenez nodded casually, as if hostage negotiation was another tick he had to put on a form before he sent in the SWAT team to avenge his fallen officers. We didn't have a cell or house phone number. So I picked up the microphone and addressed Mary Bennett through the command vehicle's loudspeaker, watching the front of her house on the monitor.

"Sergeant Bennett, this is Lieutenant John Canali of the Providence Police Department. I'd like to talk to you."

The surrounding officers readied their weapons; expecting her to answer with gunfire.

Silence. I tried again.

"Mary —"

"Fuck off," a voice called from inside the house.

"I want eyes on target," Jimenez ordered on the secure police channel.

"What do you want us to do?" I asked the shooter.

"Fuck off."

"Mary, I want to help you."

Jimenez glared at me.

"I *can* help you. Please. Tell me what you need."

No answer.

"Sergeant Bennett, please talk to me."

Again silence.

"I know you did what you thought you had to do," I told her in my best deep, calm. soothing voice. "Just let me know you're alright. Please."

Nothing.

I kept going. I told Bennett how I admired and appreciated what she'd done for her country. How no one could understand her struggle unless she came out of the house and shared her experience. I told her that many of our officers were vets. They had no desire to harm a fellow soldier. They were only trying to protect innocent life, like she did in Iraq.

My tone was right, but I couldn't find the words Bennett wanted or needed to hear to open the lines of communication. I longed to hear her say *something*, even if it was another "fuck off."

An hour passed slowly. Painfully. Dangerously.

"Prepare to breach," Jimenez radioed.

"I need more time," I begged as the SWAT team made their final preparations, remembering that I'd used the same words with Drake and Destiny.

"You're out of time," the Commander said dismissively, ordering the assault.

I heard a long series of loud pops, followed by the sound of glass shattering. The house oozed tear gas from every window. It poured out below the front door and surrounded the house. The six-member SWAT team stacked by the door, masks on. Despite the smoke, the sun's dying rays highlighted their position.

"Go! Go! Go!" Jimenez barked into his mic.

"Left!" a voice on the radio screamed. "Left!"

I saw it on the monitor: Bennett appeared from a smoke-shrouded bush by the side of the house. She shot the entire SWAT team before they could turn to face her.

I heard a crack from somewhere behind me; a police sniper trying to end the carnage. No such luck. Bennett had maintained her position for a second, maybe two. I watched her weapon disappear into the bush.

The radio burst into life. Every cop within range opened fire. The fusillade shattered windows and splintered wood, sending hundreds of bullets God knows where.

Jimenez barked a series of commands. Two SWAT officers — one staggering badly — dragged a pair of teammates away from the house. Another officer crawled away, leaving a bloody trail behind him. One more lay where he fell, dead.

"She's upstairs!" a radio voice yelled. "Top left! Top left!"

"No eyes on target," another voice responded frantically.

"Pull back!" Jimenez ordered. "Pull back!"

I heard a whizzing sound and hit the deck. Return fire slammed into the command vehicle. A monitor exploded to my right.

"Where the fuck is she?" someone yelled.

A minute of sustained gunfire passed, interrupted by slight pauses as officers reloaded their weapons and continued the barrage. I'm not sure how many bullets pierced the command vehicle, or how much time passed before Jimenez ordered cease fire. It seemed like an eternity. And then, after a few scattered shots, silence.

The dead SWAT officer lay dead on the pavement in front of the house, a growing puddle of blood framing his head. Two who'd escaped the assault were beyond help, headed for the morgue. One and only one officer emerged from the aborted entry unscathed.

The ambulance sirens faded. I heard the whir of the helicopter rotors, fading in and out with the shifting wind. I got off the floor reluctantly, shocked at the SWAT's team's bloody failure. If Bennet wasn't having flashbacks before, she would now. As would the cops who witnessed he grisly debacle, myself included.

Jimenez looked over at me — perhaps hoping I had some idea how to end the incident. Or maybe he was just lost. I shared the feeling. I'd failed to establish communications with the shooter. I'd failed to prevent the death of at least three men. I had no clue what to do next — except more of the same.

"Commander," I said, brushing glass shards from my uniform. "I'm out of my depth here."

Jimenez looked at me sympathetically; a sad, silent acknowledgment that we were were all up shit creek without a paddle.

"Everyone out!" he yelled. "Stay down!"

The entire team slinked out of the vehicle, mercifully uninjured. We ran down the street to safety, heads lowered, expecting to be picked off one-by-one. We sheltered around the block by a squad car, a disorganized bunch of defeated cops. My phone buzzed.

"Destiny wants you to know —" Drake began.

"Are you still in town?" I interrupted. "Turn on the TV. I've got a female soldier who's shot multiple officers."

"Shit," Drake swore, pronouncing the word in two separate syllables. "Where are you?"

The Commander didn't notice me leaving. But I sure as hell noticed the expression on Drake's face when he arrived at the police perimeter a few minutes later. The words "grim death" sprang to mind as he flashed his badge and ducked under the crime scene tape.

"Get me the National Guard," Jiminez shouted into his cell phone.

"Where's her DD214?" Drake asked, looking around for someone who could help him, catching nothing by empty stares. "Her service record," he clarified to the one shell-shocked officer who seemed to pay attention.

"Who the hell are *you*?" Commander Jimenez demanded.

"Sergeant Drake is the head of the Georgia State Police Crisis Negotiations Team," I said.

"He has no jurisdiction here," Jimenez declared.

Someone with some serious stones started up the command vehicle and drove it to our position. We reentered its confines, surveying shattered monitors, crunching glass shards littering the floor.

"I need that service record," Drake said to an officer who sat at one of the two functional computers.

Seeing Commander Jimenez aimlessly prowling the truck, Drake decided to take control of the situation.

"My name is Sergeant Moses Drake," he said forcefully, silencing the truck's interior. "I was an Infantry Commander for the United States Army. I'm an FBI trained hostage negotiator and the head of the Georgia State Police Crisis Negotiations Team. I've got 20 years in and 15 hostage negotiations under my belt. I'm going to put this as plainly as possible. If we don't handle this right a lot more men are going to die."

"I repeat," Commander Jimenez said, turning to face Drake, straightening his posture, "you have no jurisdiction here."

Drake drew a deep breath and smiled, undaunted.

"Sergeant Bennett is a trained soldier armed with a gun she knows like the back of her hand," he said, replacing some of the authority in his voice with calm deliberation. "She's been taught that the first person to violence in combat wins. She's already won twice. You keep up this pressure and I guara-damn-tee you she'll win again."

"Go on," Jimenez said impatiently, as if Drake needed his permission to continue.

"Your shooter was sexually assaulted in the Army. The last person she wants to hear from is a man. We need a female negotiator. Preferably one who's served."

"So a *woman's* going to talk her out?" Jimenez asked. *"After what she's just done?"*

"Maybe," Drake said, staring at the shattered monitor. "Maybe not."

Jimenez would have told Drake to pound sand if he'd had the firepower he needed to take out Bennett. The Providence cop was low on trained officers, low on options. At least until the National Guard arrived.

"Find someone," Jimenez ordered after a long pause. "Try it."

Once they understood the gravity of the situation, the personnel department quickly located a suitable candidate: Officer Joanne Grant. My spirits lifted — until Grant arrived in the truck. She was a small woman, brown-haired, in her early twenties. To my ancient eyes she looked like a teenager dressed up as a cop, weighed down by her gear and a responsibility she'd never imagined she'd have to shoulder.

Drake seemed unconcerned about her appearance or demeanor, restoring some measure of lost confidence. Not that I had much to begin with. The slaughter I'd just witnessed had taken the wind out of my sails, setting me adrift in a sea of uncertainty. I felt ashamed by my failure to communicate and yes, scared.

"Let's take this outside," Drake said, not wanting to be second-guessed by the SWAT Commander.

The three of us sheltered behind the command vehicle, the generator's steady hum forcing our little group to huddle closely.

"What's the plan?" Grant asked, her eyes darting around.

Drake shared Mary Bennett's service record and the details of her restraining order. I gave Grant a crash course in hostage negotiation, stressing the need to get Bennett talking. Which begged the question: what would they talk about? What could Grant say to convince Bennett to surrender to the police after murdering five men and severely injuring three more?

Grant fired-up a cigarette, assimilating her instructions and, I suspected, stalling for time.

"Did you smoke before or after combat?" I asked, trying to loosen her up.

"I wasn't in combat," she admitted. "I just came under fire a few times. It was scary as shit."

"And then there was the paperwork," Drake added, his enormous arms crossed over his huge chest.

"The waiting," Grant added, exhaling a plume of smoke into the cooling afternoon air, her cigarette hand shaking slightly. "Those AARs took fucking forever."

"AAR?" I asked

"After Action Report," Grant said, glad to have a topic of conversation where she had some expertise. "You have to go over what happened. Every detail, from everyone. It takes forever."

An idea hit me, lifting me from the pits of despair.

"Wait," I said. "This is combat for Bennett, right?"

Both of them nodded.

"It's over. The action, it's done. Well it will be if everyone pulls back. No more threats. No more combat. All that remains is . . ."

"Paperwork," Grant finished.

"Waiting," Drake added.

"The AAR," Grant said.

We stood there, thinking it through, knowing that none of us had a plan B.

"How are we going to get the Commander to pull everyone back?" Drake asked.

"I'll order him to."

I nearly jumped out of my skin. Chief Lamar was standing next to us — displaying ninja stealth I silently added to his resume.

"Chief Lamar," I said in case Drake and Grant missed the large amount of metal pinned to his uniform.

Lamar nodded towards the command vehicle. All four of us entered. The Chief's eyes widened at the damage. Jimenez greeted his boss with an expression somehow mixing anger with embarrassment.

Lamar put his hand on Jimenez's shoulder. The Commander's face relaxed slightly. The two top cops conferred in the vehicle's one quiet corner. Grant sat at the main desk and put on a headset, fumbling with the cans. Drake and I stood behind her.

We watched the police withdraw, slowly disappearing from a monitor, until all that was left was the fallen SWAT officer and dead quiet. Chief Lamar gave us the go-ahead.

"Use your Army rank," Drake cautioned. "Don't tell her you're a police officer."

"Sergeant Bennett, this is Staff Sergeant Joanne Grant," she said over the truck's still functioning loudspeaker.

I could hear the stress in her voice as her words echoed down the deserted street. "The action is over. Stand down."

Nothing.

"We need to start the AAR," Grant added with slightly more conviction.

"I do not have eyes on target," a sniper radioed.

"Sergeant Bennett," Grant said, sounding like an Army Sergeant in charge of her troops. "You are hereby ordered to deliver your After Action Report directly to me, in private. Stand down and report at this time."

It may have been the longest ten seconds of my life. I could almost feel the sniper's finger on the trigger, waiting to eliminate the threat.

"Ready to report," Bennett called out. "Moving Sergeant."

The key fit the lock and the door opened. It was over. Or at least it *should* have been. As Bennet emerged from the house a single shot rang out; a head shot that instantly ended the Army Sergeant's life. She crumpled to the pavement not ten yards from SWAT Officer Lu's dead body.

Something inside died with those officers and Sergeant Mary Bennett. I stopped believing in the simple, reassuring idea that all's well that ends well. I started believing that *nothing* ends well. The best I could hope for: a small victory against the forces trying to destroy me, and everyone I cared about.

The weight of that idea left me dog tired. Over the days that followed, I struggled to find something to sustain my desire to continue work, rescue my son and dodge the proverbial hangman's noose. A conundrum that became more and more difficult as my battle with Sporcatello, the FBI, Chief Lamar, Drake, Destiny and my own family raced to its inevitable conclusion.

Chapter Seventeen

Climbing my stairs after the Onleyville massacre felt like I had twenty pound weights tied to my ankles. My shoulder was throbbing with pain, rendering my right arm all but useless. I thought nothing of food or undressing or showering or even turning on a light. I popped a pain pill, stumbled to my unmade bed, lay down on my good side and fell asleep.

The next thing I knew my phone buzzed. The third time it rang, curiosity got the better of me.

"Officer Canali, this is Harold Overton from the Fraternal Order of Police."

"Hello Harry," I asked, vaguely remembering his daughter, a humorless ER nurse who didn't even smile when the Red Sox won the pennant.

"I'm calling to inform you that the Providence Police Department is charging you with dereliction of duty. You know what that means?"

"I get the day off?"

"It means you allowed unauthorized personnel to take over negotiations without the express permission from the Commander."

"The Chief was there," I objected. "He gave me permission and the Commander knows it."

"Noted and logged. You've been suspended with pay pending the results of a full investigation."

"So it's OK to miss my shift."

"I assume you want us to launch an appeal on your behalf. My secretary will give you the necessary paperwork."

"That would be great," I said shading my eyes from the light streaming in the window. "Did you know that I became a cop because I love paperwork?"

"Yeah sure," Overton said. "Lieutenant Canali . . ."

I waited for the union rep to tell me how the Fraternal Order of Police had my back. How they'd fight to clear my record and restore my good name.

"You let us down," he said.

I disconnected.

I sat on the couch and considered turning on the TV. I couldn't face the interviews. PTSD experts analyzing Sergeant Bennett's suffering. Strategists condemning the SWAT team's frontal assault. Anti-gunners calling for an "assault weapons" ban. Pro-gunners expressing "hopes and prayers." Chief Lamar walking the line between sympathy for the devil and fury at the fate of his fallen men. Bereaved friends and family memorializing the victims, putting their grief on public view. The faces of the murdered men.

I felt numb. It wasn't shock, although that was part of it. It was more a sense of impotence. I couldn't do what I needed to do in any area of my life. And there was so much to do.

"If you're going through hell, keep going."

The man who uttered those words, Prime Minister Winston Churchill, was no gym rat. I was. It was the one place where I could clear my head. I was wriggling into my workout clothes when Mother called with a four-word invitation.

"Freeman Parkway. Two o'clock."

I drove to the gym, put Beethoven's Ninth on my BOSE headphone and went to town on my lower body and left arm, barely noticing the ab-tastic fitness instructor inflicting death-by-sit-ups on an overweight sixty-year-old.

The music failed to distract me. I kept thinking about Sergeant Bennett's final moments on Earth. Her small frame crumpling to the pavement. The resignation on her face. I don't know if I was remembering her expression or imagining it. Either way, the mental screensaver joined the FBI bombing and the Molton Lane shootout in the file marked "horrors I'll revisit whether I like it or not."

I took my time in the shower, using breathing and visualization techniques to calm my mind. By the time I rolled up to Mother's I was ready to deal with her BS. Or so I thought . . .

The Hispanic girl opening the door was the latest in a line of maids whose job depended on a level of perfectionism that would challenge a brain surgeon. Benny, my father's occasional bodyguard and driver, greeted me just inside the hallway.

"You packing?" Benny asked.

I gave him my "whaddayakiddin?" look and tapped my left side.

"Your father's in there," Mother said breezing past me, pointing at the living room as if I was an exterminator asking the location of a cockroach infestation.

My father looked out of place, surrounded by "significant" paintings, furniture, glass work and ceramics.

"Hi Johnny," father called from a leather couch so buttery it made me wish I'd started day with a piece of toast. "Tough day yesterday huh?"

"Tough is just a word," I said, leaning down to let hug him me.

I sat on a hard-backed chair next to the sofa, impressed by the furniture maker's skill; the plain wood was as comfortable as the Bentley's thrones. Mother entered the room dressed in African-inspired clothing tailored to hide her overfed frame. She sat across from us in a steel and leather seat.

"We've got to fix this mess with Luke," Mother said, staring at me as if I'd shoved a Baggie of cocaine into Luke's backpack.

"I'm taking care of it," I said.

"Just like you took care of those officers?" she asked, more to needle me than gain information. "*How* many men died?"

"Too many," I replied, tight-lipped.

"Men who'd be alive right now if you knew one thing about human nature," she said. "Which you don't."

"I know evil when I see it."

I shouldn't have escalated the confrontation. I should have sat quietly and taken my lumps. But I'd never done it before and I saw no reason to start then.

"You're pathetic," Mother said with disgust.

"*Basta!*" Father growled.

Normally, the more the shit hit the fan, the calmer my father became. Not that time. For once, maybe the only time ever, his command stopped Mother's abuse dead in its tracks.

"Can we focus here?" I said, breaking the heavy silence.

"Stop distracting me," Mother said, repositioning herself in her chair.

I sighed and shook my head.

"We're here to decide how best to help Luke," Father said, using his *consigliere* voice. "Our first job is to keep Luke out of jail."

"Where are we with that?" I asked.

"They're keeping him in Moran 'til Tuesday. I can't make any headway. But the feds might be willing to cut a deal."

"Give them *nothing*," Mother spat.

"What do they want?" I asked.

"Leo Sporcatello's head on a pike," Father said.

"So what *else* is new?" I inquired, seriously.

"What does Luke know about Sporcatello?" Mother asked.

"*Niente di utile,*" Father said.

"For God's sake Franco, *speak English!*"

"It means nothing useful," I said. "What *can* we give them?"

"Forget the FBI," Mother said dismissively. "Leo Sporcatello can make Luke's arrest go away. John needs to give Leo whatever he wants."

I looked at my father. Of course he knew about the mob boss' promise to disappear Luke's felony drug charge in exchange for information on the federal investigation. But how did *Mother* know? Father *never* discussed mob business with Mother. Unless I was wrong. It was possible that my parents had hidden mob-related discussions from me. Maybe for a long time.

"It's not that easy," I said, cautiously. "Leo will take his pound of flesh no matter what. And then some."

"*Nothing's* easy for you," Mother said, renewing hostilities. "You *always* find a way to make things difficult."

"Leo might be able to get Luke out from under this thing," Father said. "But he's right. There are a whole lot of ways this can go wrong. We gotta be careful."

"Too bad you weren't careful on our wedding night," Mother said, staring at me.

"For God sake, *give it a rest*," I practically hissed.

"What did the FBI say about Max?" Mother asked me.

I'd told exactly two people about the FBI's interest in Max Herndon's finances: Leo Sporcatello and Veronica Herndon. Dad knew from Leo. Again, how did Mother know?

I remembered my conversation in Max's study the night Luke's parentage finally came into the open; Herndon's warning that my mother's deviousness was worse than I could imagine. But I couldn't put two and two together.

I looked at a Warhol painting on the wall behind my mother. A Campbell's soup can. An original, no doubt. Worth a fortune, even by Mother's standards. And then I figured it out: how Mother knew about the FBI's interest in Max Herndon and my deal with Leo Sporcatello to rescue Luke.

"You're in business with Max," I declared.

"*Nonsense*," Mother said angrily, unconvincingly.

"You're laundering mob money through your charities," I said, more to myself than anyone in the room.

"*How dare you!*" Mother barked. "What do you know about *anything*?"

"I know how you're paying for the lifestyle to which you've become accustomed. How many charities do you run? I guess charity starts at home."

"Who the Hell are *you* to judge *me*?"

"Someone with morals?"

"Oh Johnny," Mother said, sighing like she did when she proofread my grade school English essays. "You're *so* naive."

"So that's it," I said, summarizing. "I spy on the FBI for Leo, Luke gets off the hook and everyone lives happily ever after."

"No it's not 'it'," Mother said. "You leave this whorehouse thing alone. You've caused enough trouble as it is."

"What do you mean 'enough trouble'?" I asked, livid. "*They were using children for sex.*"

The maid entered the living room, bringing my mother a cup of tea. Mother accepted the china cup and saucer, looked at me and smiled knowingly.

"You see?" she said. "Not all those children are victims. Some go on to lead even more productive lives."

"Even *more* productive lives? My *God* Mother, *are you saying your maid was a child sex slave?*"

"Welcome to the real world John Canali," she replied with a nauseating measure of satisfaction, like she'd beaten three-of-a-kind with a straight flush. "Ask your father about it. Better yet open your eyes. And for once, *do what you're told.* Or there *will* be hell to pay."

Father somehow pulled himself off the couch designed to relax occupants into a coma and motioned me to follow him to the door. Mother didn't even look at us as we left.

"Your mother's scared," Father said, firing up a cigarette on the front steps.

"For herself. Jesus Dad. How long have you known about Mother and Max?"

"A while."

"*And you're OK with her using a child sex slave as a maid?*" I asked with self-righteous indignation.

"There are a lot of things I'm not OK with," Father said.

"Judge not lest ye be judged? What the fuck."

"Let's go with that."

Father gestured down Freeman Parkway, We walked away from Mother's brick pile, Benny following us at a discreet distance. A block later we stepped aside for an anorexic jogger heading for the Boulevard.

"I'm telling you Johnny," he began, "this ain't no simple thing."

"No kidding?"

"You don't have anything on the FBI that Leo needs. You don't have anything on Leo that the FBI needs."

"Copy that," I agreed. "Seems like the whole damn city knows about Max's 'financial irregularities.' And Leo's occupation is hardly a state secret. So why are they playing me?"

"Because that's what they do."

We paused outside a Victorian home straight out of Disney's *The Lady and the Tramp*. The sounds of a quality piano playing Mozart's *Eine Kleine Nachtmusik* drifted through an open window,.

"A bit ham-fisted," Father pronounced.

"We can't all be as good as you," I half-joked.

"Or you," he replied, continuing our walk. "What did I teach you about pawns?"

"That you can't win without them. That you never know when you're going to need one."

"Right now you're a pawn," Father said, flicking his cigarette butt into the street and firing-up a replacement. "The feds are trying to corner Max. You're what they call an asset."

"Lucky me."

"If Max flips," Father continued, "Leo's going down. The FBI won't need you. The whole Herndon family will disappear into witness protection. Best case, they take Luke with them."

"If Max doesn't flip?"

"The FBI will keep Luke behind bars, to put the squeeze on you and Max. It may or may not work, but they got nothin' to lose."

"What about you? You could give them something."

"I'd be dead so fast it'd make your head spin.."

"Leo tried to have me killed," I announced.

"I heard. I would have been next. Still might be."

"Jesus. That's the guy you *work for?*"

"Things change Johnny," Father said, his voice weighed down with regret. "One day you're someone's friend, the next day your their enemy, the next day your back in their good books. You gotta roll with the changes."

"What if someone slips a pair of cement overshoes on Max and takes him for a swim?"

"Then Leo's our best bet to get Luke out of this jam. Unless we have something else the FBI wants. A big fish that would give the media a massive hard-on and make the feds happy."

"Other than Leo? And Max? Who?"

"Whom," Father corrected, smiling and nodding his head gently, waiting. The answer came slowly. When it arrived I laughed out loud.

"*Mother?* You'd *do* that?"

"Would you?" Father asked, as we stood admiring her brick mini-mansion.

"Now *there's* a question," I said. "Save my son from jail or send my mother to prison."

"Not much of a choice if you ask me," Father said coldly, nodding to tell Benny they were leaving. "Talk to Veronica before we make a move. See which way the wind's blowing. And Johnny, no phones." . . .

Veronica saved me the dime, as my father used to say. She called less than fifteen minutes after I sat down for lunch at the Wayland Square Diner. She slid into my booth just as I scarfed the last triangle of the world's best turkey club.

"That thing in Onleyville," Veronica said, taking off a motorcycle leather jacket that cost more than a Harley. "I'm *so* sorry. How's your shoulder?"

"Yeah. Me too. Great."

"Do you want to talk about it?"

"My shoulder?" I joked. "Some other time."

Veronica gave the waitress holding a coffee pot the high sign.

"Max is gone," she said, turning back to face me.

I chewed slowly. Veronica and her non-incarcerated sons weren't in an FBI safe house. So Max was either missing-missing or dead-missing. Veronica didn't look particularly upset. I put my money on Max getting out of town while the getting was good, and maybe not behind Veronica's back.

"Where is he?" I asked.

It was Veronica's turn to clam up. She smiled at the waitress pouring her a cup of coffee blacker than Leo Sporcatello's heart.

"You knew Max was laundering money for the mob," I said, dipping a lukewarm french fry into ketchup and pointing it at her.

"I told you," Veronica said, watching her java swallow the contents of two half-and-half creamers. "I take care of my own."

"It's the Rhode Island way," I said. "I assume you've stashed some money in case the feds freeze Max's assets."

"You know Sam Greenberg?" Veronica asked, blowing gently over the lip of her coffee cup, staring into my eyes.

Who didn't? The white shoe lawyer made his name defending our last Mayor; an enormously popular, deeply corrupt politician who spent two years at Club Fed before becoming a radio talk show host.

"I've got him on retainer," she said.

"What now?" I asked, pushing my plate away.

"I want you should do me a favor," Veronica said, throwing down a *Godfather* quote. "Cut a deal with Leo Sporcatello. I'll tell him where Max is once Luke's in the clear."

"Wait. What? You'd trade Max's life to save Luke from prison?" I asked, failing to mention that I was considering sacrificing my mother to liberate our son from jail.

Veronica nodded. She set down her coffee mug on the formica tabletop. Before I knew what was happening, she stood up, leaned over and kissed me.

Our lip lock was more than a business deal sealed with a kiss. It was a reboot. All the emotions and desires I'd thought were dead and buried, that *had* been dead and buried, welled-up inside. I felt lost. I felt found. I felt like nothing in the whole world mattered as as long as I could feel her lips against mine.

A couple of construction workers cheered as our kiss ended. Veronica looked like the cat that ate the canary. I felt like the lion that wanted to eat the cat.

"Leo will come for you," I said slowly as she retreated to her side of the booth.

"I sent the other boys to a cousin. My house is a fortress. And I know my way around a gun."

I raised a skeptical eyebrow, remembering Luke's contempt for his mother's anti-gun *animus*.

"Say hello to Mia for me," Veronica said, standing up and placing a twenty on the table. "Tell her I'd love to take her to lunch sometime."

"That could be the worst idea I've ever heard," I said, motioning Dot to refill my coffee.

"Come over to the house after you give Sporcatello my offer. I'll make you dinner."

"*That* could be the worst idea I've ever heard."

"Or the best," Veronica said, cocking her head seductively as she left.

Either way, I felt powerless to turn-down Veronica's invitation. Which made the call to Mia something of a challenge.

"*Caro* are you OK?" Mia asked, sensing the stress in my voice. "That woman she is the devil."

It took me a second to figure out that she was talking about Sergeant Bennett, not my mother or Veronica.

"Are you free tonight?" I asked.

"No *mi amore*. Unless you want to join us . . ."

"No thanks."

I felt slighted that Mia put her S&M session ahead of me. Then again, I'd learned that she was a much nicer person when she'd scratched that itch.

"How about lunch Tuesday?" I suggested.

"Of course. You want to talk now? Or are you *occupato*?"

"No. Yes. Now's not good. I have to tie-up a few loose ends. *Nessun riposo per i malvagi,*" I said, somehow recalling the Italian translation for "no rest for the wicked."

"*Alloro non dormirò mai.*"

Translation: if that was true I'd never sleep. True or not, I had miles to go before I slept. I had to find Tommy Mulvaney.

Chapter Eighteen

According to local legend, there were five Tommy Mulvaneys. There had to be. Tommy was everywhere. He popped up at christenings, bar mitzvahs, political rallies, restaurants, block parties, little league games, car shows, concerts, funerals and open houses. Wherever people gathered, Tommy gathered with them.

He was welcome. Rhode Islanders from all walks of life greeted the personable seventy-something with open arms. He was easily identified by his dark green sports jacket, coke bottle bottom glasses, warm smile and lilting Irish accent, developed and perfected after a boyhood trip to his ancestral home.

Tommy shared Chief Lamar's ability to remember everything about everyone. Unlike Chief Lamar, Tommy used his eidetic memory to bring people together. Also unlike the Chief, Tommy deployed his mental superpowers with charm, finesse and discretion.

To make ends meet, Tommy sold information — dirt — to prosecutors, lawyers and criminals. He knew all the players. Their weaknesses and strengths. Their place in the pecking order. What they'd done, what they were doing and what they wanted to do.

If anyone could lead me to the animal who killed ex-sex slaves for money, it was Tommy. I arranged to meet him at Starbucks. I stopped by the bank for some folding money before entering the Chestnut Street outpost of Don Schultz's coffee empire.

"Officer Canali," Tommy said, rising from a table to shake my hand. "Black, right?" he asked, handing me a cup of coffee.

"You never cease to amaze me Tommy."

"I never cease to amaze myself," he said flashing his trademark smile.

We sat down in matching armchairs, close enough to hear each other, far enough away from other tables to not be overheard. Tommy peered over his glasses and pressed a button on his iPhone.

"Airplane mode," he said, placing the phone face down on the table.

"Nice case," I said, admiring the paisley pattern.

"Laura Ashley."

"Did she fall or was she pushed?" I asked, referring to the designer's fatal journey down a flight of stairs.

"Coffee OK?" he asked

"Perfect," I answered, not wanting to diss Starbuck's Pike Place blend, named after one of America's oldest farmers' markets — which probably sold coffee that didn't taste like it was roasted with a blow torch.

"What can I do you for Johnny?" Mulvaney asked.

"Straight to business?"

"You look like a man in a hurry."

"Nah Tommy. I got all day."

"Is that so? When they gonna let you back on the force?"

"Wow. News travels fast around here."

"That's because it never has far to go."

"I have no idea when I'll be back. After the inquisition. Maybe never."

"You wanna tell me what happened yesterday?"

"I do not," I said in an Irish accent.

"Okay," Mulvaney said, laughing gently at my imitation of his imitation. "What do you want to know?"

"You heard about Molton Lane?"

"Sure. You did a good thing there."

"We saved a few kids Tommy. But we were late to the game. Some kids weren't so lucky. You can guess what happened to them."

"Tell me."

"They disappeared."

"Really? That's terrible. Really terrible."

"I want to know who killed them. I want to know where the bodies are buried. *If* they were buried."

"That's some heavy shit."

"True."

Mulvaney paused to consider the implications of my request. His demeanor changed, from happy-go-lucky and friendly to quiet and deadly serious. He pretended to look around, buying time to search his mental archives. His darting eyes and suddenly blank expression told me Tommy knew something he didn't want to share.

"These are horrible crimes, Tommy," I said, leaning towards him, staring into his blue-grey eyes. "Only a monster could do this. And he'll *keep* doing it until someone stops him. He probably *likes* doing it."

Mulvaney gave me his best "what the hell kind of world do we live in?" look.

"All that is necessary for the triumph of evil is that good men do nothing," I said, hitting him with FBI Agent Pistone's brow-beating quote. "Are you a good man, Tommy?"

For most people, Tommy Mulvaney *was* a good man: the kind gentleman who remembered their hopes and dreams, setbacks and accomplishments. A man who had a kind word for everyone. Someone who knew someone who knew someone who could help someone do something, in the great Rhode Island tradition.

Customers on the dark side of Mulvaney's network knew a different Tommy: a shrewd businessman who never let his personal opinion interfere with his commercial interest. A wheeler-dealer whose success depended on turning a blind eye to all manner of criminality. Appealing to Mulvaney's better nature was a losing proposition. I'm not sure why I bothered.

"I've got a grand that says you can help me," I said, getting down to brass tacks.

Mulvaney nodded, relieved that my ask had gone from a moral duty to a commercial transaction.

"I can't give you a name," he said, shaking his head sadly, contemplating the loss of a big payday.

"I'll take what I can get."

"You sure? I don't have much to tell you."

"I'm sure," I said slipping an envelope with ten hundred dollar bills under the table.

"They call him the Ghost," Mulvaney said covertly pocketing the cash.

"*Who* calls him the Ghost?"

"You never heard of him? He's sort of a legend. You know, an urban myth."

"But he exists."

"I know someone who knows someone who's seen him."

"You got a description?"

"Not really. He wears a ski mask. Only talks on the phone through one of those devices that makes your voice sound funny."

"Can I talk to this someone who's seen him?"

"I can't do that, for a number of reasons."

I briefly considered — and then rejected — putting some pressure on Mulvaney. The man was more connected than the light bulbs on a Christmas tree. I had enough trouble with people in high places as it was.

"*When* did this happen?" I asked. "Where?"

"Summer, two years ago. I don't know where. This someone says his friend brought the package to the Ghost's car —"

"The *package*?" I said, thoroughly disgusted that Tommy was describing a child about to be murdered as a commodity even though — make that *because* — it was true.

"Give me a break John," Mulvaney said, putting hands up in front of his chest. "I'm trying to give you your money's worth."

"What kind of car was it?"

"No idea."

"Go on."

"Like I said, this Ghost guy wears a mask. And a long-sleeved shirt."

"Height? Weight?"

"I can't help you there. But listen to this. There's this bug in the car, banging up against the inside of the front window. The Ghost reaches up to smack it . . ."

Mulvaney smiled triumphantly, leaving me to guess the importance of a squashed bug in a professional murderer's car.

"The friend of a friend sees a tattoo," I said pointing to my forearm.

"Bingo! You should have been a detective."

"Tell that to my mother."

I could see Mulvaney filing away the insight into my family dynamics.

"What did the tattoo look like?" I asked.

"He only saw it for a flash, a second really."

Mulvaney paused to retrieve a nip bottle of Canadian Club whiskey from his coat. He poured its contents into his coffee.

"He saw the number 308," Mulvaney said, leaning back and gulping his cooled coffee. "Just that. That's all I got. I told you it wasn't much."

"It's enough, Tommy," I said, doing my best to hide my excitement, if that's the right word. "Thank you."

"Glad I could be of service. Hey, you don't happen to know where Max Herndon is do you?"

"I bet that information is worth a lot more than a thousand dollars."

"You're right about that," Mulvaney said, waiting to see if we were about to haggle over price.

"I don't know where Max is," I said, honestly. "If I did I wouldn't tell *you*."

I chose my words carefully, in case they got back to Leo Sporcatello. The intended implication: "I wouldn't tell *you* where to find Max Herndon, but I *would* tell Leo. I needed the *mafiosi* to believe I was his boy — whether I was or wasn't.

"You don't ask you don't know," Mulvaney said, smiling pleasantly.

One thing I knew: the Ghost. The kid killer in question was none other than Providence Police Officer and SWAT team member Henry Bastien.

During my SWAT training, I'd noticed that Bastien didn't play well with others. He didn't banter with the boys. He couldn't see that winning every competition alienated him from his team. He was always the last to find a seat for lunch.

I'd figured Bastien's die-hard demeanor and lack of social skills went with the territory. He was, after all, the guy who had to keep a two-legged target in his rifle's sights for an eternity, then calmly pull the trigger and end someone's life.

Thinking back, I remembered Bastien's fanatical devotion to the tools of his trade. It was all he ever talked about: guns, magazines, ammunition, scopes, bipods and other firearms-related bits and pieces. He described his choices with religious fervor.

No wonder, then, that Officer Bastien had the caliber of his go-to sniper rifle tattooed on his right forearm: .308.

As Mulvaney and I shared harmless gossip about mutual acquaintances, a part of my mind wrestled with my pledge to give Sergeant Drake and Destiny the name of Yanira Dupree's killer. It struck me as a particularly bad idea. Just because Bastien fit the bill as a child murderer for hire didn't necessarily make him one. Tommy's intel was third hand. Someone could have been feeding Tommy false intel to frame the SWAT sniper.

Even if Bastien *was* the monster who'd taken out little Marie Dupree and God knows how many other innocent souls, the amorality of handing over the sniper for torture and an ugly death left me feeling distinctly queasy.

I was surprised at the sudden resurgence of my conscience. I'd been a trigger squeeze away from murdering car salesman Mark Mingle. I'd shot two people to death on Molton Lane without so much as a hihowareya. And I harbored deep, pathological disgust for anyone sick enough to rape a child, never mind providing children for others to sexually abuse.

But something had changed. The Onleyville massacre had drained much of my simmering, self-righteous, homicidal fury. I felt an underlying obligation to the dead officers and Mary Bennett to avoid further bloodshed.

Tommy drained his laced coffee and said his goodbyes, stopping to greet a lawyer with greasy hair and patent leather shoes. I peered into my coffee cup, looking for a plan. I decided to break into Bastien's house and find evidence that the man who'd sworn to protect and defend Providence's residents was murdering children for money.

It was a dumb idea with no guarantee of success and dozens of ways to go wrong, including death-by-booby trap and a thoroughly unpleasant journey into the justice system. Still, a bad decision is better than no decision. Or so they say.

I found Bastien's address online and headed out to Coventry.

Coventry was the birthplace of Nathaniel Greene, the Revolutionary War hero who rose through the ranks to become General Washington's second-in-command, lending his name to the state's only commercial airport. In the intervening years, half the town was industrialized, home to a large population of poorly-paid immigrants. When the mills died, the town returned to its bucolic roots.

Judging from his last name, Bastien was a descendent of the French-Canadian workers who'd migrated from our neighbor to the north. Google maps pinpointed his house: a Cape Cod style single family dwelling off the main road surrounded by a small amount of woodland.

Bastien was on duty in Providence. As far as anyone knew, he lived alone. I was good to go. I parked my car on a nearby side street and hiked the rest of the way to his house. I walked straight up to the front door. There weren't any cars in sight, no indication of anyone inside. Just to be safe, I rang the doorbell with a knuckle, not wanting to leave fingerprints.

After a few minutes I walked around the back, looking for outbuildings, freshly turned soil or a well worn path into the surrounding woods. Nothing. I was about to break a window and fake a burglary when I decided to try the back door. It was open.

No alarm sounded. It was as if Bastien was telling the world he had nothing to hide. There certainly wasn't any mess to conceal. Officer Bastien's kitchen was immaculate, as were the living room and bedrooms. I put on a pair of rubber gloves from my car's emergency kit and scanned the interior for hidden cameras, even though I knew they'd be impossible to find. And then I started looking for hiding places.

I searched drawers and closets, carefully replacing any items I had to move aside. I checked behind pictures. I pulled up area rugs. I looked for fake ceilings. Nothing.

Bastien's enormous black-and-gold gun safe stood in a small addition to the back of the house dedicated to his relentless pursuit of ballistic perfection. He'd stocked a long bench against a wall with a wide selection of neatly arranged gun smithing tools. None of the instruments and gauges had any obvious blood spatter or stains. Which was just as well; the idea of children being tortured or killed with the metal tools turned my stomach.

I gave up searching for hiding places and returned to the main living area. I focused my attention on the decor, trying to get a feel for the house's owner. There wasn't a single personal item anywhere. No family photos, no artwork, no knick-knacks. No bills. No computer. The refrigerator was stocked with energy drinks, eggs and a few other basics. There was nothing in the trash can. The whole place was as clean and empty as a hotel room.

"A ghost leaves no trace," I said quietly to myself.

Only one thing offered insight into Bastien's personality: a small bookcase in the living room. Aside from a dozen or so paperback spy novels, Bastien's literary collection consisted entirely of hardcover books dedicated to firearms. The books were perfectly arranged by height. All except for one, a fraction taller than the coffee table-sized book to its left.

I slid out *Firearms: an Illustrated History* and thumbed through it. I was about to put the book back when it revealed its secret: a Spiderman comic wedged in between its thick pages. I carefully turned the flattened front cover. There was a childish scrawl on the top of the first page: "Property of Daniel Martinez."

Daniel Martinez was a six-year-old boy who disappeared on a cold winter's day, triggering a massive, highly-publicized search. His father was an MS-13 gang member. Rumor had it the boy was killed as a part of a vendetta or a warning of some sort. Daniel was never found.

I took a photo of the comic with my phone, replaced it on the shelf, took a photo of its position and left . . .

The Public Safety Complex was funereal. No one was happy to see me. No greetings, no commiserations, no eye contact as I made my way to the Chief's office. I felt like a ghost.

"Come to beg for your job?" Chief Lamar said as I once again sat facing Providence's top cop.

"No sir. I'm fully confident the official report will examine my actions impartially and clear me of all charges."

"Are you?"

"Yes sir," I said, betting that the Chief's lack of empathy rendered him unable to detect sarcasm. Not caring if it didn't.

"I'm here to update you on Molton Lane," I said.

I took out my iPhone and brought up the photo of the Martinez boy's childish writing on the Spiderman comic. I handed the phone to the Chief. He put on his reading glasses and peered at the image.

"Where did you get this?" has asked

"Inside a book on firearms at Officer Bastien's house."

Lamar busied himself considering the accuracy and implications of my accusation. I held out my hand for the iPhone. For a long second I thought the Chief wouldn't return it.

"What's this got to do with Molton Lane?"

"He's the Ghost," I said.

"The what?"

I waited for a sign of recognition on Lamar's face. When it didn't arrive, I continued.

"He murdered Martinez. I have no other evidence but every reason to believe Bastien killed other kids. Sex slaves who passed their 'sell-by date'."

Lamar paused, contemplating the ramifications.

"I'll need some hard evidence to get a search warrant," he said. "Something obtained *legally*."

"I'm not a detective," I said, shrugging my shoulders.

"No you're a negotiator."

"Did Officer Bastien kill Sergeant Bennett?" I asked, changing the subject.

"She made a threatening move," Lamar said, stony faced.

"Of course she did."

The Chief and I sat in silence, thinking about the previous day's shit show from our different perspectives.

"Bastien's arrest needs to happen fast," I said. "Or bad things will happen. Trust me."

We both had a small smile at that one.

"I hope this information pans out," Lamar said. "For your sake."

Chief Lamar looked at me like I was an animal in a zoo. It wasn't a million miles away from how I felt. But I wasn't the only one who was trapped.

Luke was behind bars, driven by an addiction he couldn't control. Veronica had built a gilded cage for herself and her family; a cage she was determined to protect at all costs. Mia couldn't get out from under the long shadow of her father's business — assuming she wanted to. Drake and Destiny were prisoners of a burning desire for vengeance. My mother was a captive of her character, or lack thereof. My father could never distance himself from his criminal client.

I was trapped by my moral code, such as it was, and the responsibility I felt for all of them. There was only person in my immediate circle who was free to do as he pleased: Leo Sporcatello. The mob boss had risen to power though an endless series of choices, living on the edge of extinction, influenced by the actions of others, determined to be the one calling the shots. To be the master of his own fate.

Ultimately, Leo would be the one who decided what happened to all of us, and thousands of others. It was up to me to force the mobster to give us a chance at freedom. Or so I thought.

"Listen closely, Canali," the Chief said, preparing to dismiss me from his presence. "Do not approach Officer Bastien under any circumstances. You hear me?"

"Yes sir, I do."

Like the Chief said when he promoted me, I'm a good listener. I just don't like what I hear.

Chapter Nineteen

As I entered my fourth decade, the wisdom of one of my father's favorite sayings became increasingly clear: getting older's not for sissies.

I'd recovered relatively quickly from previous injuries: broken bones, twisted tendons and pulled muscles from ice hockey, dirt biking and other high-risk activities. The gunshot wound was different. My shoulder pain came and went, but it never left. The pills could barely touch it. I mastered tasks with my left hand, but I still felt like half a man.

The doctor told me the injury would take months to heal, but I couldn't help feeling I wasn't getting any better. Eating was difficult. Sleeping was difficult. Driving was difficult. *Life* was difficult.

Thankfully, not dying has its advantages, generally speaking. Forget gaining wisdom. The older you get, the faster time passes. The faster time passes, the easier it is to be patient.

Waiting for the raid on Officer Bastien's house was the exception that proved the rule. Time slowed to a crawl. I wouldn't have been more anxious if I'd been about to jump out of a perfectly good airplane. One night, four days after my meeting with Chief Lamar, I couldn't stand another minute rattling around my apartment. I took a double dose of pain meds, hopped in the Honda and headed to Mineral Spring Avenue . . .

Venetti's Music was in a strip mall, wedged between a dance studio and a Chinese restaurant whose menu was best sampled at three A.M., if at all. The sign above the music store — the owner's signature in black-on-white typeface — was the only bit of elegance in an otherwise hang dog neighborhood.

"Buonasera poliziotto Canali," Sergio Venetti called out from behind his desk, a tiny bell over the door echoing through the otherwise deserted interior.

Sergio Venetti was the most courteous human being I'd ever met — and the only man I knew who considered a bow tie appropriate daily wear. The mustachioed maestro treated all his customers and students with respect and encouragement, no matter how limited their budget or musical ability.

Venetti's own talent was towering. The Italian-born pianist was famous for his mastery of Chopin's fiendishly difficult *Etude in G# minor, Opus 25, Number Six.* His promising musical career nose-dived in his mid-twenties when an outed lover's suicide triggered an onstage nervous breakdown, leaving Venetti unable to perform in public.

"Buonasera professore," I said, looking around the store. "Have you sold the Steinway yet?"

"*My* piano? *Never!*"

The Mahogany Model D enjoyed pride of place in the store's center, bathed in the soft glow of a dimmed overhead light. It stood aloof, apart from lesser instruments and electronic pretenders. Rumor had it Venetti blackmailed a gay businessman into selling him the German-built piano on the cheap.

In truth, he'd purchased the Steinway from my mother. She sold the piano to Venetti for pennies on the dollar after my teenage self stumbled through a dinner party performance, mangling Mendelssohn in front of the Rhode Island Philharmonic's Musical Director.

I remember the day the movers rolled the Steinway down a portable ramp. Mother ignored my crestfallen outrage; she'd given up on my musical education. She couldn't bear looking at the piano after such public humiliation. As soon as I could drive, I began secretly visiting the Steinway in Venetti's store, using my allowance to continue lessons under my teacher's supervision. My erratic musical instruction lasted through the ups and downs of high school, college and career.

And there I was, twenty-six years later, giving Venetti the same greeting I'd used the first time I darkened his door. Getting the same response.

I walked over to the Steinway and lowered myself onto the bench. I removed my sling, opened the fallboard, dropped my hands on the keys and stared at them. And there I sat, motionless, incapable of movement.

"Cosa no va?" Venetti asked quietly from behind his desk. "Too much pain?"

I couldn't answer. I looked at the piano and shook my head. I heard the eighty-two-year-old musician get up. He stood behind me, placing his hand on my bad shoulder.

"Sometimes all we have left is the music," he said quietly.

I reached across my chest and placed my left hand on top of his, feeling the fragile bones beneath his warm skin.

"Play," he commanded. "Play what you feel."

I removed my hand. I took a few deep breaths that sounded like sighs, and probably were.

"I leave you alone," Venetti said, retrieving his fedora hat and long wool coat from the closet. "Lock up when you finish."

I turned and nodded my goodbye. He smiled; a sad look from a man who was no stranger to struggle. When I heard the door close, I began playing Beethoven's *Piano Sonata No. 14 in C# minor*, a piece I'd spent years trying to master. As the so-called Moonight Sonata's first quiet notes rose up from the piano, I was surprised how easy it was to ignore the signals coming from my shoulder. How easy it was to play.

Venetti's voice came to me from somewhere in the past: "Listen for the silence *between* the notes. Control what you *don't* play."

As my hands pressed the keys, I left barely perceptible pauses between certain notes, adding longer moments of hesitation between key changes. Suddenly, for the first time, the *adagio sostenuto* revealed its secret. The *sonata quasi una fantasia* was a funeral march. For me, at that moment, it embodied the struggle to keep going, to stay afloat in an ocean of sadness.

I remembered FBI Agent Lacroix's unseeing eyes as she lay on the shattered remains of the FBI's Command Vehicle. The motionless body of SWAT team officer Lu lying on the street, abandoned, dead, alone. Sergeant Mary Bennett, crashing to the pavement like a sack of potatoes.

I thought about the victims of Molton Lane — and all the other victims of all the other Molton Lanes. Young children being used, abused and discarded by devils disguised as men. I thought about the fear and misery of the children's short lives. The loneliness of their deaths. I remembered the boy who'd offered me sex outside the sex slavery house. I saw his drugged face in my mind's eye, staring at me, expressionless. I mourned the death of his innocence. And my own.

I didn't mean to cry. I didn't feel sad, exactly. But tears streamed down my face, warming my cheeks and neck, soaking into my shirt. As I ended the first movement I felt a rifle muzzle press against my neck and then retreat.

"Hello Johnny."

"How long have you been following me?" I asked, my fingers automatically finding the keys for the second movement.

"Coming after me was a big mistake," Officer Bastien said. "Your last."

"Well it sure wasn't my first," I said, resuming the piece. "You should have heard me play this as a child."

"I bet you were a cute kid."

Any doubts I had about killing Officer Bastien disappeared. Unfortunately, so had my chance of doing so.

I should have negotiated for my life. I was trained to change minds. To make homicidal men and women abandon their plans. To surrender peacefully. I couldn't. I was too angry to think straight. All I could do was play, leaping straight into the Sonata's stormy third and final movement. I poured my desperation into the music, my fingers commanding the Steinway's keys.

Arpeggios flew off my fingertips like flocks of birds darting across a darkened sky. I could see the musical finish line in the distance. I approached the Sonata's conclusion feeling strangely fearless.

"How many kids did you kill?" I shouted, daring Bastien to admit the enormity of his crimes.

"Eleven," he yelled back, his answer flat, emotionless.

"How many for money?" I demanded.

"Nine."

"Where are the bodies?"

"Gone."

"Did you kill Marie Dupree?"

"Who?"

"Yanira's mother."

"Who?"

That was it: the end of our "conversation." And, soon, me.

There were worse ways, worse places to die. I only hoped Bastien would leave my body in front of the piano. I wanted my mother to know she'd failed to keep me from something I loved.

I struck the Sonata's last chord, sending an electronic shock from my shoulder to my fingertips. I hadn't missed a single note of the enormously demanding eight minute *presto agitato*. Whatever else I'd done in my life, at least I'd done that. Sergio Vendetti would have been proud.

As the sound faded to nothing, a gunshot ripped the silence into a million pieces. I waited for oblivion. Instead, I heard a single word: *"Abbanstanza!"* Enough.

I turned to see Officer Bastien on the floor, blood pouring from his side in a single stream, his rifle kicked out of reach. Sergio Venetti stood behind him, aiming a large revolver at the child murderer's body.

Bastien screamed, then moaned, gasping for air. I got off the bench, reached in my pocket for my telephone. Venetti aimed the gun at me and shook his head.

"No," he said sternly, motioning at the door with the gun. "Go."

I picked up my sling and stumbled out of the store, the tiny bell sounding Bastien's death knell. I fumbled for my keys, filled with a terrible, wonderful sense of satisfaction. I dared to take the time to replace the sling and drove to my father's house, watching for anyone following, checking for surveillance outside his back door.

"What do you need?" Father asked with wide-eyed paternal concern.

"An alibi."

"Go to the Roundabout. Have a few drinks."

I kept quiet about the meds in my system, hugged him and got back in my car. I had more than a few drinks. Moe poured me in a taxi. I don't remember anything past that, save the lingering taste of bile in my mouth . . .

I woke up to the sound of knocking on my door. I had no idea how long someone had been rapping on the cheap wood. My head hurt so much I figured I'd have to get better to die. I made a firm decision to stay exactly where I was — until I heard Mia calling my name.

"Gianni, please. I know you are there. Open the door."

Even Mia's pleas wouldn't have motivated me to move a muscle if the mobster's daughter hadn't kept knocking. The sound was like a hammer pounding on my head.

"*Basta*," I called out weakly.

She didn't hear me. There was only one way to stop the aural assault. I managed to stay vertical long enough to unlock the door and stagger back to bed. As my head hit the pillow, I closed my eyes and fought the urge to throw up.

"Johnny? *Stai bene?*"

I felt the pressure of Mia's body as she sat next to me. Her hand stroked my hair, slowly, rhythmically. That too was painful, but not as much. After what seemed like hours of misery, I fell asleep. I awoke some time later feeling marginally better, vaguely human.

"The bourbon she doesn't like you," Mia said, her hand still stroking my hair.

"Water."

I raised myself just enough to sip the bottle she held to my mouth. Mia carefully slid down onto the bed next to me, placing her arm and legs over me like a warm blanket. Normally, a cuddle like that would have been a prelude to sex, or a coda to its aftermath. For the first time in our relationship, holding each other was its own thing: a physical connection that bonded us without obligation.

I felt the rising and falling of Mia's breasts against my side. Something inside me broke. In my hazy stupor I realized that I'd been holding out. Rational thinking had kept me from realizing how lucky I was to have this dark, beautiful creature in my life, with all her faults, baggage and danger.

I pulled her closer. She sighed. We fell asleep in each other's arms.

I awoke for the third time to the smell of cooking. Mia was at the stove, dressed in my bathrobe, pushing something around with a spatula. I came out of the bathroom, thought about shutting the curtains on the gathering gloom, then sat at the table. I chugged a glass of water. Mia refilled it. A few minutes later she brought me a plate of mushroom risotto.

"You cook?" I croaked.

"I cook."

"Who knew?"

Mia's smile warmed my heart. We ate in silence. When I'd eaten as much as I could stomach, which wasn't much, Mia got up, pulled me to her and held me for an eternity. She took me by the hand and led me back to bed.

"I need to see your father," I said hoarsely.

"Soon," she said, my head resting on her chest.

"Rough night," I declared, unnecessarily.

"I know."

I looked into Mia's dark eyes, trying to see what she knew. Unable to read her mind, I settled back into her embrace.

"Do you remember Las Vegas?" she asked. "The first night?"

"I remember the dealer," I half-whispered. "Chinese guy. Stupid smile. I gambled like a total fool. Reckless as fuck."

"Yes you did."

"You were wearing something slinky. Versace. You still have that dress?"

"You remember walking back to the room after you lost all that money? There was a piano."

I remembered. I sat there in the empty hallway, playing for Mia. Disappointment evaporated in the early morning light streaming through smoke-stained windows.

"Schubert," I said.

"I thought to myself, how does this policeman play so beautiful music. How is that possible . . ."

I said nothing, willing her to stop.

"You were there, at the store, last night, yes?"

I wondered if she was making a statement or asking a question. Not caring either way.

"He deserved to die," Mia said, as simple as that.

"Yes he did," I agreed weakly.

"And now?"

"Now I must save my son."

"You're a good father, Gianni."

"And a good lover," I said, putting my hand on her breast.

"The best."

"What about the others?" I asked, instantly regretting it.

"When I was a little girl," Mia said quietly. "My father killed my mother. For cheating. Before he left for the states, he treated me badly. *Molto male.*

I felt her beating heart next to shoulder.

"I don't know why I do it," she said. "The — you know. It makes me forget things."

I didn't press and Mia couldn't continue. She cried, her tears cascading onto my head.

"It's OK *Cara*," I said knowing it wasn't true, and never would be.

She held me tightly until the tears stopped. We made love tenderly. There was nothing else to say. Nothing else to do. When it was over, it was my turn to hold her.

"*Dimmi tesoro*," Mia said, running her hand over my torso, her head rising and falling with my breathing. "What do you need from my father?"

I didn't want to answer.

Despite Mia's knowledge that I'd been there when Sergio Venetti sent Bastien to hell, our relationship was based on leading separate lives. I still didn't know if I could trust her. Mia was, after all, Leo Sporcatello's daughter. The stakes couldn't have been any higher.

"Veronica," I began, feeling Mia bristle slightly. "She wants to make a deal for Luke."

Mia's body relaxed.

"She knows where Max is," Mia said, as if it was as obvious as the perfect nose on her face.

I suppose I should have been surprised that Mia knew her father's business. Angry? Disappointed? I wasn't any of those things. The truth had been there all along. It was just a question of admitting it.

"Yes," I said. "She knows."

"You are willing to make the deal?"

"It's not my deal. Not my decision."

"Isn't it?"

"I suppose it is."

"And you have decided."

"I have."

"Then it is done."

"Is it?"

"It is," she said, her hand sliding down my body. "But I am not."

"Are you ever?"

As I felt Mia's hot breath descend down my body I surrendered, mentally and physically, my hangover somehow making things more intense.

As I'd admitted to Mia, I'm a terrible gambler. But sometimes life forces you to the table. Sometimes you have to stop worrying about winning or losing, focus your mind and play the game.

By the same token, sometimes the music of two people together, in love, is all there is.

Chapter Twenty

The City of Providence gave the policemen mowed down in the Olneyville massacre a sendoff befitting their sacrifice: a full dress memorial service at the cavernous First Baptist Church on College Hill. My invitation got lost in the mail.

No surprise there. For one thing, I was suspended from the force. It wouldn't do to have a disgraced cop standing at attention amongst somber politicians, stoic police and grief-stricken mourners. For another, my brother and sister officers considered me at least partially responsible for the death of three SWAT team members. For failing to talk Sergeant Mary Bennett into surrendering before her fatal flanking maneuver. A view I shared.

On the day of the service, I arranged to meet Drake and Destiny on Little Compton's town beach.

The narrow beach was deserted, save a couple of empty vehicles and a rusty camper van looking out to sea. The wind was blowing hard, sending sea foam skittering onto the shore.

"Y'always wonder 'what if'," Drake said.

We leaned on the rented SUV's rear fender, facing away from the wind towards the estuary behind the beach. Destiny stood a few yards away, her red hair whipping in the wind, taking pictures of the view with her phone.

"Do that for a while," Drake said, "then let it go. Move on."

I contemplated the irony of Drake's advice. It was the same advice I'd given my former partner after he'd double-tapped Rico Nardelli. More than that, the negotiator and his beloved couldn't let go of their need to seek and destroy Yanira and Marie Dupree's killers. Or could they?

"We're leaving tomorrow," Drake announced.

"Thank God," I said.

Destiny sheltered with us behind the SUV. Drake pulled her closer.

"Did you hear about the officer killed last night?" Drake asked, putting me on red alert.

"Shot by a robber in a music store," I said.

I knew then that I had to tell Destiny and Drake that Bastien was The Ghost, the man who'd killed Marie Dupree before her ninth birthday. I hoped it would give them some kind of closure, mute their desire for revenge.

"Officer Henry Bastien," I said. "The officer in the music store. He killed Yanira."

"Damn! A cop?" Drake asked incredulously.

I described the events leading me to the man who'd murdered Destiny's friend's daughter and, by his own admission, ten other children. Leaving out Tommy Mulvaney's name and my role in Bastien's bloody finale.

I told Drake and Destiny that there was little chance the children's bodies would ever be found — without mentioning Bastien's declaration that they were "gone."

"Is anyone looking?" Destiny asked.

"I don't think so."

"That's quite a coincidence," Drake said skeptically. "Bastien getting shot the day after you found that comic book."

"*Fuck*," Destiny spat, her freckled face suffused with disappointment and anger. "I hope to God he suffered."

I stopped myself from describing Bastien's last moments on earth, writhing in pain, bleeding to death on the floor of Venetti Music. None of us said anything for a minute or so, listening to the sound of the surf pounding the beach.

"This cop, did he kill Marie too?" Destiny asked.

"I'm not sure."

We all knew I was clueless. Worse, we all knew that whoever murdered Marie Dupree was covering up the sex slavery on Molton Lane. It had to be someone further up the food chain. Someone working for Leo Sporcatello.

"This isn't over," Drake announced.

"Drake, Destiny. Stop. Go home. You won't win. You *can't* win. For fuck's sake, let it go."

"*You* didn't," Destiny said. "*You* killed Yanira's murderer."

I wanted to tell Destiny I wasn't a killer. That I played by the rules and so should they. It would have been a ludicrous statement, given my homicidal spree at Molton Lane. By the same token, the truth about Bastien's fatal finale — that `I was there when my music teacher shot the killer cop in the back to save my life — was a secret I'd take to my grave. Unless I had to testify. Which I hope to God I didn't.

And then there was the fact that I hadn't delivered Bastien to them. That I'd left it to Chief Lamar to arrest the sick fuck. There was no sugar-coating it: I'd betrayed my promise to deliver Yanira's killer.

My phone buzzed in my back pocket. Veronica.

"Luke's out of prison," Veronica said. "They finally gave him a hearing. I posted bail."

"When can I see him?"

"He's sleeping. I'm taking him straight to rehab when he wakes up. You can visit him there. Eventually."

"Don't tell anyone where you're taking him. He'll be safe."

"Have you had your meeting yet?" she asked.

"This afternoon. You still want to go through with this?"

Veronica hung up. We both knew what I was going to do . . .

Working out at the gym, preparing for my sit down with Leo Sporcatello, I caught sight of Agent Pistone coming off one of the machines. The scruffy-looking FBI agent was remarkably fit, dressed in a tight fitting Under Armor T shirt and shorts.

"Funny meeting you here," I said.

"Right?"

We walked outside.

"Busy?" Pistone asked, firing up a cigarette.

"Working on my memoir."

"Am I in it?"

"Sure. You're a hero. The federal agent who set up and busted my son out of his love for justice."

"Your tax dollars hard at work."

"Get to the point Pistone."

"Just for the sake of argument, let's say you knew where Max Herndon is. You'd tell us wouldn't you?"

"Of course," I answered moving to his left side, avoiding his second hand smoke. "Why wouldn't I?"

"I think we both know the answer to that one."

I hoped the FBI Agent was talking about my relationship with Leo Sporcatello's daughter, not my upcoming meeting with her father. I couldn't be sure. For all I knew, the Bureau was tapping my phone.

"Here's the thing," Pistone said, watching a young man throw his gym bag into an Audi. "We might be willing to drop the charges against your son in exchange for information on Max's whereabouts."

"Might?"

"Would," he clarified.

"That's a generous offer," I said, trying not sound sarcastic.

"But?" Pistone said, ignoring the Bureau's betrayal.

"I don't know where Max is. If I did — if I do, you'll be the first to know."

"If you know where he is and don't tell us we won't be happy."

"Your happiness is important to me."

"On the flip side, that job offer still stands — *if* you help us apprehend Mr. Sporcatello."

"Threats and bribes. My father's recipe."

"You want to negotiate?" Pistons said, grinding out his cigarette against the wall and pocketing the stub.

"Why would I trust *you* after what you've done to me? To my son."

"Because you don't have a choice?" he answered.

"Just for the sake of argument, let's say I know another Max Herndon. Someone else who laundered Sporcatello's money who can help you build a case. What would that be worth?"

"Big fish?"

"Big enough. Media friendly."

Pistone stretched his triceps, trying to hide his excitement.

"Name?"

I laughed.

"You give me the name and I'll see what I can do," he said.

"You see what you can do and I'll think about giving you the name."

"You do that. Just don't take too long. Things are moving quickly."

"Aren't they always?"

I headed back to my apartment to dress for a third meeting with Leo Sporcatello. I chose blue jeans, a polo shirt and a leather jacket. I left the sling on the bed.

We met at *Cosi Fan Tutti*, an Italian delicatessen on Federal Hill. Sporcatello was sitting at one of the outside tables — with Mia. The idea that Mia Sporcatello kept her distance from her father's business was well and truly dead. I could only hope the same wouldn't happen to me.

Leo was wearing fine cut Italian clothes: wool slacks, a dress shirt and a black cashmere sweater that cost as much as my entire wardrobe. Well the bits Mia hadn't donated to the cause. The boss' daughter wore a floral print dress, a small sweater covering her shapely shoulders, and black high heels. Leo called me over with a friendly wave. I scanned the surroundings.

I recognized the handsome man who'd inspected my junk for hidden weapons at Sporcatello's seaside retreat. Leo's bodyguard was sitting across from an elderly woman who looked like the Queen of England, of all things. The rest of the crowd seemed the usual combination of tourists and regulars.

I kissed Mia on both cheeks, only slightly distracted by her Narcisco perfume and the proximity of my teeth to her earlobes.

"Officer Canali," Sporcatello pronounced as I lowered myself into the chair opposite.

"*Mr.* Canali," I corrected, leaning across the table to shake his hand with my right hand.

"A temporary measure," Sporcatello declared, pouring me a glass of wine. "*Per cent'anni,*" he toasted.

"I'd settle for an hour of good luck," I said, sampling the wine.

The sun continued its game of hide-and-seek, occasionally emerging from cloud cover to warm De Pasquale Plaza. Leo enquired about my health, I told him I was on the mend, knowing that my posture told him I had a ways to go.

"Are you hungry *Caro*?" Mia asked. "*Tu non mangi muori*," she said with a devilish smile.

"I don't think I'll die of starvation."

"You know why they call this Federal Hill?" Sporcatello asked, pretending to be oblivious to our flirting.

"Papa not another *lezione*," Mia chided.

"It was named after a celebration of the *ratifica*," Sporcatello said. "The ratification of the federal Constitution by the nine of the thirteen states."

"But not Rhode Island."

Sporcatello nodded.

"General West led a thousand armed farmers to stop the celebration," he said. "Fortunately there was no *spargimento di sangue*."

"Bloodshed," Mia translated, unnecessarily.

"Do you think you could have negotiated that?" Sporcatello asked.

"I bet the farmers smelled the food, had something to drink and decided to party instead," I replied, avoiding a straightforward answer.

"Who knows? But it was two years before Rhode Island joined the United States."

"Your point being?"

A momentary flash of anger crossed the mobster's face; he wasn't used to being hurried along.

"You can't deny the inevitable," he said. "All you can do is negotiate terms. So," he said leaning forward, all business. "Where is Max Herndon?"

"Fix this thing with Luke."

"You don't trust me?"

"Who do *you* trust Leo?"

"I trust Mia," Sporcatello, patting her hand, confirming his daughter's role in his criminal enterprises.

Mia showed no obvious emotion, no loving look at her father. She was busy watching a pair of police officers entering the restaurant.

"Friends of yours?" Leo asked, clocking the objects of her attention.

I recognized Officers Swanson, the rookie cop, my former partner and mafia hit man. Sporcatello must've known he had Swanson in his back pocket. For all I knew, his new partner too. The whole damn department.

"All the guys love me," I said.

"What's not to love?" Mia said breaking her stare to speak on my behalf.

"I don't know where Max is," I said. "But I know someone who does."

"Who?"

"Veronica Herndon," I said, banking on the chance that Mia had already shared that piece of information with her father.

"Of course," Leo Sporcatello said. "And she sent you to arrange this?"

"She'll tell you where Max is after you get rid of the charges against Luke."

I was about to close the deal when my gaze fell on a small blond in a tight skirt standing at the delicatessen counter. It took me a moment to see past the wig and oversized sunglasses. Destiny.

Sporcatello hadn't survived the slings and arrows of outrageous fortune without developing a keen sense of danger. He turned to see Destiny at the very moment she confronted Officer Smithson.

"*You!*" she screamed. *"You bastard! You raped me!"*

For a second, I thought Destiny appeared at the restaurant in disguise to confront her abuser. The surprise in her voice put paid to that theory. Which meant one thing: her accusation was either a planned distraction or an unfortunate coincidence. Either way, she was there to kill Leo Sporcatello.

Destiny pulled out a small gun and emptied it into the cop's chest, point blank. Sporcatello's bodyguards sprang from their chairs and rushed to their asset. They pulled the boss to the ground and jumped on him, guns drawn. They looked around for threats, preparing to rush Leo Sporcatello out of the kill zone.

Out of the corner of my eye I saw Sergeant Moses Drake striding up the Square, like an enraged bull heading straight for a matador. Drake pointed his GLOCK at the armed gaggle surrounding the mobster. Mia was crouching under the table near the huddled protection team. The next thing I knew my gun was in my hand aiming at Drake's center mass.

I hesitated. An instant before I could pull the trigger, both bodyguards opened fire. A least a couple of rounds found their target — with no appreciable effect on Drake's progress. The older female bodyguard, the one who looked like aging royalty, broke from the group, stood up, moved sideways and continued firing. She only stopped when Destiny shot her from behind.

Mia looked straight at me, her beautiful features frozen in fear. I glanced beyond her and saw Destiny aiming her gun at my lover and her *mafiosi* father. I wondered if Destiny had reloaded her pocket pistol. I told myself it was unlikely but didn't matter. I walked towards her, firing as I went. I shot her several times.

I turned back towards Sporcatello and Mia. They were scurrying from the scene with their armed entourage. Sergeant Drake changed his target from the moving Sporcatello scrum to me.

We pulled our triggers at roughly the same time. I don't know if I hit Drake but his bullet missed me, kicking up shards of pavement by my feet.

I ducked behind a concrete fountain in the middle of the Plaza. When I peered out at Drake, Sporcatello's would-be assassin was looking around the Plaza like a mother who'd lost a child. He was dazed, confused, doomed.

The barely walking wounded cop turned and staggered back towards the street. Officer Swanson emerged from the restaurant and followed him. My ex-partner kept his sights on Drake as he stumbled towards Atwell's Avenue.

Swanson was fully cured of his post-assassination angst; he unloaded on Drake. If Drake hadn't reached permanent retirement by that point he achieved it immediately.

I came out from behind the fountain, searching for God knows what. The restaurant and the surrounding area was total chaos; there were dozens of people running and screaming, blood and bodies everywhere. But no Leo or Mia Sporcatello.

Responding officers arrived a minute or so later, shouting commands. I put my hands up and waited . . .

It took the Providence Police ten confusing minutes to restore a semblance of order and establish a perimeter. It took them the rest of the night to process the crime scene, logging the exact position of the bodies and shell casings, interviewing witnesses, directing traffic away from Atwells.

I spent the time refusing to answer questions, letting the EMTs check me for bullet holes and sitting in the dank inside of a cruiser, awaiting my fate. I leaned my head against the cold window and fell into a dreamless sleep.

"You OK?" Chief Lamar said, leaning into the car.

"Are these cuffs necessary?" I said, my voice thick with exhaustion.

Lamar pulled me from the car and instructed a sour-faced Detective Cruse to unshackle my wrists.

"How you feeling?" Lamar asked.

"Long day."

"It isn't over yet," he said, guiding me to the passenger door of his car.

"I'm not saying anything. On or off the record."

"Get in."

I got in and waited.

"I need a favor," Lamar said, eyes front as we drove off, waved past the roadblock.

"Where are we going?" I asked.

"Home."

"If I knew you were coming I'd have baked a cake."

"Not your home," Chief Lamar said, his expression grim. "Mine."

Chapter Twenty-One

"You look like shit."

Chief Lamar glanced at me as we drove down the Interstate, followed by a line of cars waiting to resume a more sensible speed. I don't know what I looked like, but I felt like a wreck. All I wanted to do: go home, shower and sleep some more. That and get another gun. I had no idea what the Chief had in store for me; I wasn't happy about going into unknown situations without ballistic protection.

"You did good," the Chief said, violating the rules of grammar for dramatic effect.

"I'm the man," I declared. "The man who shot a Georgia State Trooper."

"There was no 'almost' about the way you took out his accomplice. Five shots, center mass."

"Awesome," I said slowly.

"From everything I've seen and heard it was a clean shoot."

"I don't think that word means what I want it to mean."

"Well I'm sure Leo Sporcatello was happy you were there. He's got a lot of friends."

"He who has a thousand friends has none to spare," I said, quoting Ralph Waldo Emerson.

"He who has one enemy will meet him everywhere," Lamar replied, once again matching me Waldo for Waldo.

If the Chief was reminding me that Leo Sporcatello was still my enemy, there was no need. Saving Leo's life changed nothing. The Italian mobster would always act in his own self-interest. No matter what.

We pulled off onto Route 114, a winding four-lane divided highway leading through Barrington to Bristol; a thoroughfare known for its money-spinning speed traps.

"How you holding up?" Lamar asked.

"I'm just hoping you're not 'taking me for a ride,' if you know what I mean."

"That's ridiculous."

"Wouldn't be the first time," I said, wondering how Porsche salesman Mark Mingle was enjoying his second lease on life. "What's happening at your place?"

"It's my wife. Susan. She's locked herself in the bathroom."

"*That's it? That's* why you've dragged me away from a multiple murder scene in the middle of the night?"

"It's been twenty-four hours. She's been there since last night."

"I'm glad you've got your priorities straight," I remarked sarcastically. "So your wife is holding herself hostage in the bathroom. Well, at least she's got fresh water and a place to piss."

I looked out the window, both annoyed and relieved.

"What makes you think your wife hasn't come out of the bathroom while you've been cleaning up another one of Sporcatello's messes?" I asked.

"My brother-in-law's there, trying to talk her out."

"And you think *I* can convince Mrs. Lamar to leave her safe space?"

"You're the negotiator," Lamar said without any apparent irony.

"Not anymore. Or did you forget about Onleyville?"

"You do this and I'll make sure you get your job back."

"Is that a threat or a promise?"

"Yes."

"Is that a joke or an observation?"

"Yes," Lamar said, allowing himself a small smile.

"How long have you been married?"

"Eight years."

"Kids?"

"We had a son. Christopher. We lost him to leukemia two years ago. He was four."

"I'm sorry for your loss. How long have you been trying for another baby?"

"Two years. I'm 'sub fertile.' Stress related."

"IVF?"

"Five times. No luck."

"Does our health care plan cover that?"

"Some quack sterilized Susan," Lamar said resentfully. "So no. We're broke . . . She found out I had an affair."

"Shit happens," I repeated, hoping I didn't sound flippant.

"With a man," Lamar revealed as we peeled off the highway onto rustic roads lit by occasional street lamps.

I sighed. The odds of luring Lamar's wife out of the bathroom were somewhere between slim and none, and Slim had just left town.

"Do you want to stay married?" I asked the Chief.

"Susan doesn't know it but . . ."

"It wasn't your first rodeo."

"Yes. I mean no."

"I'll ask you again," I said, too tired to play anything but bad cop. "Do you want to stay married?

"How could any woman put up with that?"

"That depends on the woman. And you. So?"

"I don't know."

We pulled into a gravel driveway and stopped in front of a colonial style house. A couple of small SUVs were parked ahead of us.

The interior was a well-ordered place with what used to be called a woman's touch: a Van Gogh copy of his famous flowers painting in the hallway, bright blue throw pillows on the couch, frilly curtains and a bowl of lemons on the kitchen counter.

"Hey Bud," Lamar called, hanging his keys on a nail next to the door. "I'm back."

Lamar's brother-in-law looked how I felt: tired and haggard. His weary face told us Mrs. Lamar was still locked in the bathroom.

"Who's he?" Bud asked suspiciously.

"A friend."

The look on Bud's face told me he shared my doubt that Chief Lamar had friends.

"Do you want me to stay?" Bud asked.

"No. I'll call you when she's out. She hasn't said anything."

Lamar looking relieved.

"Good luck," Bud said, closing the front door behind him.

Lamar led me through the living room into a small corridor.

"She's in there," he said pointing at a flimsy bathroom door.

"Susan, are you O.K.?" Lamar called out.

"Leave me alone," a weak voice answered.

"I've brought someone to talk to you."

"Leave me alone."

I nodded towards the main room. Lamar took the hint and left me with his wife.

"Hey Susan. My name is John. John Canali. It's just you and me now . . . How you doin'?" I asked, laying on the Rhode Island accent for comedic effect.

Nothing.

"Can you tell me what's going on?"

Still nothing.

"Your husband told me some of what's happened. I want to hear it from you."

Silence. A problem that served as an unwelcome reminder of Sergeant Bennett's response to my entreaties. Oh yeah, I was a real conversationalist.

"You don't want to come out do you?" I asked.

I was hoping for "that's right" — a starting point. No such luck. I got the distinct feeling that Mrs. Lamar wasn't going to say anything. *Couldn't* say anything.

I remembered a story from my FBI training. The agent who designed the Bureau's hostage negotiation protocol talked a couple of armed robbers into surrendering by monologuing through a closed door. Given Mrs. Lamar's stony silence, it was my best shot.

"Susan, your husband told me you lost your son Christopher a couple of years ago," I began, sitting on the floor outside the door, lowering myself loudly enough for her to hear that I was settling in. "That must've been tough."

"I lost my son too," I continued, "but in a different way. His name is Luke. Someone else raised him. There were so many things I never got to see. His first smile. Learning to crawl. To walk. At least you had that. But I know it's not enough. It will never be enough."

I paused.

"And now you're afraid that you've lost your husband. Lost everything. I don't think that's true Susan. Not entirely."

I searched my memory for Chief Lamar's first name and came up blank.

"Your husband loves you," I declared. "Yeah, I know. I know about his affair with a man. That's got to hurt. That's got to hurt a lot. I bet you're thinking you could never compete with that. But it's not a competition Susan. It really isn't.

"Think about it. I know it's hard right now, but think about it. You shared a good part your life with the Chief. The best part? I don't know. There are ups and downs in every marriage. But I'm sure there were good times. No one can take that away from you. Not even your husband. What he's done doesn't change that. You loved him Susan, didn't you?"

I heard her shifting positions.

"Of course you did. And there's nothing wrong with that. Sometimes we love people who get lost, and it's not our fault. And sometimes we love people we shouldn't."

I shouldn't have gone on. I should have kept my mouth shut. I don't know why I didn't.

"You know who I love? A mobster's daughter. Me. A police officer. Then there's my high school sweetheart. Who's — get this — married. *And* she's the mother of my son. Who's a drug addict. What do you think about all that?"

I sighed.

"I think you've probably given up on your marriage. I understand that. It's normal to want to protect yourself. But don't give up on Martin," I urged, finally remembering my boss' Christian name.

"I'm not saying your marriage will survive. Not the way it was. Not the way you wanted it to be. Not the way he promised. But he's a good man, Susan. Someone who wants to do the right thing but sometimes finds he can't. He has to live with that. Like you, right? Like me. I've done the wrong things for the right reasons. Lots of times. I hate myself for it. Hate the world for making me do it . . .

"I shot a man today Susan. A man I admired and respected. A man who helped me out of a jam. I didn't want to shoot him but I had to. I wish I'd had a chance to talk to him. To stop him from making a mistake. I saw it coming. I knew what he was going to do. I denied it, ignored it. And then it was too late.

"You knew something was wrong with Martin, didn't you? You probably put it down to grief. Never imagined that he'd want someone, something else. Right?"

Silence.

"It's not too late, Susan. Not too late to find something positive in this mess. Some way to live with Martin, to keep loving him, even if it's in a different way. And if not that, some way to live by yourself. With yourself."

I took off my jacket and placed it on the floor next to me.

"I should tell you about my mother. You want to hear about my mother? Susan?"

No reply.

"My mother doesn't know how to love. Oh she loves art and music and theater and Japanese movies. Stuff. Things. But she doesn't know how to love another person. I don't blame her. I feel sorry for her, even when she hurts me. Well I do *now*. Because I realized it's her loss as much as mine. Maybe more.

"When I first met the Chief he reminded me of my mother. I thought 'this guy's an asshole. He doesn't give a shit about anyone but himself.' But it's not true. Martin loved Christopher. Loved him with all his heart. And he loves you too. He could've broken down this door, pulled you out and sent you to the psych ward. He could've denied he'd had sex with a man. Told everyone it was the ranting of his poor, mentally ill wife.

"I know you're angry," I said, switching gears. "You have every right to be. Who wouldn't be? I'd hate him too if I were you. Locking yourself in the bathroom means you don't have to deal with it. With him. You don't have to deal with anyone.

"I know how people suck. They're selfish. Arrogant. Insensitive. Sometimes you have to get away from them. Otherwise the anger and disappointment eats you up. But like everything else, anger passes. You ever heard the old Persian saying 'this too shall pass?' It will. Then what, Susan? That's up to you isn't it? Not him. You.

"Right now you don't have to think about the future. You don't want to. I understand that. So how about this? How about I get your husband to leave tonight? Give you some space to come out, get some food and think things through. You hungry, Susan?"

"Tell Marty to go to his lover," Lamar's wife said in a matter-of-fact way.

"No," I said, relieved to finally to hear her voice. "He'll stay with me. And I'm not gay, by the way."

Lamar appeared from the living room. I shook my head in case the Chief thought I was about to share my apartment.

"I'll come out once he's gone," she promised.

"OK Susan. It's a deal. We'll both leave now. But do me a favor. Flash a light when you come out. That way I'll know you're O.K."

She didn't answer, but I heard her stand up and turn on the faucet.

"Am I really leaving forever?" Lamar asked in a child-like voice as I put on my coat and headed for the door.

"I don't know," I said as we both stood by the cruiser, waiting for Lamar's wife to flick the lights.

She appeared at the window, lit from behind, a small figure standing stock still, looking out into the night. She turned off the light.

"Let's go," I said, opening the cruiser door, waiting for the Chief to get in. Which he did, eventually.

"She's going to take me back," Lamar announced once we'd rejoined the main road.

I thought about agreeing with him, but didn't. Life may work out best for people who make the best out of how life works out, but that doesn't mean it always works out. It didn't look like it was working out for the guy who'd smashed into a pole ahead of us, waving us down.

"Will this day ever end?" I asked.

Lamar put on his car's light bar, radioed in the accident, got out of the car and headed for the wreck. Most of the crashed vehicle was still in the road. I checked for traffic before joining the Chief.

The driver was a tall guy dressed in a pair of dark slacks and dark T-shirt. He stood by the side of his car, looking surprisingly calm, as some people do when they're in shock.

"Anyone else in the car?" Lamar called out, walking towards the driver.

He stared at the Chief wordlessly, then looked down the road over Lamar's shoulder. I heard it before I saw it: a car coming up behind us. Fast.

When the guy jumped out of the way I dove for the side of the highway. Lamar wasn't so quick. Or lucky. The oncoming car smashed into the side of the wreck, right through the Providence Police Chief.

It was a medium speed crash — severe enough to make mincemeat out of the Chief but not so hard that the speeding vehicle got hung up on the wreck.

The late model Buick backed up, releasing the Chief's mangled body from the steel-on-steel embrace. It hit the pavement with a sickening thud. The "stranded motorist" ran to the vehicle's passenger side and got in.

I reached for my gun — the gun I didn't have — and yelled for him to stop. He didn't.

And that was that. The Buick disappeared into the night, leaving Lamar's crumpled, lifeless remains lying on the concrete.

I pulled the Chief's corpse to the side of the road and sat down next to him. I should have gone back to the cruiser and called for help, I should have started the search for the fleeing vehicle. I couldn't. I couldn't move a muscle.

I listened to the cruiser's cooling engine ping and crickets chirp. It suddenly occurred to me that *I* might have been the killers' target. Then I remembered the set-up guy staring at the Chief like he was a dead man. Not me. The Chief. What had Lamar done to sign his death warrant?

I knew only one criminal with the balls to order a hit on Chief Martin Lamar: Leo Sporcatello. Maybe Lamar was in hock to Sporcatello for the IVF treatments. Maybe he thought Lamar set him up. Who knows? It didn't really matter.

I decided Sporcatello had to pay for his crimes. I knew my decision would end any chance of a future with Mia. But that chance had been an illusion — like the belief that Drake and Destiny would let the Duprees' death go unavenged.

As a siren approached, I knew I wouldn't be weak. I wouldn't question my nature or wrestle with my conscience. Not anymore. I'd take my time and act decisively. No hesitation. No regrets. No remorse.

Anyway, that was the plan. As poet Robert Burns observed, the best laid plans of mice and men often go awry.

Chapter Twenty-Two

My father had a lovely smile. Poorly arranged, nicotine-stained teeth did nothing to detract from his broad grin and dancing eyes. His smile told me everything was going to be alright — even when it wasn't.

Father was beaming at me from across a picnic table at "The Shack," locals' nickname for The Dune Brothers restaurant.

"What a beautiful day," my father pronounced, biting into his fin and haddie toast. "Almost makes winter worth the effort. What's the matter Johnny? You're not hungry?"

"Not really," I said, picking at my market salad.

"You've had one hell of a ride," he said.

"Ya think?"

"Only when I'm paid."

"I'm paying," I said slapping a ten dollar bill on the table.

My father made a big show of putting the note in his sharkskin wallet.

"Go ahead," he said. "Shoot."

"I'm taking Leo out."

My father looked around, then stared at me, making sure I wasn't kidding. When he saw I was serious, he resumed eating. Slowly.

"That's a hell of a thing, Johnny. A hell of a thing. Seeing as you're in Leo's good books right now, what with saving his life and all. And what about Mia?"

I winced at the mention of Mia's name.

"You kill Leo and Mia's gonna take you right off her Christmas card list."

"*Amor vincit omnia*," I said ironically. "Love conquers all."

"Not that," my father said, his laughter highlighting the surreal nature of the whole enterprise. "So Johnny, you wanna explain this to me?"

I laid out my reasons for wanting to take out Leo Sporcatello. Some of them emotional, some of them practical. At certain points, I felt like I was trying to convince myself that murdering Sporcatello was as sensible as my father's Clarks shoes. If so, I did an excellent job. Whatever it was that led me to homicidal intent, my determination grew and solidified. As I finished my presentation and pushed aside my salad, I avoided the 800-pound gorilla in the room: my actual plan to kill Leo Sporcatello.

I didn't have one. If I did, I wouldn't have shared it with my father. I didn't want to make him a co-conspirator — any more than he already was. When I finished, Father lit a cigarette.

"You gonna try and talk me out of it?" I asked, breaking the silence.

"Johnny, when you were a little boy, you always did the opposite of what your mother told you. I told you to go along, to make your life easier. You never did."

"I listened to you."

"I never had much to say. I was busy fighting my own battles."

"Which you won."

"Yeah? Where did it get me?" he asked, pointing at the city across the river.

"I will always be proud of you Dad. You're my hero."

"Some hero," my father said wistfully.

"The only one I've got."

There it was again: his reassuring smile, tempered with parental concern.

"I assume you're telling me all this in case you fail," he said, flicking ash into his mostly empty coffee cup. "Making sure I'm ready if Leo comes for me."

"Yes."

"What have I told you about failure, Johnny?"

"Failing's easy," I said, imitating his Rhode Island accent. "Anyone can fail. It's success you gotta worry about."

"Right?"

"If this works, there's going to be chaos," I said.

"True."

"If it doesn't, go to the FBI," I said. "They'll protect you."

"Can the feds protect me from knowing my only boy is dead?" my father asked, his pain making my heart hurt. "Are you *sure* I can't convince you to stop? I can be a pretty persuasive guy."

"If you were going to try and talk me out of it you wouldn't be asking."

"Final answer?"

"Yes."

"Then you better not fail."

"Dad, I have a question for you."

"Ask."

"Are you proud of me?"

"Oh Johnny," my father said, tears welling up in his aging eyes. "You're the best thing that ever happened to me. Maybe the only good thing that ever happened to me. I love you son."

"I love you too Dad. I've done some bad stuff."

"You did what you thought you had to do. If you have to do this thing, I understand."

"Do you?"

"I remember the day I met Leo. Your Mom had kicked me out of the house. I was working out of a dump in North Providence. I was 32. Didn't have a dime to my name. Leo walked in, looked around, and smiled. He knew he had me."

"You didn't have a choice."

"With Leo Sporcatello knocking on my door? No."

"You did what you had to do."

"Sure. But that doesn't make it right. Anyway, it is what it is. Next stop Veronica?"

"Next stop Veronica."

"One piece of advice, Johnny: trust no one. I'll talk to the FBI. Get an agreement in writing. Max for Luke."

"I was hoping you'd say that."

That afternoon, Agent Pistone handed me the agreement in the FBI's safe house. The gratitude on Pistone's face was mixed by something not a million miles away from pity.

"You think I'm a dead man," I said, folding the papers.

"You gonna join up?" Pistone asked, implying that a job with the feds was the best if not only way to avoid an untimely demise.

"I'll let you know." . . .

Veronica led me to the same home office where Max told me he knew Luke was my son. Veronica's skirt and blouse may have been all business, but it did nothing to kill my desire to gather her up in my arms. We sat in the chairs opposite Max's throne, facing each other. I gave her the FBI document. She shook her head as she read the second page.

"I'm not going into witness protection, John. I won't do that to my family."

I didn't say anything.

"I thought we agreed that Leo Sporcatello is our best bet to get keep Luke out of jail without losing everything," she said, looking up.

"Leo's not our best bet if he's dead."

Veronica had to think about that one. It didn't take her long to recover enough composure to see my murderous intent.

"I don't get it," she said, her brows furrowed. "If Leo's dead the FBI won't have any reason to trade Max's testimony for Luke's freedom. They won't go easy on Max or drop the charges on Luke."

"True."

"If Leo's alive and the FBI has Max, we'll have to go into witness protection," she repeated, confronting me with the chance not-to-say-likelihood that I'd fail to kill Leo.

"It's all a matter of timing," I said. "You sign the FBI agreement and tell them where Max is hiding. Once the feds have him, once he's safe, you've completed your part of the bargain. *Then* I'll take care of Sporcatello."

"What could possibly go wrong?"

"I've been thinking about this. Even if Leo gets Luke off the hook, he won't let it go. You'll owe him. I'll owe him. One way or another, he'll find a way to collect. We both know Sporcatello won't rest until he eliminates Max. He's a threat, a loose end. You're a loose end too. Luke. Me. The boys. All of us. You remember that family murdered in East Greenwich? That was Leo cleaning up, sending a message.

"Even if he leaves you alone, the FBI won't. They've got investigators all over Max's books by now. They'll take their pound of flesh. Nest egg or not, you'll be out of this palace so fast it'll make your head spin. Have a look at the agreement. Handing Max to the FBI limits the damage to a fine. A hefty fine, but it won't ruin you."

Veronica paged through the document.

"Why didn't you say all this before I sent you to negotiate with Leo?" Veronica demanded.

"Because I wasn't planning on killing him."

"And now you are."

"If this works, you get Max back, Luke stays out of prison and Leo Sporcatello is history. If it doesn't, you get Max back and you raise your kids in Topeka. At least you'll be alive."

"This doesn't work, I lose you."

It was my turn to be surprised. Killing Leo Sporcatello would end things with Mia — a sacrifice that tore at my heart in ways I didn't want to think about. But I hadn't considered the possibility that Veronica would be waiting for me if I made it out alive.

"You pay's your money you take your chances," I said, acting cool, feeling hot.

"Let me get this straight. I'm betting on my high school boyfriend killing a mafia boss."

"Yes."

"What have you done with John Canali?"

"He's here. Somewhere."

"O.K.," she said, grabbing a pen from Max's desk.

"I'll text you Agent Pistone's number," I said as she signed both copies of the agreement. "Don't call Max. Don't call the FBI until I text. When Max is safe, text me the letter k."

Veronica held the papers out. She looked into my eyes as we both held them.

"Be careful," she said, letting go.

"I don't think that's an option."

"Neither is this," Veronica said, leaning forward and kissing me.

It was a kiss full of promise, like a movie hero's love interest giving him something to remember her by before the big showdown. I didn't *feel* like a good guy. I felt like a condemned man. And a cheat. Especially when Mia hugged me in my apartment.

"Thank you *Caro*," she said, holding me tight. "Thank you for saving me."

I don't think I've ever felt more guilty in my life. When we disentangled, Mia made her way to the stove and started unpacking groceries.

"I'm making you something special," she said, smiling, wiping tears from her eyes. "A *celebrazione*!"

"Be careful," I said, sitting at the table. "I might get used to your cooking."

A part of my mind was in denial. Watching Mia preparing a meal, looking as content as I'd ever seen her, the idea that I'd soon be murdering her father seemed a million miles away. I silently grieved for what could have been. Quiet nights in. Nights out. Trips to exotic locations. A lifetime of making love.

"What's the matter *Caro*? You look sad."

"I'm just tired," I half-lied.

"Of course you are," she soothed, ruffling my hair and placing a steaming bowl of Ribollita soup in front of me. "We'll eat, drink, make love and sleep."

And so we did, and it was more peaceful, more wonderful than I had any right to imagine. I drank a little too much and thought as little as I could. I somehow managed to put Leo Sporcatello out of my mind — until Mia fell asleep next to me, resting quietly in my arm.

I tried not to plan Leo Sporcatello's murder. And failed. In between scenarios I thought about what would happen after I'd done the deed. Mia would never forgive me. That much was true. But how could I forgive myself for violating my oath to faithfully and impartially discharge the duties of a peace officer? I consoled myself with the fact that I wasn't a police officer. My suspension was still in force. So what was I? Luke's father.

The next morning, Mia made me breakfast.

"You're not hungry?" I asked, dipping sourdough toast into egg yolk.

"I never eat with a *subronza.*"

"Hangover?" I asked incredulously, noting that Mia looked as fresh as a daisy.

"Papa wants to thank my brave *amore*. He says he will never forget what you did for us. He wants to take us for a boat ride on Saturday."

And there it was: my chance to kill Leo Sporcatello and, conveniently enough, dump his body into the ocean.

"Just the three of us?" I asked.

"And Luigi. Of course."

"Does Leo go anywhere without him?" I asked as innocently as possible.

"No."

My heart sank. I'd have to kill not one but two men in cold blood. Or die trying.

"You don't trust my father?" Mia asked, laughing gently.

"Should I?"

"You'd be the only one."

I didn't say anything. Maybe I should have. By the same token, I probably shouldn't have visited my mother that afternoon. But I did . . .

Mother was busy readying herself for a cocktail party. I sat outside her dressing room in an overstuffed chair, contemplating a piece of pottery I'd silently dubbed cauliflower on acid.

"Mother, I've been thinking about that money you gave me."

"You're leaving town?" she asked hopefully.

"I'm considering it," I lied. "But I think I should stick around. For Luke."

"Don't be silly. He hardly knows you."

"Which is why I want to stick around."

"So you're returning the money," she said wearily, as if it was a done deal.

"Actually, I'm going to use it to buy a sports car."

"Ridiculous. You drive like a cowboy."

"You wish."

"What?"

"I said, 'you wish'."

"*Consuela!*" Mother called out. "Where did you put my Peretti earrings?"

The maid scurried into her dressing room.

"They're here, where you left them," the small servant replied.

"Are you talking back to me?" Mother asked indignantly.

"No Madam."

"Is there a reason you stopped by John? I'm already late. *Consuela,* did you clean this mirror?"

"Yes Madam."

"Turn off the light," Mother commanded.

A beam from Mother's iPhone bounced off the mirror into the bedroom.

"Look you stupid girl. You see those smears?"

The bathroom light came back on.

"I'm so sorry Madam," *Consuela* said, running out of the room for window cleaner.

"There's no particular reason I stopped by," I said. "I just wanted to see my dear old mother."

Consuela ran back into the dressing room. I heard the sound of spray cleaner squeaking as she sprayed cleaning fluid onto the mirror.

"That's better," my mother pronounced. "Now get me the Chanel bag. The small black one with the gold chain on the hook by the door. Have they found Max yet?"

"No."

"Good. Let's hope they never do. Well I've got to go."

Mother entered the bedroom dressed in something impossibly expensive.

"Before you go, a quick question," I said. "Do you think I should ask for my old job back?"

"Of *course* not. You should try and make something of yourself. Although what, I have no idea."

"I could write a crime novel."

"And I could become a brain surgeon. Honestly John, it's time you grew up and did something useful with your life."

"I thought I was."

"We all know how *that* turned out."

Mother made for the door. She looked back at me, telegraphing the fact that it was time for me to go.

"Let me know what you're going to do," she said. "Return that check. And do *not* expect me to subsidize you going forward."

"I'm going to get something from my room. I'll see myself out."

"*Consuela* will keep an eye on you," Mother said.

My bedroom looked nothing like I'd left it. Mother had removed any evidence of my existence, turning it into guest quarters befitting a luxury hotel, complete with Patresi sheets and stark paintings. The closet held a few of my possessions, carefully labeled, boxed and shoved into a corner.

I found what I was looking for: a finely-crafted leather sports bag. The bag had a false bottom, an addition I made to hide high school contraband. I'd left it behind when I'd bought something less expensive and more discreet.

I left the house feeling like a thief. I got over it, knowing that the bag wouldn't be empty for long. Happy that something I'd used to pull the wool over my mother's eyes would once again serve an important purpose.

Chapter Twenty-Three

To paraphrase legendary football coach Vince Lombardi, timing isn't everything, it's the only thing.

I wanted Max in protective custody so the FBI would drop the charges against Luke before I killed Leo Sporcatello. But not too soon. If the mob boss found out that I'd negotiated a deal that put his money-launderer-in-chief into the FBI's hands, I'd be the one sleeping with the fishes.

As far as *that* danger was concerned, the clock was ticking. It wasn't safe to assume that I was the only one keeping tabs on the FBI for Leo Sporcatello. If someone inside the FBI dropped the dime on Veronica's agreement to surrender Max, my I was screwed. And my father, Veronica, Luke and the rest of the Herndon clan.

In the days running up to my boat ride with Leo Sporcatello my head was on a swivel, scanning for his soldiers. I varied my routine; eating at new places, avoiding my usual haunts. The day before the sea cruise, I packed my false-bottomed bag for the job ahead and texted Veronica: do it at two. It was time for her to tell the FBI where Max was hiding.

I planned on waiting for my fateful encounter with Leo Sporcatello chilling in front of the TV. No such luck. I was summoned to the Public Safety Complex for an unexpected sit down with the new Interim Police Chief.

The City Council gave the top cop slot to Jack "Double D" Johnson; the fat fuck who'd sidled-up to me the day Rico Nardelli decapitated Jorge Gonzales, the father of the boy used as a sex slave on Molton Lane. I had no idea what Johnson wanted, but I was in no mood for surprises. I got one anyway, even before I made it to the station.

Motoring through the run down neighborhood west of the Complex, I noticed a U-Haul truck parked by the side of the road. I couldn't believe I'd stumbled on the same vehicle I'd seen on Molton Lane; the truck that had disappeared in the aftermath of the decapitation and assassination. I recognized the license plate, committed to memory without thought at the time of the incident.

I parked and approached the vehicle. It was driverless, unattended, unlocked. I rapped on one of its metal sides. I heard a metallic echo, then silence. I took a few deep breaths, braced myself and opened the cargo door. Empty.

I climbed inside the cargo bay and examined the scuff-marked interior. There was nothing to identify the truck as transport for helpless children on the way to hell — except a small word written near the floor in marker. AYUDA! Help.

I sat down in the truck, stunned. I don't know how long I sat there or what I was thinking — if I was thinking. My reverie was interrupted by a short black-haired man standing on the street at the end of the cargo bay. Gesturing wildly, he unleashed a string of Spanish expletives, ordering me to *vamos rapido*.

I had no way of knowing if the agitated Spanish speaker was involved in the child sex trade; U-hauls are passed from customer-to-customer on a daily, sometimes hourly basis. But the fact that he started barking into his cell phone as I jumped off the truck and headed back to my Honda left me with a bad feeling. I hoped to God my description wouldn't work its way up to the boss of bosses.

I decided against giving my good friends in the Detective Division a heads-up. If the FBI had potential leaks to Sporcatello, the Providence Police had a direct line — as witnessed by the two uniformed hit men the mob boss sent to kill me for poking my nose into the Dupree murders.

As I resumed my drive to HQ I took comfort in an old Italian expression: *il pesce inizia a puzzare dalla testa*. The fish stinks from the head down. Cut off the head and you stop the stink. A more likely, less comforting saying occurred to me: *il pesce grande mangia il pesce piccolo*. The big fish eat the small fish . . .

Interim Chief Johnson hadn't changed anything about his predecessor's office — save removing all evidence of Chief Lamar's existence. A small mountain of paperwork sheltered under a box of donuts. The new chief's enormous body gave the space a distinctly claustrophobic feel.

"Lieutenant Canali," Johnson said, gesturing at one of the chairs opposite his recently commandeered desk.

"Chief," I said warily, sitting down.

"Thanks for coming in. I'll get right to the point."

"Well it *is* lunchtime."

Johnson glanced at the clock then gave me a dirty look, gradually replaced by an empty smile.

"Good news," he said. "You've been cleared of all charges. You're back on the force. Same rank and everything."

"Let me see if I've got this straight," I said slowly. "You're reinstating me in recognition of the fact that I faithfully discharged my duties. And my ongoing contribution to the job of preserving law and order."

"Something like that."

"Alternatively, someone put a word in your ear. Food on your table. Something like *that*."

I was pointing out the obvious: my return to the force was a gift from Leo Sporcatello. Double D was Sporcatello's boy. Leaving the mob boss free to call the shots at the Providence Police Department. The bad old days were back.

"By the way," Johnson said, letting me know that the subject of my employment was closed. "My kid liked what you said about the Jedi being the bad guys in Star Wars. Me too."

"The Force runs strong in your family," I said Yoda style.

"I know, right?" he said, waiting for me to leave.

I did so gladly, heading off to pick up my badge and a department issued handgun. Once again, I was a sworn peace officer. A cop fully committed to killing a pair of citizens without arrest or trial. The thought should have weighed heavily on me. But my encounter with the U Haul truck had eliminated any moral qualms. My mind was made up . . .

At 2:15pm, I received Veronica's "k" text telling me Max was in protective custody. I said a small prayer, asking God for forgiveness and protection, and headed to Leo's summer house for our final showdown.

The walk from my car to Leo Sporcatello's front door was a long one. The gun-toting sports bag felt heavy in my hand. Luigi answered the door, stepped back and eyed me with deep disdain.

"I love you too," I said stepping inside the foyer, glad for the ocean breeze flowing through the door.

The bodyguard wore Ralph Lauren's best yachting clothes: tan khakis, a light green shirt and Topsiders. He pointed at the table for me to disarm. I put the bag down and held my palms up. Luigi nodded and started to frisk me. Thankfully, he spared me the painful ball grab of our initial introduction.

"*Gianni!*"

Mia's boating clothes were something else entirely: a pair of tight white shorts and a salmon colored silk shirt tied at the midriff. Her greeting was a lot more enjoyable than Luigi's, on one level. On another, her tight embrace was a painful reminder of what I was about to lose.

Luigi picked up my bag, placed it on the table and began rifling through its contents.

I'd stuffed as much as I could into the bag's leather interior: a bathing suit, full change of clothes, sunscreen, water bottle, a tin of Mia's favorite smoked almonds, a large beach towel, a hardback mystery book, my wallet, iPhone, baseball cap, travel humidor, cigar lighter and a five inch folding knife wedged into an inside seam.

As I'd hoped, Luigi found the "hidden" knife. He opened it, tested the razor sharp edge on his fingernail, closed the blade, wagged a finger at me and placed the knife on the table. Mia was unfazed, waiting impatiently for her father's bodyguard to give me the all clear.

"*Babbo's* on the boat," she said as I was released from inspection.

Mia smiled happily, practically dancing as we walked arm-and-arm through the house.

"Ignazia has prepared a beautiful lunch."

"Is she coming with us?"

"Of course not. This is an intimate affair."

Luigi carried the sports bag, walking a few steps behind us as we made our way to the dock.

"*Benvenuto a bordo!*" Leo called out as we clambered onto his 70 foot motor yacht.

He shook my hand vigorously, noting that I'd ditched the sling for the job ahead.

"Are you happy to see me or is that a gun in your pocket," I joked, pointing to the bulge in his tailored shorts' front pocket.

"Yes," Leo said, pleased with both the joke and his response.

Mia and I settled into the leather sofa on the aft deck. Luigi placed my bag on the deck in front of us, then returned to the dock to cast off. The boat's enormous engines rumbled mightily as Sporcatello took us out to sea. I checked my watch; an hour and ten minutes had expired since the FBI had nabbed Max Herndon. I watched the mobster and his bodyguard nervously, like a hawk, in case either man received an emergency phone call.

Luigi joined the boss on the elevated bridge; Mia and I sunned ourselves, unobserved. Mia pulled off her shorts and removed her top, revealing her barely there black bikini. She stretched out on the sofa and put her head back, letting the wind whip her dark hair.

She was posing. I wasn't complaining. I was thinking about timing. When should I do the deed? I'd already decided to shoot Leo Sporcatello. But I needed to kill his bodyguard first. The two men needed to be close to each other. On the bridge? No. The bodyguard was going back and forth to the galley, preparing our food. At lunch then . . .

After an hour of steady motoring, Leo put the boat on autopilot, slowly cruising out to sea. The water was as flat as Kansas; a sea breeze kept us cool underneath the shaded deck. I had a hard time concentrating on our meal. The food was perfect, the wine refreshing. Mia looked fabulous and Leo was in fine form, recounting a recent trip to Japan. Luigi hovered nearby, playing waiter.

"Cigar?" I asked, after somehow managing to finish my seafood salad.

"I have some in the cabin," Leo said, preparing to get up.

"Don't bother," I said, quickly getting out of my chair. "I have something special for you."

I could feel Luigi's eyes watching me. I put my hand on the 10-round SIG in the bag's hidden bottom. I turned to look at Leo and Luigi's position, lining-up my shots, making sure Mia wasn't in the line of fire. I froze when I saw a gun in Leo's hand, pointed in my direction.

I had to hand it to the mob boss: his instinct for danger had saved his ass yet again. And put mine in a sling. I could only hope that my final moments on earth wouldn't involve torture. I'm a bit of a pussy when it comes to having bones crushed and body parts removed. Especially mine.

"*Gianni,*" Sporcatello said, beaming, "a present for you."

I waited for my present to arrive at 830 feet-per-second; the Holland Tunnel-sized hole at the end of the gun's barrel promised death by .45. I had one chance. Shoot the bastard. Something in Sporcatello's expression made me hesitate.

"What's that?" I asked.

"What does it look like?"

"A 1911," I replied, remaining crouched by my bag

"Not just *any* 1911," he corrected, turning the gun around and walking towards me. "A Cabot."

I slowly lay my gun back down inside the bag and stood up. I accepted the handgun, turned it over in my surprisingly steady hand and admired its beauty. The artist had carved scenes of heaven and hell onto every inch of the pistol's metal surface: angels, demons, tormented souls, the grim reaper and more. It was a pistol better suited to a Mexican drug Lord than a Providence police officer but I was in no position to complain.

Mia smiled at me. I smiled back.

"It's fantastic Leo," I managed.

"It's not department issue," Leo admitted. "But I don't think you will have any trouble should you carry it for your job," he added, confirming his grip on my employers. "Anyway, I have something also for you."

Leo nodded his head at Luigi. The bodyguard opened the cabin door and disappeared inside its refrigerated interior. He reappeared, pushing a bound and gagged man ahead of him. Max Herndon.

Leo waved Mia to his side and studied my face. I was too shocked to react — until I realized that everyone was waiting for me to say something. My first thought — hihowareya — didn't seem appropriate.

"A gift from your friends at the FBI?" I said finally, eyeing the polymer pistol in Luigi's free hand.

"Sadly no," Leo said shaking his head.

"Veronica," Mia said, rolling her eyes.

Max's eyes widened. He made some kind of moaning noise through the duct tape sealing his mouth. Luigi tightened his grip on his captive.

"*Gianni*," Sporcatello said. "I heard about your deal with the FBI. That's no good. But I understand. Your boy, yes? You have no cause to worry about him any more. I fix that problem."

"Thank you," I said.

What I wanted to say: fuck that shit. Die motherfucker. Meanwhile, I mentally prepared plan B: shoot Luigi and Leo with my fresh acquired Cabot 1911. A plan that required bullets. I had a sneaking suspicion Leo wasn't the kind of mobster to give a loaded gun to someone who'd arranged to hand a rat to the FBI.

It also doubted my ability to retrieve my SIG from my sports bag before Luigi put a few rounds into my back. A guess that seemed all the more accurate when the bodyguard stepped away from Max and pointed his gun at me, finger on the trigger.

"Do something for me *Gianni*," Leo instructed. "Shoot Mr. Herndon. And then we are all square. Square, right?"

With his free hand, Luigi forced Max to his knees. Then stepped to the side, continuing to aim his pistol at my torso.

"Wait, this gun is loaded?" I asked, incredulously.

"What good is an unloaded gun?" Leo asked.

"Not much," I agreed, thanking God that Leo Sporstcatello had finally made a mistake, hopefully his last.

I pointed the pistol's muzzle at the deck and pulled back the slide a few inches. Sure enough, a .45 caliber round sat in the chamber, ready to go. I got a firm grip on the gun and aimed it at a wide-eyed Max, ready to shift the sights sideways and shoot Luigi.

Max's bowed his head. His shoulders slumped as he awaited execution. It was a sad, pathetic, horrifying sight that almost short-circuited my ability to think. But not quite.

Action beats reaction. Even with Luigi's finger on the trigger, I knew I could shoot Leo's bodyguard before he could unleash a round in my direction. And then shoot Leo. One, two. Then return my sights to Luigi for another shot. Then back to Leo to serve-up seconds.

So there it was: the moment of truth. I had the motive, means and opportunity to rescue Max and kill Leo Sporcatello and his male model bodyguard.

I like to think my love for Mia stayed my hand. That I couldn't bring myself to shoot her father in front of her, no matter how loathsome he was. Then again, maybe it was cowardice. Fear that I'd miss and wind up dead? *Something* stopped me. It was a mistake.

"Oh for God's sake," Leo said, nodding at Luigi.

The bodyguard aimed his gun at the back of Max's head and pulled the trigger. The gun's rapport echoed out to sea. Max Herndon's lifeless body fell to the deck.

Shocked out of my paralysis, I raised my new gun to shoot Luigi. I was too late. Before I could squeeze the trigger, Luigi took two rounds to his chest. I looked over at Mia. She had a smoking gun in her hand, wrenched from her father's pocket.

Leo looked over at Mia as well — just in time to see his daughter fire three shots into *his* body.

Leo fell where he stood. Mia pointed the gun at her father's head and fired the *coup de grace*. She left her father, walked over to Luigi and fired her gun dry into his motionless body.

"Mia!" I yelled.

She looked at me, expressionless, blood and bits covering her perfectly tanned body. I watched, mesmerized, as she lay her gun on the table's bloodstained tablecloth and climbed the stairs to the bridge.

I heard the engines roar. I followed her a minute or so later, nauseated by the carnage behind me and the growing swell.

"We are going to get rid of the bodies," she said, wiping her stomach with a white towel.

"Why?" I asked, noticing that I still held the Cabot in my hand. "Why'd you do it?"

"Not your business," she replied defiantly, looking out to sea. "By the way, I'm pregnant."

- FIN -